# THE PAPER
# MAGICIAN

# THE PAPER
# MAGICIAN

## CHARLIE N. HOLMBERG

47N◉RTH

Text copyright © 2014 Charlie N. Holmberg
All rights reserved.

Published by 47North, Seattle

www.apub.com

Amazon, the Amazon logo, and 47North are trademarks of Amazon.com, Inc., or its affiliates.

ISBN-13: 9781477823835
ISBN-10: 1477823832

Cover design by Ryan Hobson

Library of Congress Control Number: 2014930971

Printed in the United States of America

*To my husband, Jordan, who is the source of
all the magic in my life.*

# CHAPTER 1

FOR THE PAST FIVE years, Ceony had wanted to be a Smelter.

However, while most graduates of the Tagis Praff School for the Magically Inclined got to choose what material they dedicated their craft to, Ceony had been assigned. "Not enough Folders," Magician Aviosky had explained in her office.

Less than a week had passed since Ceony had heard this, and she still felt the tears that had stung the back of her eyes. "Paper is a wonderful medium," Mg. Aviosky had continued, "and one that's lost credit in recent years. With only twelve acting magicians left in that discipline, we have no choice but to direct a portion of our apprentices that way. I'm sorry."

So was Ceony. Her heart had broken at those words, and now, standing before the gate of Magician Emery Thane's lair, she wished it had stopped beating altogether.

Her hand gripped the wooden handle of her suitcase as she stared up at the monstrosity, even worse than her fitful dreams had imagined it to be. If it weren't bad enough that Mg. Thane—the only Folder this side of the River Thames—lived on the wild outskirts of

London itself, his abode looked like the creation of a campfire story. Its black walls stood six stories high. Scraps of worn paint peeled beneath the fingers of a sudden, foreboding wind that picked up the moment Ceony stepped foot onto the unpaved lane leading away from the main road. Three uneven turrets jutted up from the house like a devil's crown, one of which bore a large hole in its east-facing side. A crow, or maybe a magpie, cried out from behind a broken chimney. Every window in the mansion—and Ceony counted only seven—hid behind black shutters all chained and locked, without the slightest glimmer of candlelight behind them. Dead leaves from a dozen past winters clogged the eaves and wedged themselves under bent and warped shingles—also black—and something drip-drip-dripped nearby, smelling like vinegar and sweat.

The grounds themselves bore no flower gardens, no grass lawn, not even an assortment of stones. The small yard boasted only rocks and patches of uncultivated dirt too dry and cracked for even a weed to take root. The tiles composing the path up to the front door, which hung only by its top hinge, were cracked into pieces and overturned, and Ceony didn't trust a single one of the porch's gray, weathered boards to hold her weight long enough for her to ring the bell.

"I've been shot to hell," Ceony murmured.

Mg. Aviosky, her escort, frowned beside her. "Never trust what your eyes see at a magician's home, Miss Twill. You know that."

Ceony swallowed against a dry throat and nodded. She did know that, but she didn't care to, not now. The dark, foreboding mansion seemed a reflection of herself and everything that had gone wrong the last few days. Perhaps she had jinxed herself last night when she had gathered all the paper she could find in the hotel and burned it sheet by sheet in the fireplace while Mg. Aviosky consulted a map in the receiving hall. Or perhaps Mg. Thane was proof that Ceony's imagination needed a great deal of expanding.

Ceony bit down a sigh. She had come so far during her nineteen years of life, and now everything she had achieved—at steep odds, no less—seemed to flit away from her, leaving her cold and empty. All her aspirations were now to filter down to simple paper. Ceony would spend the rest of her days writing ledgers and reading outdated books, her only cheer in life penning letters home that would open themselves upon arrival. Of all the materials Mg. Aviosky could have chosen—glass, metal, plastic, even rubber—she had chosen *paper*. Mg. Aviosky obviously did not realize that the reason Folding had become a dying art was because the skills it enabled were so completely useless.

Refusing to be pulled along like a schoolgirl, Ceony straightened her back and trudged up the lane toward the gates. The fence itself was little more than spears shoved into the ground butt-first and tied together with barbed wire. The wind's strength built with every step, threatening to blow Ceony's hat off as she reached for the gate's catch—

The scenery around her changed so abruptly Ceony jumped, nearly dropping her suitcase. Her hand rested on a simple chain-link fence, and not one built from the refuse of old battles and dilapidated prisons. The sun broke through the clouds above, and the wind settled down to the faintest, most uneven breeze. The house before her shrunk to three stories, built of simple yellow brick. The shutters, all open, were white, and the porch looked sturdy enough for an entire team of horses to prance upon.

Ceony lifted her hand, wide eyes taking in the transformation. She half expected that breaking her connection to the gate would restore the dreary illusion, but the house remained the same when she released the catch. The path to the door was unpaved, but an array of red, violet, and yellow tulips lined it instead of jagged rocks.

Blinking, Ceony unlatched the gate and stepped closer. Not tulips. At least, not real ones. Every flower in the yard looked to be crafted of Folded paper, each blossom perfectly creased. The buds appeared real—so much so that, when a cloud passed over the afternoon sun, they all closed their petals ever so slightly. Like flowers trying too hard to be flowers.

With a quick glance, Ceony noticed the strips of paper hanging from the chain-link fence, and beyond them whole sheets of paper taller than any person and wider than the buggy that had brought her here. *An illusion.* Ceony recalled attending a lecture on espionage at the school last winter where the speaker had mentioned using paper dolls to mask one's appearance, but she had never imagined using the tactic for an entire *house*, however it was done.

Mg. Aviosky stepped up beside her, casually pulling off her silk gloves finger by finger. The transformation didn't jar her one bit, but she didn't gloat, either.

Ceony half expected Mg. Thane to show up at the door there and then, but the door—now of solid wood and painted such a light brown it looked orange—remained closed and quiet.

*Perhaps he's not evil at all,* Ceony thought with a frown. *Just mad.*

Passing the paper flowers, Ceony stepped up to the door, Mg. Aviosky not a pace behind her, and knocked firmly with her knuckles, trying to stand as tall as her five-foot-three frame would allow. She absently touched her hair, which was the color of uncooked yams and hung over her left shoulder in a loose braid. She had purposely chosen not to do it nicely that morning, just as she didn't wear her best dress or her student's uniform. She had nothing to be excited for—why dress up? It was clear Mg. Thane had made no special allowances for her.

The knob turned without the faintest trace of footsteps on the other side, and when the door opened, Ceony screamed and fell back a step.

A skeleton greeted her.

Even Mg. Aviosky seemed surprised, though she only showed

4

it by pursing her lips and adjusting the round-framed glasses that sat atop a rather prominent nose. "Well," she said.

The eyeless head of the skeleton looked up and down almost mechanically, and Ceony, with a hand over her heart, realized all six feet of it was comprised of paper—its head, its spine, its ribs, its legs. Hundreds, perhaps thousands of pieces of paper, all white, rolled and Folded and pinched together to connect in a variety of joints.

"He's mad," Ceony said, aloud this time. Mg. Aviosky sniffed loudly in a subtle attempt to scold her.

The skeleton stepped aside.

"Any more surprises?" Ceony asked no one in particular as she entered the house, staying as far from the skeleton as the narrow doorframe would allow. The house started in a long hallway that smelled of old wood and branched off in three directions, two to the right and one to the left. The first right opened onto a small front room that, despite being filled with clutter, was deftly organized: everything from candlesticks to books shoved in a most orderly fashion onto shelves, with clay ocarinas, marble sets, and more books crammed into straight lines across the mantel. Ceony noticed every detail of the room, as she was prone to do—such as the threadbare cushion on the couch, which told her Mg. Thane preferred to sit on the far-left side and scooted back. A small wind chime hung in the corner—an odd place for a wind chime, as no wind would pass through the front room unless he opened the window, and even then, very little. She surmised that Mg. Thane liked the look of it, but not the sound.

Mad, indeed.

A perfect stack of unread mail sat on a side table in the corner next to what looked like a music box and some sort of blacksmith's puzzle, which rested in perfect alignment with the stack and the box. Ceony had never known a pack rat to be so . . . tidy. It disturbed her.

The closed door to the left of the hallway hid whatever room lay beyond it, but instead of walking farther into the house to see what the second right revealed, she shouted, "Magician Thane! Your guests are here and would greatly appreciate a real person at the door!"

"Miss Twill!" Mg. Aviosky said in a suppressed sort of hiss as the paper skeleton shut the front door. "Manners!"

"Well, the absence is rude, isn't it?" Ceony asked, hating how childish the words sounded in her mouth. She cleared her throat and sucked in a deep breath. "I'm sorry. I'm a little on edge."

"No need to remind me," Mg. Aviosky quipped just as a real person emerged from that second right, some sort of ledger in his hands.

"There *are* guests at the door," the man said, closing the ledger. The ensuing burst of air rustled his wavy black hair. In words pitched at a light baritone, he added, "And I would have thought the knock gave it away."

Ceony gripped her suitcase all the harder to keep herself from starting, or from thinking too hard on the man's words, for she couldn't decide if they had been meant in mockery or not.

Mg. Thane looked much younger than Ceony had expected, perhaps about thirty or so, and he hadn't taken the effort to dress up, either. He didn't wear his magician's dress uniform, or anything particularly fancy at all, just plain slacks with an unadorned high-necked shirt, over which hung a lightweight, oversized indigo coat that dropped clear to his ankles, with loose sleeves that fell nearly to his palms. He seemed quite average, his skin neither light nor dark, his height neither short nor tall, and his build neither thin nor broad. His dark hair fell just below his ears in a sort of kempt-but-unkempt way. He had black sideburns down to his jaw, and his nose had a slight bump to it, just above the middle of the bridge. The only thing extraordinary about him was the brightness of his eyes—green as summer leaves and shining as if someone had hid a light behind his forehead.

Mg. Thane glanced at Ceony without the slightest smile, gesture, or draw of the brow, but in those bright eyes Ceony could tell the man was rather amused. Whether with her or with himself, she couldn't be sure. She ground her teeth together.

"Magician Thane," Mg. Aviosky said with a nod of her head, and Ceony wondered how well they knew one another, "this is Ceony Twill, whom I telegraphed you about."

"Yes, yes," Mg. Thane said, setting down the ledger on the stack of unread mail by the couch, aligning the book's corners just so. He turned and met Ceony's stare. "Ceony Twill, eldest of four and top of her graduating class. How many students made it out of that prison this year?"

Ceony adjusted her hat, if only to give her free hand something to do. "Twenty-two."

"Still an accomplishment," he said, almost offhandedly. "Hopefully you can put those study habits of yours to good use here."

Ceony only nodded. She did have good study habits—she prided herself on them—but schoolwork had always come easily to her. She had a sharp memory, and often remembered things after reading them through only once or twice. It was a blessing that had pulled her through many difficult and dull lectures. Hopefully it would help her here as well.

Mg. Aviosky cleared her throat, breaking through the silence before it could settle. "I have her new uniform in my case. Do tell me you prepared the bonding."

"Of course," he answered, dismissing the question with a slight wave of his hand. He looked at Ceony. "I suppose you'll want a tour of sorts."

Ceony felt herself shrink. How easily this man could crush her future with a wave of his hand! For once she bonded to a material, there would be no turning back—a bond was for life. She searched for a possible escape route should she need one and spied the paper skeleton immediately behind her and shrieked for the second time. Who needed ghosts to haunt a house when one could form his own demons out of paper?

"Jonto, cease," Mg. Thane said, and the skeleton collapsed in a heap of paper bones right there on the floor, his carefully Folded skull resting right at the top.

Ceony stepped away from it. What sort of morbid man constructed a butler out of paper? Was there no one else to answer the door?

"Do you live alone?" Ceony asked.

"As it suits me," Mg. Thane replied, leading them down the hallway. "The study," he said, gesturing to the closed door on the left, "and the dining room is through here," he added, pausing at the second right in the hallway.

Ceony followed with slow steps and peeked around the corner, half expecting another paper atrocity to jump out at her.

Instead she found a short hallway with mirrors hanging across from one another on either wall, a bench, and a simple stunted dresser with an empty vase on top of it. Tightly Folded paper triangles lined the walls close to the ceiling in teal and yellow where the hall opened into a small, well-stocked kitchen. A marble countertop surrounded a single-basin sink. Dark-stained cupboards loomed to either side, but gave enough room to work in. A metal grating above the sink carried a small set of pots and pans, their dark bottoms denoting that they were well used. Around the edges of the grating wrapped a paper vine that looked very similar to the skeleton's—Jonto's—bones. Did it have a use, or did the paper magician merely grow bored being cooped up here, away from real people? How much of the paper décor in this house was actually used for spells, and how much of it was pointless ornamentation?

Would Ceony spend her days as little more than a glorified decorator?

Shaking the thoughts from her head, Ceony eyed the rest of the kitchen. Mg. Thane had a more narrow stove than what she was accustomed to, and an old-fashioned one at that, but not poor. Ceony felt somewhat assured knowing that between her lessons on Folding she could escape here to cook. After all, had she not received her scholarship, she would have attended culinary school as an alternative. The tuition for that was a tenth of what the Tagis Praff School demanded, and Ceony had a knack for food. She felt confident she would have been enrolled.

Ceony moved past the kitchen to the dining room. Hundreds of paper birds hung from the ceiling by filament threads, looking nearly alive. They dangled quietly, out of the way, suspended above a simple square table that sat atop a brown woven rug. Near it stood a tall, dark-stained hutch neatly cluttered with dishes, books, napkins, jars, and jugs—everything fit together so tightly that removing just one item might make the rest avalanche. Along the top of the hutch rested strange paper balls and cones made of smaller balls and cones and smaller ones yet. They hurt Ceony's eyes. The house would be cozy were it not so crammed with things.

She wandered to a thick stack of parchment at the edge of the table and rested her hand on it, thinking of the paper illusions lining the cottage's fence. "The front you put onto your home is horrid," she quipped.

Mg. Aviosky passed Ceony a warning look as she stepped into the dining room. Mg. Thane merely replied, "Yes. Pleasant, isn't it?"

He passed her and opened a door with a long handle, which revealed a steep set of stairs leading up. "If you'll follow me."

Ceony did so, suitcase still in hand. The ninth step creaked under her weight, and her knees hurt by the time she reached the second floor.

"Your room," Mg. Thane said, pushing a door open, "if you want to set down your luggage."

Ceony stepped into the room, a stark contrast from the rest of the house, as all its shelves were empty. No stacks, piles, or knickknacks, but judging by the indentations in the carpet, the room had recently held furniture that had been moved or removed. Mg. Thane must have only just prepared for her arrival, despite having a week's notice.

Even stranger, no paper ornaments adorned the walls or the ceiling—they had been left starkly bare. A simple twin-sized bed rested against the only window. A set of three shelves had been built into the wall beside it, and a simple writing desk with one drawer rested a couple paces from the bed's foot. There was a small closet, large enough for Ceony's few changes of clothes, and a small table with a new candlestick and holder upon it.

It offered her a little more space than her dorm room at Tagis Praff, albeit with fewer shelves. Still, she thought her dorm room somewhat warmer and more hospitable, though that may have been because she'd earned her place there. She'd *wanted* to be there.

"Thank you," she managed, setting her suitcase down. She briefly thought of the 1845 Tatham percussion-lock pistol she had stowed away in there—a graduation gift from her father, for she had *planned* on being a Smelter—and decided to unpack later, away from watching eyes. Mg. Thane must have expected as much, for the tour continued on.

"Down here," Mg. Thane continued as Ceony shut her bedroom door behind her, "is the lavatory, my room, and the library," he said, stopping at the end of the hall and another set of stairs. To Mg. Aviosky he said, "I've set up the bonding in here," and gestured to the library.

Ceony's steps slowed. So the tour ended at the bonding.

She eyed the door at the end of the hall, identical to the one in the kitchen that opened onto the stairwell. "What's on the third floor?" Ceony asked. Perhaps something uplifting lingered up there. Perhaps she'd find a window to leap from. Judging by the height of the ceilings on the first and second floors, the third was by far the tallest, which was strange for a backcountry house like this one.

"The big spells," Mg. Thane answered, his expression plain but his bright eyes smiling. Did he know how much those eyes gave away?

Ceony made a note not to tell him. She needed all the advantages she could get if she were to survive here.

With Mg. Thane barring the stairs to the third floor with his shoulder, Ceony dragged her feet after Mg. Aviosky into the library, which appeared only slightly larger than her bedroom and had bookshelves only on the sidewalls, albeit ones that stretched clear to the ceiling. As Ceony expected, books had been crammed into every available space, spine against spine, some forming double rows so she couldn't see what titles lay in the first. The shelves seemed recently dusted—very recently, for the moment Ceony thought it she sneezed, which made her notice the path of dust highlighted by a large window on the far wall. Her eyes landed on a loop of paper chains that surrounded the window, as well as the pinewood table beneath it, which held stacks of paper in varying sizes and colors organized from lightest to darkest, and then from roughest to smoothest. A small telegraph hung off its back-right corner.

The table's single chair had been turned around, and upon it rested a short easel bearing a canvas of thick, plain paper, eggshell white and fine grained. No ornamentation, no hoopla, just a plain sheet of paper.

Studying it, Ceony realized what it was.

Her grave.

She knew about material bonding—it was one of the dozens of subjects she studied over the last year of rigorous courses at the school. It was nothing fancy, just an oath that tied your spirit into the subject, allowing you to conduct magic through it and *only* it. A woman could not, for instance, cast spells with both glass *and* fire. Only one. Ceony couldn't bond paper and still hope to be a Smelter, enchanting jewelry and bespelling bullets as she had often daydreamed during her lessons.

It wasn't fair, but there was no use in further complaining. They all knew it. Mg. Aviosky knew it, and Mg. Thane likely knew it, too. Ceony had earned the right to choose her material, but because those before her had neglected Folding—the weakest of the magics—she had been forced into it.

Mg. Thane handed her a smaller piece of standard white eight-by-eleven paper. Ceony pinched it between her fingers and turned it over, but it bore no instruction. No writing of any kind graced its surface, nor did any Folds, magical or otherwise.

"What is this for?" she asked.

"Feel it," Mg. Thane said, clasping his hands behind his back once more.

Ceony continued pinching the paper, waiting for some sort of clarification, but Mg. Thane merely held his stance. After several seconds Ceony pressed the simple paper between her palms and rubbed her hands back and forth, thoroughly "feeling" the paper.

The paper magician's eyes smiled, and he took the slightly wrinkled paper back without comment. "Do you know the words?" he asked, softer. Perhaps her eyes were as easy to read as his.

Ceony nodded, numb. The long talk she had had with Mg. Aviosky in the buggy surfaced in her mind. *"It's this or nothing. It has to be that way, for balance,"* Mg. Aviosky had said. *"Don't let rumor and comedy dissuade you, Miss Twill. Folding takes a keen eye and deft hands—you have both. The others have accepted this fate; so must you."*

Accepted this fate. But had they? Were the words only meant to persuade Ceony to be more willing to sign away her dreams?

The two magicians watched her, Mg. Aviosky with her usual blank-canvas countenance and Mg. Thane with a strange sort of humor to his eyes.

Ceony pressed her lips together. As far as magic went, she knew it was paper or nothing, and she'd rather be a Folder than a failure.

She lifted a clammy hand and pressed it to the sheet of paper resting on the chair. Closing her eyes and gritting her teeth, she said, "Material made by man, your creator summons you. Link to me as I link to you through my years until the day I die and become earth."

Such simple words, but they did the deed.

Ceony's hand grew warm, and heat flashed back through her arm and body, then left just as quickly.

It was done.

# CHAPTER 2

"I ALWAYS FOUND BONDING incredibly anticlimactic," Mg. Thane commented as he picked up the easel from the chair. "Do you want to save it?"

Ceony blinked a few times and held her bonding hand to her chest. "Save what?"

He shook the large paper in his hand. "Some find it sentimental."

"No," she said, perhaps a little too sharply. Mg. Thane didn't seem to notice and placed the paper against the wall, and the easel atop the table perfectly parallel to the paper stacks.

Finding no empty table space, Mg. Aviosky crouched on the floor and opened her hard plastic briefcase, crafted by the hands of a Polymaker—a type of magician who had come into being only thirty years ago, after a rubber magician had discovered plastic itself. From the briefcase Mg. Aviosky pulled a crisply folded red apron and a short, black top hat: the garb of an apprentice.

Despite the gnawing inside her stomach and the pieces of heartfelt dreams collecting in a heap at the base of her skull, Ceony accepted the clothing with a quiet reverence.

Unlike the green student apron, the apprentice apron had pleats across the thighs and thin scarlet trim around the collar. The fabric covered more of the bust as well. It tied behind the neck and around the ribs and had two small half-circle pockets at either hip.

The top hat, stiff and shiny, was a mark of experience. Students didn't have top hats. Even though the road Ceony had stepped onto would be narrow and unexciting, at least the apron and hat proved her worth. Proved she had achieved *something*, for graduating from Tagis Praff, especially in a single year and at the top of her class, had been no easy feat.

"Thank you," she said, hugging the apron to her chest.

Mg. Aviosky smiled, the sort of smile she had always given Ceony at the school. The smile that made Ceony like her so much. *If only I could study under her*, Ceony thought. Given the choice, she would rather enchant glass than paper.

Mg. Aviosky squared her shoulders, dispelling that notion rather abruptly. "I'll see myself out," she said, "unless you have another paper servant to do it for me."

Mg. Thane's eyes smiled as he said, "It's no bother to escort you, Patrice. Ceony?"

"I'll . . . stay here, if you don't mind," she said. Ceony had the feeling that, should she get to the buggy with Mg. Aviosky now, she'd run away and never come back. And, though she despised it, Ceony knew she needed to wait for her new responsibility to settle before she could trust herself near any easy exits. She had bound herself to paper indefinitely, and it did her no good to push through a year at Tagis Praff just to throw it all away now.

Mg. Thane nodded once, then handed her back the wrinkled piece of paper he had had her "feel." Confused, Ceony accepted it. It took a couple of seconds—enough time for Magicians Thane and Aviosky to reach the library door—for her to realize something had changed about the parchment.

She turned it over in her hands. It still bore no Folds, no writing, but it *felt* different in a way difficult to describe. It still felt like paper, of course—a medium lightweight that a sketch artist might find useful—but something beneath her skin tingled at the feel of it. Was this the result of the bond? Was this why Mg. Thane had insisted she touch the paper before, so she would notice the difference now?

Somewhat confused, Ceony set the paper on the chair and hurried to the library door, peeking out to see Magicians Aviosky and Thane moving down the hallway, discussing something too quietly for Ceony to hear. She couldn't help but follow them. Ceony crept through the hallway as the magicians vanished down the stairs, then crept down the stairs as they vanished into the dining room, making sure to step over the creaking ninth step. She scuttled after them and saw that as Mg. Aviosky finally stepped outside, Mg. Thane followed her, keeping the front door propped open with his heel. They spoke in hushed tones, so naturally Ceony suspected it was about something she was not meant to hear. Mg. Aviosky never did trust her to do as told.

She padded quietly down the hall, eyeing the unmoving pile of Jonto's paper bones near the door. She still couldn't make out her teachers' conversation, but dared inch no closer.

Instead, she turned the knob to Mg. Thane's study and let herself in.

This room had more organized clutter than all the others, highlighted by a circle-top window on the far wall, facing the bespelled front gate. Yellow paper curtains had been drawn back to reveal glass that had not been washed on the outside for quite some time. Beneath the window sat metal shelves bearing more books, folders, and ledgers similar to the one Mg. Thane had been holding earlier. Kitty-corner to that shelf rested three cedar-wood triplets, four shelves high, weighed down with neat stacks of paper pressed into one another to minimize empty space. Yet more papers had already been Folded—starter Folds, perhaps, to save time. A great deal of trinket spells likely started with those V-shaped Folds. Ceony assumed a great deal of her apprenticeship would be spent making starter Folds of no importance for Mg. Thane to use at his leisure. She sighed.

A second, square window, blocked on the outside by some sort of ivy, had various paper chains hanging down in front of it, some tight-knit with sharp angles, others made of large loops torn on the ends and fitted together so loosely that a simple tug would pull the entire thing apart. Some chains were blue, some pink, others multicolored. The color didn't matter, of course. Ceony knew that much from her History of Materials course at Tagis Praff.

She noticed small scraps of paper in the pale-green carpeting. Mg. Thane hadn't cleaned in here, or perhaps he had only recently worked on a spell to further terrorize Ceony before her arrival. She scanned for such a spell, but the room held so much *stuff* she could barely tell a tabletop from a desk. The walls, in contrast, were mostly bare, save for Mg. Thane's framed Magician's Certificate and more shelves of folders pressed into the corners behind the desk.

She heard the front door shut, but Ceony didn't hurry herself. She crouched down and picked up the paper bits from the carpet, unfolding them in her fingers. Felt that subtle, curious tingle beneath her skin once again. She wondered at the paper bits. None was larger than her thumbnail, and all appeared to be in strange symmetrical patterns.

The door to the study opened. "Amusing yourself?" Mg. Thane asked, his tone light.

*At least he doesn't have a temper*, she thought. Out loud she said, "You were making snowflakes." She studied a paper cut in the shape of an elongated heart. "That's what these are from, aren't they?"

He nodded, his face calm save for a glitter in his green eyes. "Very astute."

Ceony stood and brushed off her brown skirt, which covered her from rib to calf. She would have thought he mocked her had his eyes not gleamed their sincerity. What a confusing man.

"Ceony," Mg. Thane said, leaning against the doorframe. He folded his arms against his chest, his long sleeves drooping down from them. "I presume I can call you by your first name." He didn't wait for a response. "Folding is not as dreary as I'm sure you believe it to be. It may not be as exciting as Smelting or as innovative as Polymaking, but it has its own outlets for creativity. May I show you?"

Ceony hid a frown and tried very hard not to look incredibly bored at the suggestion. After all, she would be apprenticing under this man for at least two years, if not longer. She needed him to like her. She forced a polite smile on her face and moved toward the door.

Mg. Thane stepped out into the hall, but as Ceony followed after him, her eyes glimpsed something on the cluttered desk that made her pause. Something that wouldn't have caught her eye at all if the envelope had not matched the stationery set tucked securely into a side pocket of her suitcase.

She stepped back and reached for the wire note holder that had been packed with various letters and postcards, each aligned with its neighbor along the left edges. She selected the peach-colored envelope near the holder's center and tugged it free, too stunned this time to feel the tingling sensation in her fingertips. The address was not to Mg. Thane, but to the Magicians' Cabinet . . . and in her penmanship. She had addressed it there because her donor had been anonymous, and she hadn't known how else to contact her.

Or, apparently, him.

She didn't need to open the letter to know what it said. She remembered it word for word.

To my anonymous donor,

I cannot begin to express to you my utmost gratitude for the scholarship I've received by your hand, though I have no name to address my gratitude to. It has been my dream since I was a young girl to learn the secrets of magic, but due to my family's financial situation and some bad luck on my part, I had truly believed only a few days ago that my dream was unobtainable. However, I am happy to say I've officially enrolled in the Tagis Praff School for the Magically Inclined, and I plan to make you proud by graduating within one year.

Words are not adequate for my joy and thanks to you, but I plead for your patience as I try. You may have very well changed my life and my family's lives for the better, and for good. Because of your generosity I feel capable of achieving anything, for nothing worldly can possibly hold me back from my ambitions now.

Please know that you have made a vast difference in my life. I only pray one day I might learn your name and find some feeble way to repay you.

Sincerely and with the warmest regards,

Ceony Maya Twill

Feeling a bit stiff, a bit light-headed, she said, "You . . . were my donor?"

Mg. Thane, just outside the doorway, lifted an eyebrow.

Ceony turned the letter over in her hands. "This is my thank-you letter," she said, heart quickening in her chest. She felt a blush creeping up her neck. "My scholarship. It . . . it came from you."

The man merely tilted his head to the left. "Tuition at that place is ghastly, isn't it?"

"Why?" she asked, swallowing to keep her voice from shaking. The walls of her throat grew sore. "Why . . . sponsor me?"

From the beginning Ceony had known she could only attend

magic-preparation school—a requirement for all apprentices—if she received some sort of financial aid. She had studied hard during secondary school and was a nominee for the Mueller Academic Award after her acceptance to Tagis Praff, but lost the scholarship without explanation. Heartbroken, she had packed her bags and readied herself to move to Uxbridge, where she would take work as a housemaid for a year or so to pay for culinary school. Four days before her departure, Tagis Praff contacted her with an anonymous scholarship offer of fifteen thousand pounds, enough to cover one year's tuition, books, and board. A miracle—no bank would allow a shanty nobody from Whitechapel's Mill Squats to take out a loan for such a grand sum. She knew that from experience.

She cried after receiving that telegram. She wrote this letter the next day.

And Mg. Thane—a man she had not met until that morning and whom she had pegged as some sort of lunatic sorcerer—had been the one to give her the money, without interest or return. Without even a name.

Mg. Thane didn't answer her inquiry. Rather, he simply asked, "Shall we?" with a sweeping gesture of his arm. A gesture that closed the matter. If Mg. Thane had wanted to discuss the scholarship, he would have listed his name when he gave it to her.

Shaken, Ceony set the letter down. Rubbing the back of her neck, she followed the magician out into the hallway and through the kitchen and dining room. *He* might have closed the matter, but she wouldn't just let things stand pat. On the stairs she asked, "Did you request me?"

"I assure you that your assignment was pure coincidence. Or perhaps a bit of bad humor on the part of Magician Aviosky. If you can call it humor. I've always found her rather . . . dry."

*Some coincidence!* Too stunned to think of a reply, Ceony traced Mg. Thane's path back to the library, where her apprentice's uniform rested on the floor. She slipped on her red apron but left the top hat. It was more for public show, besides.

Mg. Thane pulled around the chair and had her sit on it. Retrieving several pieces of paper from the table, along with something that looked like a cutting board, he sat on the short green carpet and folded his legs under him, his long coat puddling about him almost like the skirt of a woman's gown.

"I-I can get you a chair," Ceony offered. Part of her still held the disappointment of becoming a Folder, but another part felt strange sitting before Mg. Thane now, knowing what he had done for her and not knowing any of the reasons. Knowing that letter she had drafted and redrafted four times to her donor had actually gone to him. No etiquette class or textbook had ever explained to her how to handle a situation like this.

"Nonsense," Mg. Thane said as he hunched over the board, seemingly unbothered by the hair falling into his eyes and the long sleeves hindering his hands. "I have a personal motto to never Fold on one's lap."

Ceony's blundering thoughts paused at that. "*One's* lap, or your own?" she asked.

Mg. Thane glanced up at her and she spied laughter in his eyes, even if it didn't quite sound in his throat. "I think a person would think me quite peculiar if I were to Fold in his lap, wouldn't you say?"

"They might think you peculiar besides," she said, only processing the words after they had passed from her lips. She flushed. Her well-practiced snarkiness had tasted so much sweeter before the man's revealed philanthropy. Perhaps the best way to handle the situation with her donor-gone-teacher would be to act like nothing extraordinary had happened just minutes ago. That would be easiest.

It helped that Mg. Thane smiled before returning his eyes to the board before him. "Everything is made of Folds," he explained as he worked, Folding a square sheet of orange paper in half, then in half again. "But you know that. The trick is getting the Folds right. Everything must be aligned just so, or the spells won't work. Just as you can't enchant a mirror if it doesn't reflect a perfect image."

"Or bake a cobbler if you don't have the right ingredients," Ceony said softly. Mg. Thane only nodded, but she felt even that small approval was important. Ceony watched his average-looking hands move the paper this way and that, rotating it and flipping it over. It bent under his touch like water, and he never struggled in getting the paper to obey his direction. Ceony studied the movements, storing their images in her memory.

Mg. Thane Folded the paper into what looked like a kite, then opened it into a tall diamond. Not too complex. Still, Ceony couldn't see the bird among the paper until he had nearly finished. Not a bird like those hanging in the kitchen, but one with a long neck and tail, and broad, triangular wings creased to perfect points.

He held it out in his palm and said, "Breathe."

Ceony inhaled, but the command hadn't been for her.

The paper bird shook its head, and though it had no legs, it hopped once on Mg. Thane's hand before flapping its orange wings and taking to the air. It flitted around the library, bobbing through the air almost like a real bird. Ceony watched it with wide eyes. It circled the room twice before perching upon a high shelf holding an assortment of calligraphy books.

She had heard of animation, of course, and seen Jonto for herself, but actually watching the magic unfold was, well, *magical*. She had never seen this sort of spell before. No paper magicians taught at Tagis Praff. And, as Mg. Aviosky had said, England had only twelve registered. Thirteen, once she completed her apprenticeship. But that was two to six years away, and Ceony still had difficulty imaging herself as a true Folder.

But she dearly wanted magic, even magic as simple as this.

"And you can do that with anything?" Ceony asked.

"You may use your imagination," Mg. Thane replied, "but creating something completely new is time-consuming. You must discover which Folds work and which don't."

"How many do you know?"

Mg. Thane only chuckled quietly to himself, as though the question were absurd. In his hands he had already created another creature, a tiny frog of green paper. He commanded it, "Breathe," and it bounded away, pausing every so often to look about and choose a new direction. Ceony half expected a long tongue to shoot from its mouth to taste for flies, but of course the simple creature hadn't been created with one.

"Jonto," Mg. Thane said, now Folding a sheet of white parchment, "was particularly tricky. He took me months to get right, especially with the spinal column and the jaw. Human anatomy is a mite bit complicated, especially when it comes to figuring out what sort of Folds something like a shoulder joint prefers. But though he is made of one thousand, six hundred and nine pieces of paper, he animates as a whole. Make it whole, and it will rise whole. That's your first lesson of the day."

His hands stilled, revealing a stout fish between them, puffed out in the middle to form a three-dimensional body. Folds similar to the orange bird's wings formed its pectoral fins. Mg. Thane picked it up, whispered to it, and released it. The fish soared upward through the air as a real fish would in water, its tail fin paddling back and forth until it hit the ceiling—which Ceony noticed had been covered with long pieces of white paper tied together with a simple string. The white fish used its puckering mouth to bite down on the string and untie its looping knot.

To her amazement, snow began to fall. Paper snowflakes cascaded through the air, some as small as Ceony's thumbnail, some as large as her hand. Hundreds of them poured down as the paper ceiling gave way, all somehow timed just right so that they fell like real snow. Ceony stood from her chair, laughing, and held out her hand to catch one. To her astonishment it felt cold, but didn't melt against her palm. Only tingled.

"When did you do this?" she asked, her breath fogging in the library's air as more snowflakes fell like crisp confetti from the ceiling. "This would take . . . ages to make."

"Not ages," Mg. Thane said. "You'll get quicker as you learn." He still sat on the floor, completely unfazed by the magic around him. But of course he would be—it was his creation. "Magician Aviosky mentioned you hadn't exactly jumped at the news of your assignment, and I can't blame you. But casting through paper has its own whimsy."

Ceony let her captured snowflake fall from her hand and turned to Mg. Thane, wondering at him. *He did all of this for me?*

Perhaps the man wasn't so mad after all. *Or maybe it's a madness that I can learn to appreciate.*

As the last snowflakes fell, Mg. Thane rose and pulled a thin hardcover book from the shelf behind him. He gestured for Ceony to once again sit in the chair. She complied.

He handed her the volume. The cover had a silver-embossed mouse on it and the words *Pip's Daring Escape.* Her mind quietly registered that subtle prickling beneath her skin as she accepted the book; she wondered if she would ever get used to it.

"A children's book?" she asked. At least the snowflakes had had some majesty to them.

"I'm not one to waste time, Ceony," he said. As though reading her thoughts, he eyed the scattered snowflakes with a frown, one that showed more in the tilt of his eyes than the curve of his lips. Ceony imagined he would have preferred them to fall in neat rows all perfectly aligned with one another, but real snow never fell that way. "I'm going to teach you something. Consider it homework."

Ceony slumped in the chair. "Homework? But I'm not even settled—"

"Read the first page," he said with a jab of his chin.

Rolling her lips together, Ceony opened the book to its first page, which showed a small gray mouse sitting atop a leaf. Her memory sprang to life, whispering that Ceony had seen this picture before, and her mind spun until it settled on a rainy afternoon some seven years ago when she'd been babysitting her neighbor's son. He'd been sobbing at the door for half an hour, mourning the departure of his mother. That family had owned this book, albeit a very worn edition. Ceony remembered reading it to him. The boy had stopped sobbing by page four.

She didn't mention the memory to Mg. Thane.

"'One morning Pip the mouse came outside to get some exercise, only to discover a golden wedge of cheese sitting just outside his stump,'" she read. As she moved to turn the page, Mg. Thane stopped her.

"Good," he said. "Now read it again."

Ceony paused. "Again?"

He pointed to the book.

Suppressing another sigh, Ceony read, "'One morning Pip the mouse came outside to get some—'"

"Put some effort into it, Ceony!" Mg. Thane said with a laugh. "Did they not cover story illusion at Praff?"

"I . . . no." In fact, Ceony had no idea what the man referred to, and she could already feel herself getting frustrated, despite her best attempts not to. She wasn't used to doing something wrong twice, especially when she didn't understand what she had done wrong the first time.

Folding his arms, Mg. Thane leaned against the table and asked, "What is the story written on?"

"What sort of question is that?"

"The kind you should answer."

Ceony's eyes narrowed. His tone carried an air of chastisement, but his expression seemed lax enough. "It's obviously written on paper."

Mg. Thane snapped his fingers. "There we are! And paper is your domain now. So make it mean something. And calm down," he said, almost as an afterthought.

Ceony flushed, and she cursed her light skin for making it so obvious. Clearing her throat, she reread the passage slowly, letting herself cool down.

Mg. Thane motioned with his hand for a third repetition.

Swallowing, Ceony shut her eyes and tried to take herself back to her neighbor's house, with the little boy on her knee and his beloved book in her hands. *Like you're reading it to him*, she thought. *Make it "mean" something.* Then perhaps the paper magician would leave her be. She had already thrice reformed her assessment of his sanity.

"'One morning Pip the mouse came outside to get some exercise,'" she said, reading it with the same inflections she had used seven years ago in attempts to calm her babysitting charge, "'only to discover a golden wedge of cheese sitting *just outside* his stump!'"

"There you have it. Take a look."

Ceony opened her eyes and nearly dropped the book.

There, like a ghost in the air, sat a little gray mouse with a fidgeting nose. His tail trailed behind him like a tired worm. Beside him stood a stump with a broad leaf and a golden wedge of cheese just like the one illustrated in the book. The image as a whole hovered nose level with her, and she could see through the apparition to the bookshelf on its other side.

Ceony's throat choked with words. "Wh-What? *I* did that?"

"Mm-hm," Mg. Thane hummed. "It helps when you can see an image, such as with picture books, but eventually you'll be able to read novels and have *those* scenes play out for yourself, if you wish.

I admit I'm impressed—I thought I'd have to demonstrate first. You seem familiar with the story already."

Once again she flushed, both over the praise and over being called out for having read what, in her mind, was a childish thing. The ghostly images lasted only a moment longer before fading away, as all unread stories were wont to do.

Ceony shut the book and glanced to her new teacher. "It's . . . amazing, but I admit it's also superficial. Aesthetic."

"But entertaining," he combated. "Never dismiss the value of entertainment, Ceony. Good-quality entertainment is never free, and it's something everyone wants.

"One more trick, then." Mg. Thane pulled a square piece of pale gray paper from the table and began Folding it in his hands, without a board to press against. The Folds seemed relatively simple, but by the time he finished he held what looked like a strange sort of egg carton, one that could only hold four eggs and bore no lid.

He pulled a pen out from somewhere inside his coat and began writing on it. Ceony noted that he was left-handed.

"What is that?" she asked, setting *Pip's Daring Escape* down on the cushion of the chair as she stood.

The corner of his mouth quirked upward. "A fortuity box," he answered, flipping the contraption around and lifting its triangular flaps. Standing on her toes, Ceony peeked around his arm to see him scrawling symbols, one in each Folded triangle. She recognized the shapes as fortune symbols, the ones drawn on cards at fortune-tellers' booths during carnivals.

"I'm no fortune-teller," she said.

"You are now," he replied, pinching the fortuity box in his fingers. He tilted it back and forth to show Ceony the placement. "Remember that you are much different now than you were an hour ago, Ceony. Before you merely *read* about magic; now you *have* it. Denying it won't make you return to ordinary."

Ceony nodded, wondering at that.

"Now," he said, leaning back against the table. "Tell me your mother's maiden name."

Ceony knit and reknit her fingers, for telling Mg. Thane her mother's maiden name could be a very bad thing, should he actually be mad. She had heard of a great many ancient curses that involved names during her studies, and she had been cautioned often about the power of names.

Mg. Thane lifted his eyes from the fortuity box. "You *can* trust me, Ceony. If you're worried, be assured I could look up the information and more by requesting your permanent records from Praff."

"How comforting," she mumbled, but it tempted a smile from her. "It's Philinger."

Mg. Thane opened the fortuity box like a mouth, then split it the other way, moving it once for every letter in *Philinger*. It was a fairly common last name, so he got the spelling right. "Now, your date of birth."

She told him, and again he swished the panels of the box back and forth.

"Pick a number."

"Thirteen."

"No higher than eight."

She sighed. "Eight."

Freeing one hand, Mg. Thane lifted a panel to reveal a symbol Ceony couldn't see. He waited a moment, his eyes a little unfocused, before saying, "Interesting."

"What?" Ceony asked, trying to spy around him, but he simply shifted the fortuity box from her line of sight.

"Bad luck to see your own fortune. What *are* they teaching new apprentices these days?" he asked with a click of his tongue, and Ceony could not tell if he jested, for his eyes were downcast to the box and therefore revealed none of their secrets. "It seems you have a bit of an adventure ahead of you."

*Yes. Living with* you *ought to be quite an "adventure,"* she thought. Enough adventure for anyone. Still, part of her regretted the thought the moment it formed in her brain. Surely this man hadn't personally offended her in any way . . . yet.

"That's all it says?" she asked.

"That's all I saw, at least," he said, handing her the fortuity box. It made her fingers buzz, her body once again registering the new bond it had made.

"Did you catch that?" Mg. Thane asked.

"What you did?"

"Yes."

"Yes." It had been simple enough.

"Well, go on."

Ceony held the box in her fingers. "What is your mother's maiden name?"

"Vladara," he answered. "One *r*."

Ceony opened and closed the box as Mg. Thane had done, then flipped it about for his date of birth. She had guessed right—thirty years old, and turning thirty-one next month. Finally, Mg. Thane picked the number three.

"The number three is bad luck," Ceony said as she lifted the flap.

"Only for Smelters," he retorted. A subtle reminder that she would never be one, purposeful or not. She chewed on the inside of her cheek in attempts to mask her still-brewing frustration at the fact.

A curling symbol with a wriggling head greeted her—one that was unfamiliar, for if she had seen it before, she would have remembered. Before she could open her mouth to ask for a translation, her vision doubled, and a strange image entered her mind: the silhouette of a woman, but none she knew. Strangely enough, a name pushed itself against her thoughts as well. Was that normal?

She lowered the fortuity box and narrowed her eyes at him. "Who's Lira?"

Mg. Thane's expression did not waver, nor did his stance, but for a moment Ceony could have sworn his eyes flickered dark and back. Only . . . no, they weren't *quite* as bright as before. Perhaps it was the late-growing sun outside the library window, but she didn't think so.

He tapped two fingers against his chin. "Interesting."

"Who is she?"

"An acquaintance," he said, and he smiled, all in the mouth. "I think you may have a natural talent for this, Ceony, which is a benefit to both of us. Practice with that, and with the storybook— I'd like to see its full illusion by Saturday. In the meantime, why don't you unpack your bags?"

Mg. Thane said nothing more on the subject of the fortuity box. Instead, he walked to the door and poked his head out into the hall, shouting, "Breathe!" He waited a beat, and then called, "Jonto, would you come up here and help with this mess?"

Ceony set the fortuity box on the table, wondering if Mg. Thane's "mess" referred to the snowflakes, or to her.

# CHAPTER 3

CEONY, WITH *PIP'S DARING Escape* tucked under her arm, picked up a few snowflakes herself until Jonto showed up at the door. Still somewhat unnerved by a live skeleton, regardless of its docile (and papyric) constitution, Ceony excused herself. She stowed one of the smallest snowflakes into her skirt pocket to take with her. For studying.

Mg. Thane had already vanished into his bedroom, so Ceony vanished into hers as well. She set the book and her hat on the table, then hefted her suitcase onto the bed beside the beige capeline hat she had brought with her.

The latches on the suitcase opened with two clicks. Her green student's apron lay on top, a last-minute packing decision, just in case she needed it. She set it aside and pulled out her blouses and skirts, shaking each in an attempt to unwrinkle the fabric. Fortunately the paper magician had remembered hangers in the closet; Ceony took her time hanging up each item of clothing.

She paused on the last skirt, her thoughts shifting from where on earth she would stow her under-things and pistol to the revelation about her scholarship. *Fifteen thousand pounds.* Where would

31

she be today, if not for that money? Scrubbing some aristocrat's floor, hoping she had saved enough to enroll in cooking classes?

And why had Mg. Thane given the money to her in the first place? She had never met him before today—she would have remembered. The scholarship had no title, no recurrences. Ceony couldn't believe she had merely been filtered through and selected due to good grades for a one-time donation, as he seemed to imply.

Had she?

What sort of man was Magician Emery Thane, to donate such a large sum to a complete stranger, and one he didn't even request for apprenticeship?

As Ceony returned to her suitcase, she began to wonder just how much a magician made. It must be a grand sum, unless Mg. Thane hoarded money the way he seemed to hoard all the other knickknacks in the house. Ceony hoped for the grand sum. She would feel terribly guilty otherwise. Perhaps it would be better not to pry, but he couldn't stop her from thinking on it.

For now, though, she'd put it aside and focus on the task at hand. She reached into her suitcase, filled now with her makeup, barrettes, journal, and a library card that would do her no good here, so far away from any library she knew, when again her thoughts took a turn. Her hand went to the turquoise dog collar wedged in the corner beneath her under-things. She held it up, running a thumb over its frayed ends, worn from too much chewing. She had taken Bizzy's tag off yesterday and given it to her mother, who now looked after the Jack Russell terrier in Ceony's stead.

Ceony sighed. That dog had been her dearest friend through the last few years, especially at the Tagis Praff School for the Magically Inclined. One couldn't make much in the way of friends at that school if they wanted to graduate in the designated year. There was simply too much work to do. But Bizzy didn't have homework, and she had always waited eagerly by the dorm-room door for Ceony to return after classes every day. That made her the best kind of friend.

"You have a dog? Or a very large cat?"

Ceony's heart skipped a beat and she whirled around, slamming her suitcase shut to hide her under-things and gun. Mg. Thane stood in the doorway, not yet breaching the threshold into her bedroom, holding a rather large stack of books. She should have closed that door.

Ceony clasped the collar. "Had one. He lived with me at the school, but Magician Aviosky told me I couldn't bring him here. Because of your allergies."

Mg. Thane nodded slowly, his bright eyes thoughtful. "I never was good around animals, even as a boy," he said in agreement. "I preferred bees."

"Bees?" Ceony asked.

He looked at her as though the preference was entirely normal and she was strange for questioning it. And, as he seemed wont to do, he didn't respond more than that.

"May I come in?" he asked.

Ceony nodded.

Kicking the door open with his toe, Mg. Thane stepped into the room and set the stack of books down on the desk. Ceony cringed—she had worried those would be for her.

"Some reading for when Pip tires you," Mg. Thane said, patting the top of the stack with his hand.

Arching sideways, Ceony read the titles: *Astrology for Youth, Anatomy of the Human Body Volume I, Marcus Waters's Guide to Pyrotechnics, Theories on Aviation,* and *Calming the Spirits: An Essay on the Tao.* Ceony's lips parted a little wider with each title.

"But these have nothing to do with paper," she said.

"Mmm, I can see why they accepted you at Tagis Praff," he said with a chuckle. Ceony glared at him, but he went on, nonchalant. "Paper is more than just trees run through a chipper, Ceony. These will benefit you for future lessons."

He tapped his chin and glanced to the window. "Are you hungry?" She set Bizzy's collar down. "Not especially. I ate in the buggy."

"I'll leave something on the stove for you, then," he replied, walking back into the hallway. "Do get some rest," he called, even as his voice faded away. "I have a busy day planned for you tomorrow. We don't want to let that Tagis Praff work ethic go to waste!"

Ceony glanced to the books on her desk, wondering just what sort of work the paper magician had in store for her. She had heard that many magicians forced their apprentices to do physical labor for their first year to humble them, or perhaps to break them. Ceony prayed that wouldn't be the case here. Although, she wouldn't be surprised if Mg. Thane planned to break her mentally first, what with the thickness of those volumes. At least she could be confident that weeding would not be one of her chores—she hadn't seen a single real flower in the front gardens.

Ceony unpacked the rest of her things, putting her makeup, barrettes, journal, and Bizzy's collar on the shelves carved into the wall beside the bed. She decided to keep her under-things and pistol in her suitcase, which she shoved beneath the bed. Outside, the sun made its slow descent to the west. Ceony would have to see to getting a clock in her room, if Mg. Thane granted her any wages. She would have to ask about that in the morning.

Sitting on her mattress, Ceony cracked open the well-worn bindings of *Astrology for Youth* and skimmed the first four chapters, then browsed through the figures in *Anatomy of the Human Body*, reading the captions beneath images of lungs, kidneys, hearts, and livers. Lying back on her pillow with *Theories on Aviation* on her stomach, Ceony pondered paper snow until she drifted into a hazy slumber, where she dreamed of enchanted cannons and the other spells she could have learned, had Mg. Aviosky only let her become a Smelter.

———————

Ceony woke with a start, though she could not remember why. Perhaps she had dreamed of falling, a nightmare she had at least once every other week since the age of eleven, when she had toppled off a dapple mare in her uncle's cousin's backyard. The sun had disappeared entirely from her window. If she pressed her face against the glass, she could spy the tip of the three-quarters moon above her. It was very late, indeed—perhaps an hour past midnight.

Stomach growling, Ceony blinked sleep from her eyes, stood, and adjusted her skirt, which had turned about her sideways. She also rebraided her hair over her left ear, for it surely looked a mess, not that anyone would be up to see it. Not that anyone lived in the cottage but Mg. Thane and his animated skeleton-butler.

After making her way down to the kitchen by candlelight—it felt strange to wander a place entirely dark, as Tagis Praff always had those new electric bulbs lighting the hallways, or a fire magician keeping lanterns lit—Ceony found a saucepan and bowl sitting atop the stove. The saucepan held half-stale rice, and the bowl had been filled with what looked like some form of preserved tuna. She shook her head. Was this what Mg. Thane ate normally, or was this what he served to guests? For if rice and tuna was his for-guests meal, Ceony couldn't imagine what the man ate when he dined alone. Perhaps Mg. Aviosky had assigned her here merely to ensure England's oddest paper magician got some decent nutrition and didn't wither away, leaving the country with only eleven paper magicians instead of twelve. Ceony would have to inspect the cupboards tomorrow to see just what Mg. Thane had stocked.

For now, however, she found a bowl and scooped up some cold rice, but left the tuna. She took two steps back toward her room when she heard something subtle—a drawer closing, perhaps. Curious, Ceony shoved a spoonful of rice into her mouth and tiptoed through the dining room and kitchen before spying a line of light coming from the hallway. The door on the left—her right—specifically. The study.

Ceony fed herself another spoonful. What sorts of hobbies did this man keep to be awake so late? The idea of him meddling with the dark arts almost made her laugh, but a good swallow prevented that. Ceony had a hard time imagining Mg. Thane, regardless of his level of madness, dabbling in shadow work or Excision, the forbidden magic that used human flesh as a conduit.

A shiver crept up her neck as she recalled what Mg. Phillips, her History of Magic Meddling teacher, had said about Excision:

*"Materials magic can only be performed through manmade materials, of course, but someone many, many years ago concluded that because humans begot humans, people were also manmade, and thus the dark arts began. Now, turn to page one twenty-six in your text—"*

Ceony ran a thumb over the shiver in her neck. Now such things were limited to campfire stories and history classes taught at Tagis Praff. Besides, Ceony had *seen* Mg. Thane work paper magic, which meant he couldn't possibly be an Excisioner.

She crept along the hallway where floor met wall, grateful that the floorboards didn't squeak and give her away. She heard a tune as she neared the study. Mg. Thane hummed to himself, though Ceony couldn't name the melody. It sounded . . . foreign.

He'd left the door open a crack. Ceony pushed on it lightly with her index finger, just enough to see inside.

Mg. Thane worked with his back to the door on the narrow table right behind his desk. A stack of standard-sized white paper sat at his right elbow, and his long indigo coat draped over the back of his chair. He continued to hum as he took a piece of paper off the stack and Folded it out of Ceony's sight. What was he creating, and at one o'clock in the morning?

Careful to be silent, Ceony stepped away from the door and retreated back into the dining room. She didn't like secrets, at least not ones she wasn't in on. Perhaps she would confront Mg. Thane in the morning. Or, perhaps, she wouldn't.

———————

Sometime in the early-morning hours, Mg. Thane went to bed, for he was not in his study when Ceony came downstairs to raid the cupboards precisely one minute after eight o'clock.

She wore her apprentice's apron and her hair in a braid, but again hadn't bothered to line her eyes or rouge her cheeks, as had recently become popular in town. There was just no reason to do so—who did she have to impress? Dragging a chair from the dining room into the kitchen, Ceony stood on it and looked through all the cupboards, which she found to be surprisingly well stocked. Mg. Thane had all the ingredients needed to make a chocolate cake, for instance, though Ceony noticed most were unopened. He had an enormous bag of rice beneath the sink, a half-eaten loaf of bread in the bread box, and eggs and an assortment of meat in the icebox, which Ceony found behind the counter, near the back door. The icebox also held a few handfuls of paper confetti. She wondered how they had gotten in there, or if they were part of some spell, but she merely brushed them off the bacon and grabbed the carton of eggs, a wedge of cheddar, and a bundled stock of fennel.

She had gotten down a frying pan and stoked the stove when she heard the strangest rasping sound coming down the stairs, along with the soft padding of paper on wood. Thinking it Jonto, she readied a spatula in her defense, but when the door to the stairs creaked open, something much shorter emerged from behind it.

Ceony gaped in surprise. There, wagging its little paper tail, stood a paper dog.

Dozens of pieces of paper formed its body, interlocking almost seamlessly from head to foot to tail. It had no eyes, being made of paper, but had two nostrils and a distinct mouth that opened and rasped at her in a strange sort of bark. It looked something like a Lab-terrier mix, its head only reaching Ceony's knee.

Barking once more, the dog sprinted up to Ceony and began sniffing her shoes.

With parted lips and tingles running down her back, Ceony set the spatula down by the stove, knocking the fennel stock to the floor. She crouched and stroked the dog's head. It felt surprisingly solid beneath her fingers, and its paper body made her fingertips buzz almost as though she were stroking real fur.

"Why hello!" she said, and the dog jumped and pressed its front paws against her knees, then actually licked her with a dry, paper tongue. Ceony laughed and scratched behind its ears. It panted with excitement. "Wherever did you come from?"

The door squeaked again, announcing Mg. Thane's arrival. He looked a little tired, but no worse for wear, and still wore that long indigo coat. "This one won't give me hives," he said with a smile that beamed in his eyes. "It's not the same, but I thought it would do, for now."

Wide-eyed, Ceony slowly stood, the paper dog yapping in its whispery voice and nudging her ankles with its muzzle. "You made this?" she asked, feeling her ribs knit over her lungs. "This . . . this is what you were doing last night?"

He scratched the back of his head. "Were you up? I apologize— I'm not used to having others in the house again."

*Again*, she thought, wondering. Mg. Thane seemed old enough to have had, perhaps, one apprentice before her, if that's what he meant. She had never bothered asking Mg. Aviosky about Mg.

Thane's previous pupils. And she didn't ask, not now. Not with this wonderful pup sniffing at her ankles.

He had made this for her. Because of Bizzy.

She looked from him to the dog, then back at him. She pinched the back of her arm to keep herself from crying, for her eyes had already made the decision without her consent.

"Thank you," she said, perhaps too quietly. "This . . . this means a lot to me. You didn't have to . . . thank you." She grasped the spatula. "Do you want some breakfast? I was about to make some—"

"I have good timing, then," Mg. Thane said, momentarily distracted by something up the stairs. "If you don't mind."

She shook her head no. Mg. Thane's eyes smiled and he vanished back up the stairs.

Ceony retreated back to the icebox for more eggs, the paper dog trailing behind her, sniffing the floor as it went. She watched its paper joints move together as a whole—so that's what Mg. Thane had meant.

She scooped the fennel off the floor.

"I think I'll name you Fennel," she said to it, slipping eggs into the pockets of her apron. "It may be a better cat name, but since you're not quite a real dog . . . well, it suits you."

Fennel merely cocked his head to the side, not quite understanding.

———

Mg. Thane ate his breakfast in the study, where he laid out several books and ledgers across his tidy-cluttered desk. Ceony practiced her reading illusion until just after lunch—she could get three of the fourteen pages to form in the air around her now, and Fennel tried to chase the mouse every time it appeared. The dog provided quite the distraction, but Ceony didn't mind one bit. She even fastened Bizzy's old collar around Fennel's neck. It fit perfectly.

Just after noon Mg. Thane called her into the library to show her the variety of papers kept on the table there, explaining the importance behind their thickness and grain. He seemed somewhat distracted and repeated himself here and there, but Ceony didn't point it out to him. She was merely relieved that the man hadn't assigned her physical labor. And, while the thought of such chores didn't irk her quite the way it had yesterday, she found herself almost grateful for the lesson. What Mg. Thane was teaching her had started to weasel its way into that part of her that wanted to *know*. She found herself paying rapt attention to Mg. Thane's lecture, and when she recited the details of the paper back to him at the end of the lesson, she beamed under his compliment, simple as it was.

"That's quite accurate," he said. He peered out the window, seeing something Ceony didn't beyond its glass.

"Are you stuck on something?" she finally asked as he put the sheets of paper into the wrong piles on the desk. She took them from his hands and placed them correctly, being sure to keep all the stacks straight.

"Hm?"

"Stuck on something," she repeated. "You're somewhere else today."

Unless he was always like that in the afternoon. Ceony had known him not quite a full day, so she had nothing to compare him to. She felt sure it wasn't madness, though.

"I suppose I am," he said after some thought, blinking and returning to the present. "I've a lot on my mind, what with a new apprentice and all."

"Am I your first?"

"Second and a half," he answered.

"Half?" Ceony asked. "How do you have half of an apprentice?"

"The last one didn't stay his full term," he explained without really explaining at all.

*Full term?* Ceony thought as a bead of fright washed down her throat. Was he in an accident? Quit? Laid off? Did magicians often lay off their apprentices?

Ceony bit the inside of her cheek. Surely Mg. Thane wouldn't fire her. The country was too desperate for paper magicians to lose any aspiring Folders, and she'd already bonded paper.

She hadn't considered the security of her position until now, and it made her stomach curdle. She'd worked so hard to get where she was now—even if it was on the path to becoming a Folder, not a Smelter—and she had still required the luck of receiving a scholarship.

For a moment she saw stars as she remembered the car crash, smelled burning onion as Mrs. Appleton had screamed at her after spilling that wine—

She blinked the memories away. This apprenticeship wasn't just another job; there would be no going back were she to be laid off. She'd be bound to paper and only paper, yet not legally authorized to do anything with it. She'd be a spent magician.

"You look like you've eaten something sour," Mg. Thane said, pulling a thick sheet of slate-colored paper from the upper-right pile on the desk, just beside the telegraph.

"I was just thinking of what a waste it would be, to bond something and then quit, is all."

"I agree. Well, let me show you some basic Folds, unless you covered that at Praff?"

Ceony shook her head no.

Mg. Thane dropped to the floor with his board, setting the square of paper on top of it. "Let's see how astute you actually are, Ceony," he said. A challenge, then.

She focused. The paper magician Folded the paper from corner to corner so it made a triangle. The thick parchment held the Fold well. "This is a half-point Fold—any Fold that turns a square into a triangle. And this is a full-point Fold"—he Folded the paper in half again—"any Fold that turns a triangle into a smaller triangle. With none to spare, of course."

Ceony nodded, watching quietly. He had done these two Folds when making the paper bird yesterday, before turning them into a second square and then the kite. He had her repeat the Folds and say their names, all while emphasizing that the paper's edges had to be completely aligned for the magic to take. Then his eyes took that faraway look again, becoming not quite as bright as they should have been.

"We'll start you on animation," he said, peering out the window again. "It's a good place to learn the Folds."

"I can work on this," Ceony said, "if you need to do something else."

Though deep in that space of wanting and knowing, she wished he'd stay and teach her.

What a silly thought that was.

Mg. Thane nodded and stood, his long coat rustling about his legs. She felt the disappointment keenly. When he disappeared into the hallway, Fennel poked his head in and trotted right up to Ceony's hip, where he turned around three times before lying down and sleeping. Ceony had a feeling a dog made of paper couldn't get tired, though. Must have all been in the enchantment.

She held her half-point and full-point Folds in her hands and stared out the open doorway, wondering after Mg. Thane. A thread of guilt tugged between her ribs as she remembered his working late to create Fennel for her. But surely that couldn't be the source of his . . . mental absence. And she'd been on her best behavior. Today, at least.

"I ought to make it up to him," she murmured to Fennel. "After all, any apprentice needs her magician's favor, or I'll be here six years instead of two."

Though her mind knew the Folds, she practiced them until her hands knew them, too, then resigned herself to the kitchen, where she pulled spices and wines out of the cupboards and recited *Pip's Daring Escape* under her breath, testing out different voice inflections that might coax the images on page four to life. She set one pot of water on the stove to boil for pasta and washed out last night's saucepan, setting it on the stove as well. She melted butter and added flour and milk to start a white sauce, something with lemon and garlic to go with the tied-up chicken in the icebox. When she couldn't find a lemon, she settled on tomato and basil. Everyone liked tomato and basil, and if Mg. Thane kept the ingredients stocked in his house, Ceony could be confident that he liked them as well—and that they were safe to use. Ceony had noted throughout her life that people with one sort of allergy often had others. She'd already started her apprenticeship on the wrong foot; hives would only make the other foot wrong, too.

When the chicken was nearly done, the bread sliced, and the sauce stirred into the penne, Mg. Thane emerged from his study.

"I need to give you more assignments if you have time to do this," he commented as Ceony peeked into the oven to check on the poultry. "I don't think this house has smelled this good since I've lived in it."

Ceony stifled a grin at the compliment and tucked a loose strand of hair behind her ear. "I wanted to thank you, for everything. And apologize, for my behavior yesterday. I wasn't quite myself."

"This wasn't necessary," he said, his bright eyes curious.

"It will be done in just a minute," she said, scuttling to the cupboards to locate the green ceramic bowl she had seen earlier. It rested on the highest shelf, so Ceony climbed onto the counter to grab it. "If you want to sit down, I set the table already."

Mg. Thane smiled, or did something between a smirk and a smile. It touched both eyes and lips. "All right. Thank you. But then I'm assigning you reading material and giving you two hundred sheets of paper to Fold."

Ceony dumped the pasta into the ceramic bowl and set it on the table first, then carefully transferred the chicken and roasted vegetables to a broad plate—Mg. Thane had no serving trays—and set that in front of Mg. Thane. He said nothing, but the arch of his eyebrows told her he was impressed. At least, Ceony hoped that's what it meant. It could also have meant that the magician had been saving that chicken for something else, and noted that Ceony had cooked it without permission. If that were the case, hopefully the taste would smooth out any hard feelings.

Ceony sat on her chair on the other side of the square table, then stood up again and asked, "Do you know how to carve a bird?"

"I believe Jonto does."

Ceony paled. She spied mirth in his eyes. Was that a joke?

Regardless, she picked up a fork and knife and sliced into the chicken herself. Gathering a few teaspoons of courage, she asked, "I was also wondering if my apprenticeship included a stipend of some sort, or a wage."

Mg. Thane laughed—light laughter that didn't come from the chest or the throat, but somewhere in between. "Ah, I understand. The plot thickens."

Ceony flushed. "No, what I said earlier was sincere, really. But people should talk over dinner, especially if they're going to live in the same house, and I thought my wages would be a good place to start, is all."

"The school board decides your stipend," Mg. Thane said, scooping up some tomato-basil pasta onto his plate. "So yes, you have one. I believe it's ten pounds a month, plus anything else I decide to pay you on the side."

*Ten pounds?* She focused on loading her own plate to hide her wide eyes. More than she had thought. She could send half of that home every month, should she be frugal.

She glanced back to the paper magician. "And . . . what will you pay me on the side?"

Mg. Thane held his fork loosely in his hand. "I'll not starve you, if that's your worry."

Ceony considered his tuna and rice and thought to make a point on the note of starving, but she bit back her tongue and took her seat. The paper magician made no move to say grace, and she seldom did, so she cut herself a morsel of chicken, watching him from the corner of her eye.

He stabbed his fork into two pieces of pasta and raised them to his lips. He tasted them, chewing, and his eyes brightened just a bit more. "I'd say, Ceony," he said after swallowing, "had I not been present for the lessons, I'd think you'd found a way to enchant pasta."

Ceony smiled. "You like it?"

He nodded, scooping up another bite. "It tastes just as good as it smells. That's a sign of a well-rounded person. I should congratulate you."

"On my person or my pasta?"

Light danced in his eyes. He didn't answer.

Ceony tasted her chicken, relieved it wasn't too dry. Three bites into her own dinner, Mg. Thane said, "Oldest of four."

"Two sisters, one brother," Ceony replied. "Do you have a large family? You seem like someone who suffered through a great deal of sisters."

"I've suffered through a great many people, but none of them sisters. I'm an only child."

*That explains a few things*, Ceony thought.

A few seconds of silence passed between chewing bites. Not wanting the time to grow long, Ceony asked, "When do you get groceries?"

He glanced at her. "When I run out, I suppose. Groceries are my most dreaded chore."

"Why?"

He lowered his fork and leaned his chin onto his hand, elbow on the table edge.

"They require going to the city," he stated. "And it's hot out, besides."

Ceony paused as she cut into the next morsel of chicken. "Do you freckle?"

He laughed. "Now there's a conversation turn—"

"I mean," Ceony began, "I could understand not going outside if you freckle." She glanced to her hands, spotted with freckles of her own. They had a tendency to cover any bit of skin exposed to the sun between March and October.

"I don't freckle," he said. She must have been frowning at her hands, for he added, "And there's nothing wrong with freckles, Ceony. Heaven forbid you look like everyone else in this place."

Ceony smiled and shoved some pasta in her mouth to keep the grin contained.

"And since you have so much extra time," Mg. Thane said, "your first quiz will be tomorrow morning."

# Chapter 4

Mg. Thane kept his promise by giving Ceony her first quiz the next morning—six o'clock in the morning, to be precise, and with Jonto as his messenger. Ceony awoke to the skeleton's Folded countenance grinning inches from her nose and shrieked loud enough to bring Fennel, who had been sniffing for mice in the living room downstairs. Ceony commanded the skeleton to "Cease" as Mg. Thane had earlier, and to her relief, the paper butler fell into a harmless heap of cardstock bones at the foot of her bed.

A small, almost thoughtless spell, but for the first moment since bonding to paper, Ceony felt like she might actually have some real power.

Mg. Thane quizzed her on the different paper types he had shown her in his office the day before. Thanks to her keen memory, Ceony got all of them right. The paper magician graded her with a content nod, then left her to her studies.

Her "studies" included reading the textbooks Mg. Thane had assigned her. She started with *Marcus Waters's Guide to Pyrotechnics*, as it sounded the most interesting, but the print was tiny and the book was only sparsely populated with figures, making it somewhat difficult to understand. She read only half a chapter. After a trip to the kitchen for toast, she started on *Anatomy of the Human Body Volume I*, which proved a much more fascinating—if slightly grotesque—read.

Over the next few days Ceony helped herself freely to the paper stacks in the library to practice her basic Folds. Mg. Thane had a habit of quizzing her at random times and without warning, so she fought to learn quickly. Thursday he quizzed her twice. Friday she practiced so many Folds she developed a blister on the tip of her right index finger. As a result, on Saturday Mg. Thane taught her how to make snowflakes—the same that had fallen from the library ceiling her first day as an apprentice.

"Cuts follow the same rules as Folds, more or less," he explained, sitting cross-legged on the floor of the library with his board across his lap. "You must make them precise if they're going to work, unless they're for decoration. Then it doesn't matter."

"Are these decoration?" Ceony asked, thinking of the small snowflake she had filched and hidden in her desk drawer. Last she checked, it had still felt cold.

Mg. Thane Folded a white square of paper into half-corner Folds, which turned it into a narrow triangle. "What do you think?"

She thought of the falling snow, the intricate snowflakes in all shapes and sizes scattered over the carpet. Each had been unique, just like real snow. "It's decorative," she answered.

"Very astute," Mg. Thane said, lifting a pair of scissors. "There is one cut that the snowflakes must have in order to become cold. Observe."

He held up the triangle and pressed his scissors into its thickest Fold, cutting just a centimeter below the highest point. He sliced out a small almond-shaped portion of paper and let it tumble onto his board.

"Chill," he commanded. Nothing happened to the paper that

Ceony could see, but when he handed it to her, it felt frosty. The coldness soothed her blister.

"The rest is creative inclination," he said.

By Monday the kitchen had run low on groceries.

"I can fetch them myself," Ceony said. "I don't mind."

Mg. Thane looked up from his desk, where a small ledger sat open, its cover pinned down on one side by a mug of lemon tea and on the other side by a butter knife. He held a pen in his left hand. "That's not a requirement, Ceony," he said.

"I don't mind," she repeated, smoothing the pleats in her skirt. "If I'm going to live here I might as well pull my weight." *And I wouldn't mind taking a break from this house.* "I can't keep making decent meals with the scraps left in your cupboards, if I may say so."

Mg. Thane smiled, again more in his eyes than in his mouth. "Also not a requirement. How is your reading coming?"

"I'm finished with human anatomy, and nearly finished with the Tao one."

Mg. Thane turned around in his chair and scanned the shelves behind him. Leaning down, he pulled a thick volume from the bottom shelf to his right and held it out to her. Its cover read *Anatomy of the Human Body Volume II.*

Ceony frowned and took the book.

"But if you insist," he went on, "I can call a buggy for you. Don't be out too late." He tapped the uninked side of his pen to his lips. "I suppose I should teach you animation. When you get back, then."

He handed her several bills—she was surprised that he trusted her with his money already—and went back to his ledger.

———

Her lessons in animation didn't actually start until her second week of tutelage. She began by prepping an eight-inch square of yellow paper with all its Folds, which she had to name as she completed them. The result was a crinkled square that had a starlike pattern pressed into it. Prepping the paper would make subsequent Folds easier to make, though the final creation would be more sluggish—so Mg. Thane explained.

"Now," the paper magician said, demonstrating on his own square of paper without preparation Folds, "we'll start simple. A frog."

Ceony remembered the demonstration of the paper frog from her first day. She remembered it well enough that in her mind's eye she could see Mg. Thane's fingers forming every Fold, and she felt confident she could create an identical creature without additional instruction. However, she kept this information to herself and watched the paper magician work, searching for any Folds her memory may have missed. She found none and mentally patted herself on the back.

"Breathe," Mg. Thane commanded his paper frog, and the animal shook with spirit and hopped from his hand. The paper frog made it two feet from Mg. Thane's knee before the magician commanded it "Cease" and left it inanimate once more.

Despite the seeming simplicity of the spell, Ceony's hands itched to complete it. She steadied them, not wanting to appear hotheaded, not wanting to shirk Mg. Thane's lesson. She waited for his permission to Fold.

Her back stiffened just a bit, and she glanced to her yellow square of paper, retracing memories from the past several days. When had that strain of discipline entered her head? She couldn't recall making the decision to sit as obediently as a paper dog.

She glanced to Fennel, who scratched behind one of his paper ears in the corner by the door.

Licking her lips, Ceony began Folding, regardless, following the same steps Mg. Thane had shown her. She felt his eyes on her—an oddly heavy stare—but he made no comment.

Careful to line up the paper's edges just so, Ceony formed a paper frog and held it out in her hand, examining her slightly crinkled creation. She whispered "Breathe" to it, and to her relief, the animal came alive. It wiggled one leg, then the other, and jumped sleepy jumps in her palm. A smile tickled her lips.

Fennel lifted his head and peered toward her, sniffing the air.

"Well done," Mg. Thane said. "I want you to practice making them a few times before attempting them without the preparation Folds. Tomorrow we'll start on cranes and jays."

"Only one day on frogs?" Ceony asked as Mg. Thane rose from the floor, his strange indigo coat falling around his legs as he did so.

The paper magician quirked a dark eyebrow. "You hardly need more than a day," he said, gesturing to Ceony's still-hopping frog with his chin. "You're coming along rather well for someone who wanted to be a Smelter."

Ceony started and dropped her frog, which rolled over onto its back and squirmed like a capsized beetle. Fennel rushed across the room and batted at it with his paws. "How did you know about that?"

Mg. Thane merely smiled and set his Folding board beside the desk, not an inch off of where it had been placed before, centered between the desk's front-left and back-left legs. "Don't forget your reading," he added, and he left the room.

---

As promised, Ceony received lessons on Folding birds, as well as fish, and was later quizzed on Folding frogs without paper preparation. She failed that test, but only because Mg. Thane insisted her frog had to beat his in a race, and she lost by two yards. A bizarre way to rate her performance. Ceony would have protested had her teacher not promised she could retake the "test" as many times as she wanted before he submitted her grades to Tagis Praff.

It was while Folding yet another frog for this challenge that the telegraph in the library began to click. Ceony sat at the library desk, having pushed aside several stacks of paper to give herself a decent workspace, and started at the sudden tap-tap-tap of the telegraph. Fennel, snoozing at her heels, leapt up and began barking at the contraption, though his quiet paper larynx couldn't compete with the machine. Setting down a half-finished lime-green frog and scooting her chair back, Ceony stood and hunched over the telegraph, eyes scanning the slip of paper jutting out from it.

found in solihull stop

The words whipped away from her eyes as a new hand pinched the message's corner and pulled it from the machine. Ceony didn't need to turn to know Mg. Thane stood behind her. She spied the name Alfred at the end of the message as it flew past her.

She stepped back and watched Mg. Thane read the note, his bright-green eyes holding their secrets, for once. She found nothing in his expression save for concentration and a spot on his chin where he had missed shaving that morning. He read the telegram in the space of half a breath and crumpled the paper in his hands.

"What's in Solihull?" Ceony asked. The city was over a hundred miles away, to the northwest.

Mg. Thane gave her a small smile—one of his odd smiles, for it was all lip and no eye—and said, "Just a friend." He then turned on his heel and strode out of the library, nearly stepping on Fennel as he went.

Ceony peered after him, watching him cross the hall and disappear into his bedroom. What sort of friend had been "found" in Solihull?

She stood there a moment, wondering at the light fleeing from her mentor's eyes. She had the feeling of reading a story with all its even pages torn out. What did that telegram say?

Chewing on her bottom lip, Ceony sank back into her chair and returned to her frog, only half her mind on its Folds. She had begun forming its back legs when Mg. Thane returned with a large stack of things in his hands, paper and books and ledgers and pencils. He dropped them beside Ceony and straightened up two paper stacks on the desk before speaking.

"A spontaneous lesson," the paper magician announced, taking a sheet of off-white typewriter paper from the desk. He picked up his board and sat cross-legged on the floor. Hesitating a few seconds, Ceony took another sheet of the same and joined him.

"Watch carefully, this will be quick," Mg. Thane said, setting the paper longways before him. He Folded up an inch of it, creased it with his thumb, then turned it over to Fold it up another inch.

"A paper fan," he explained, flipping the paper over again. "I'm sure you've made these before."

"As a child," Ceony said, glancing to his face.

He turned the paper over and over, Folding it up and up, somehow managing to get each Fold perfect without a ruler. "The trick is to make it even," he explained. "Every panel must be the same length and width, or the spell won't hold. You can measure it if you like, but focusing on that first Fold and using it as a guide works just as well. If there's anything left over, you can cut it off."

He finished the fan, having nothing to spare, and pinched its bottom. "It doesn't need to be secured," he added. Turning the fan away from Ceony and toward the door, he flapped it lightly. One, two, three gusts of wind spat out from the paper, too strong to be ordinary, but too weak to do any harm.

He set the fan down. "Simple enough. I want you to practice it while I'm gone."

The words tumbled over one another in Ceony's mind. "G-Gone?" she repeated. "Gone where?"

"Magician's business, as usual," he said, standing. He left his board on the floor and returned to the stack of things he'd brought in. "*The Art of Papier-Mâché*," he said, reading the title of the lowest book in the stack. He pointed to the ledger above it. "I want you to record notes on it while you read. Take thorough enough notes and I won't make you write a report."

Ceony's jaw fell. "But—"

"*A Living Paper Garden*," he said, gesturing to the next book in the stack. "Do the same. I bookmarked chapters five, six, and twelve; they have exercises in them I'd like you to do. And *A Tale of Two Cities*. It's just a good book. Have you read it?"

Ceony stared at the paper magician, words caught in her throat. He'd gone mad again. He'd tricked her into thinking he wasn't mad, and yet now he'd proved—

"And I want that paper fan perfected," he added, withdrawing his hand. "Made well, it can give gusts that would embarrass a thunderstorm. And the reading I previously assigned you."

Shaking her head, Ceony stood and asked, "How long do you plan to be gone?"

Mg. Thane shrugged. "Hopefully not too long. It's quite the bother to break one's routine too many days in a row. Do you know Patrice's contact information, just in case?"

"Patrice?" Ceony repeated, her voice a little higher. "Magician Aviosky? I . . . yes, but—"

"Excellent!" Mg. Thane clapped her on the shoulder and strode out of the library. "I'll be on my way. Try not to burn anything down."

Ceony followed after him. "You're leaving *now*?"

"I am," he replied as he vanished into his bedroom. Somehow in the few minutes between receiving the telegram and delivering the pile of homework to the library, he had managed to pack a bag. He returned to the hallway with it in tow. He swept a hand back through his dark hair, and in that moment Ceony saw a flicker in his eyes and a thinning of his lips. He was worried.

"Is everything . . . all right?" she asked, hesitating at the threshold of the library, unsure of her bounds.

"Hm?" he asked, his countenance smoothing between ticks of the library clock. "Quite fine. Do take care, Ceony." He walked down the hallway as far as the lavatory, where he turned around and added, "And keep the doors locked."

Ceony watched him disappear down the stairs and listened to the quiet padding of his shoes below. Fennel licked her sock.

Hurrying to the library window, Ceony peered outside to see Mg. Thane walk past the paper flowers in his yard and beyond the warded gate, down the dirt road. Did he have a buggy waiting for him?

Ceony didn't realize she had her face pressed to the glass until her breath fogged her vision. The paper magician stepped out of her line of sight and left her alone in his cluttered, barely familiar cottage set in the middle of no-man's-land.

*Keep the doors locked.*

Ceony's heart drooped in her chest.

# CHAPTER 5

*PAPIER-MÂCHÉ IS TRADITIONALLY DONE in two forms,* Ceony wrote in her ledger with a tired hand, *paper strips and paper mulch, to which is added either glue or starch.*

Sighing, Ceony set her pencil down and stared across her bedroom to its single window over the bed. The sun cast leafy shadows across her pillow.

Would Mg. Thane return today? She didn't have even a tenth of her latest homework stack completed if he did. Surely he wouldn't penalize her for that, but Ceony had come to learn that the paper magician only sometimes did what she expected.

The house, its doors and windows still locked from last night, sat quiet enough that if Ceony held her breath, she could hear the library clock ticking in the next room. Fennel had taken to adventuring downstairs, and Ceony had shoved Jonto's inanimate bones into a closet in the office and left him there. Now the place seemed . . . lifeless.

She glanced down. The words in the papier-mâché book blurred in and out. Yawning, she shut both it and the ledger and dropped them onto the floor, hearing a loud thunk in return. She pulled out

*Anatomy of the Human Body Volume II* and flipped to her bookmark halfway through the chapter detailing the cardiovascular system. She stared at a picture of a dissected artery, turned the page, and stared at a diagram of a heart cut longwise to show its four chambers. She read a paragraph and shut the book again.

She heard Fennel climb up the stairs, pause, then climb back down. Eager to get away from her desk, Ceony abandoned her work and went downstairs.

She found Fennel sniffing about the door to Mg. Thane's office, perhaps smelling Jonto, since Mg. Thane would never leave food sitting out. Ceony opened the door and the paper dog ran in, sniffing as he went. He stood on his hind legs to investigate the paper chains hanging from the window and, as suspected, trotted to the closet to smell after the paper butler.

Ceony glanced to the ivy-covered window. So quiet in the house. So irresponsible for a magician to leave his new apprentice on her own, wasn't it? She should report it to Mg. Aviosky.

She lowered her gaze to the desk. *Might as well take advantage of his absence before I do that,* she thought.

The tiniest smile teased her lips as she sat down in Mg. Thane's desk chair and began opening his drawers, none of which had been locked. She found nothing interesting—a few ledgers of conference notes, spare pens and pencils, a bizarre multipointed paper star that looked like it belonged on the end of a mace. A lint brush, a small sewing kit. Ceony made sure to leave everything straight and tidy before closing each drawer. She had no doubt Mg. Thane would notice a pen knocked a few millimeters out of place.

She reached for the wire note holder, running her fingers over the edge of the thank-you letter she had mailed out over a year ago. Fifteen thousand pounds.

She chewed on her lip, not wanting to dwell on that mystery for the moment. She thumbed through the other letters, reading off names, some preceded by "Mg." or "Dr." She spotted one that read "Alfred Hughes." Thinking of the telegram, she pulled it free, only to discover it was an old Christmas card without a photo. Her memory tickled at her—she'd heard that name before. A Mg. Alfred Hughes sat on the Magicians' Cabinet, didn't he? Yes . . . he did. A Siper—a rubber magician. He'd given a speech at Tagis Praff once. Mg. Thane had friends in high places.

Oddly enough, none of the letters read "Thane" on them—none appeared to be from family. Mg. Thane had mentioned being an only child, but what about his parents? His cousins? Surely he had cousins.

She scoured the bookshelves next, finding more textbooks and old novels, ledgers filled from cover to cover. The only thing that stood out was a Granger Academy yearbook dated 1888–1889. Apparently she and Mg. Thane had attended the same secondary school, albeit twelve years apart. Odd that Mg. Aviosky would assign her to a magician so young, but there were few other options for Folders. Perhaps that was why she had sat so rigidly in the buggy.

Fennel pawed at her shoes.

"I know, I have work to do," Ceony said, suppressing a sigh. She scooped the paper dog into her arms, laughing as he wagged his tail, and carefully pushed Mg. Thane's chair back under the desk.

She spent the rest of the day Folding frogs and fans, reading more about anatomy than she ever wanted to know, and doodling in the margins of her notes on papier-mâché.

---

When Mg. Thane didn't return the next day, Ceony began to worry.

She had never considered herself someone prone to worrying, and it seemed almost silly to worry over someone whom she'd only worked with for a short time, let alone someone she hadn't wanted to work with in the first place, but she worried.

She imagined that flicker in his eyes just before he'd left, thought of the privacy of the telegram. And she worried.

She thought again to contact Mg. Aviosky, but didn't. What would she say? Today, at least, she had no desire to get Emery Thane in trouble, so she busied herself with chores to take her mind off of things.

She fried fish and chips for lunch, enough for one. She wiped down the countertops and swept out the kitchen. She gathered her laundry to wash it.

Outside her bedroom, Ceony peered down the hallway to Mg. Thane's bedroom door, which he had left closed. It would be kind to wash his, too, wouldn't it?

Leaving her own dirty clothes in a pile near the stairs, Ceony let herself into the paper magician's bedroom and spied around.

His bed was larger than hers, understandably, and the window across from its foot was larger as well. Three different candlesticks sat atop the dresser by the door, which was missing three of its bronze handles. A collection of beads, some sort of jewelry box, and a variety of paper gadgets that looked like chunks of machinery sat all around them. A bottle of brandy and a glass sat on the nightstand beside a novel without a cover, a bottle with a ship inside of it, and a tall paper box painted gray, violet, and peach.

There was a shelf stacked with larger sheets of paper, writing utensils, and books; a closet full of more long coats and dress slacks; and a hamper brimming with dirty clothes.

She put her hands on either side of her face like a horse's blinders and went straight for the hamper. No snooping today. She was nineteen years old—she could respect a man's privacy.

She washed clothes until her knuckles turned red, then hung them on a line in the backyard to dry.

Ceony woke up alone again the next day. After finishing her anatomy book, she took down the laundry and folded it. Unsure of where Mg. Thane kept the particulars of his clothing, she left it on his bed for him to put away when he returned.

She paused at a bookshelf on her way out. Good heavens, the man owned a lot of books. She perused the titles, wondering why these books had been kept in his room instead of in the library. Not snooping, not really. Just curiosity.

She found only a handful of textbooks—most of the volumes appeared to be leisure reading, both by popular and unpopular authors. She found a second copy of *A Tale of Two Cities* and a poetry book by Matthew Arnold. At the end of that particular shelf she found a hymnal.

"Strange," she said, pulling the leather-bound book off the shelf. Her fingers left prints in the dust sprinkling its cover. Mg. Thane didn't seem the religious sort. He didn't say grace at dinner. The spine cracked. Ceony flipped through the pages, noting the excellent condition of the book's spine.

Then she discovered the gold-etched inscription on the cover. It read "The Thanes."

"Thanes?" she asked aloud. Who was the other Thane? Mg. Thane certainly wasn't married, and the book looked too new to belong to his parents. Perhaps the paper magician had a bastard child out in Norwich and this had been someone's clever way of blackmailing him.

She laughed at the idea and flipped back through the pages again, spying hymns both familiar and unfamiliar.

Something fell out from the back pages—pressed wildflowers.

Crouching, Ceony picked up the purple and orange blossoms with a soft touch and examined their brittle beauty. She wasn't sure what sort of flowers these were. Which of the Thanes had kept them here?

Fennel barked from the hallway. Ceony returned the hymnal to its place on the shelf and wiped her dusty fingers on her skirt. She stepped out of her mentor's room and shut the door behind her.

She didn't enter it again.

---

A few days later, at approximately six in the morning, Ceony woke to a loud pounding on her bedroom door. She shrieked and jumped to her feet, remembering first Mg. Thane's admonition to keep the doors locked—

"We're learning about paper boats today!" Mg. Thane's cheery voice said from the other side of the door. "Bright and early! Up we go!"

Ceony's pulse pounded in her neck. Pulling the top blanket off her bed and hiding her nightgown with it, she cracked open the door. Mg. Thane stood there just as he had left, fully dressed and donning that indigo coat.

"I . . . when did you get back?" she asked.

He shrugged. "Just now. Where did you put Jonto?"

"In the . . . ," she began, but instead said, "How did things go? Did you see this friend of yours?"

"Things went, at least," he answered. "And thank you for doing my laundry, but you didn't need to, as I wasn't here to wear it. Library in ten minutes."

He clapped his hands once and strode down the hallway.

Six days. The man had been gone six days, and that was all he had to say about it?

Ceony shut the door and rubbed the back of her neck. *Then again, what right do I have to know where he goes?*

Shaking her head, she dressed and combed through her hair, braiding it behind her left ear. At least he hadn't mentioned more testing.

By the time Ceony made it to the library, Mg. Thane had already taken his usual position on the carpet with his board on his lap. A few pieces of rectangular paper rested beside him. Ceony studied him as he approached. Unsoiled clothes, clean shaven, but his shoulders had a slight stoop to them, and faint circles lined his eyes. Tired, then, but from what? Why make the effort of another lesson when he should be getting some rest?

Ceony sat across from him and didn't ask. Let him keep his secrets, then.

"For a boat, we start with a half-Fold, then two double dog-ear Folds," Mg. Thane explained, Folding as he spoke.

"What good is a paper boat?" Ceony asked. "No one can fit on it, and it will sink."

"Ah, but an enchanted paper boat won't sink easily."

"Easily?"

"It will sink," he said with a nod, more toward his knees than to Ceony, "but slowly. Generations of Folders have yet to waterproof paper, but they can at least make it stubborn. Boats are useful for relaying messages when sending one through air is too bothersome. Or too risky. A little outdated with telegraphs and this mythical telephone, perhaps, but you should learn it anyway."

He flipped the spell toward her and Folded the paper's edges to form the boat's base. "Fold it like an animation. I'm sure you remember the rules."

Ceony nodded, but as Mg. Thane finished the last Folds, she saw up his loose coat sleeve to a bandage coiled thickly around his right forearm.

Something inside of her twanged, like a fiddle string had been stretched down her torso, fastened between throat and navel. With a soft voice, she asked, "What happened to your arm?"

Mg. Thane's fingers stilled. He glanced up at her, then to his arm. He pulled the sleeve down to the palm of his hand. "Just a bump," he said. "I often forget how much focus walking requires."

She frowned. That same string twisted, and she had a distinct feeling her tutor was hiding something.

She wondered if his arm hurt.

The paper magician handed her a sheet of paper and had her copy his Folds, which she managed to get right on her first try. The fact gave her little comfort.

Mg. Thane stood, board under his uninjured arm. "Now down to the river to test them out!"

Now the string pulled tight enough to snap. Muscles all over Ceony's body went rigid, especially in the neck, shoulders, and knees. "R-River? The one outside?"

Mg. Thane grinned. "There's hardly one inside, is there?"

Ceony felt herself root to the floor. Mg. Thane offered a hand to help her up, but she couldn't lift her arms to take it. Her pulse quickened and her cheeks reddened. "I . . ." She cleared her throat. "Can we test them in the lavatory? The tub? Please?"

He lowered his hand. "I suppose. You're not hydrophobic, are you?"

Ceony's face grew hotter.

"Oh," he said, sobering. "I admit that surprises me. You don't seem the type."

Ceony managed to loosen her shoulders enough for a shrug. "Everyone is afraid of something, right?"

The paper magician nodded, albeit slowly. "True. Very . . . true. The tub it is, then."

He offered his hand a second time. Ceony grasped it and let him pull her up, getting a strange tingle in her fingertips just before he released her.

She pressed the fingers against her cheek to cool her face. She followed Mg. Thane to the lavatory, where they crowded around the bathtub and cast the spells "Float" and "Endure" on the boats. Before hers had a chance to sink, Ceony excused herself to her room and picked up *Astrology for Youth*, but for some reason she had a difficult time concentrating.

---

Fennel whined an airy whine at Ceony's feet as she dropped the last fish cakes into the fryer. He wagged his tail, hopeful.

"You can't eat it, silly thing," Ceony chided the paper dog, scooting him back with her foot to open the oven. She pulled from it a shallow ceramic dish filled with asparagus. She had hated asparagus until she worked as a caterer during her last year of secondary school. Apparently anyone of importance ate asparagus, so she had coaxed herself into tolerating it as well.

The stair door opened and Mg. Thane emerged, looking somewhat less tired than he had that morning. Perhaps he had napped while Ceony cooked dinner. "Mmm," he said. "I do hope you're cooking for two."

"I'm cooking for two so long as I can burn that papier-mâché ledger without your review of it," Ceony said. She picked up a fish cake with a fork and waved it back and forth, claiming both the magician's and the paper dog's attention. "It's busywork I'd rather not finish, but if I must, I'll finish it with a basket full of fish cakes in my lap."

Mg. Thane laughed. "I'm sure this sort of bribery is disapproved by the school board. I really should read those letters they send me . . ."

Ceony let the fish cake hover, and Mg. Thane waved a hand. "Yes yes, let it burn. I'm famished."

Grinning at her victory, Ceony put the fish cake back and pulled the last of them from the fryer before taking the dishes to the table she had already set. Mg. Thane pulled out her chair before sitting in his own.

"We need groceries again," Ceony said, setting a fish cake on her plate before passing them to Mg. Thane. "And I was wondering what day of the month to expect my stipend."

"I shan't ever partake of my apprentice's cooking without discussing money, so it seems," he replied, setting two fish cakes on his own plate. He lifted his fork, again foregoing grace. "I will, however—"

At least one more word escaped the paper magician's lips, but a loud explosion in the hallway muffled the sound.

Ceony dropped the asparagus dish onto the table and whirled around, staring with wide eyes as bits of wood and paper blew in on a breeze from the hallway and drifted into the dining room. The smell of dust and paint mixed with haddock and chives. Mg. Thane leapt to his feet.

Loud footfalls like sarcastic applause sounded in the hallway. Hard shoes with heels. Ceony stepped forward, but Mg. Thane held out his arm, stopping her. All the mirth had vanished from his face. He looked altered—not cheery nor distracted, but stony. Taller, and his coat seemed to bristle about him like a wild cat's fur.

A woman stepped into the dining room. She was stunning—tall with long, waving hair such a dark brown it looked almost black, coffee-colored eyes, and fair skin without the slightest trace of freckles. She donned a black shirt well fitted to her rather ample figure, and tight pants with panels over the knees. She wore two-inch gray heels that fastened with two cords around her ankles.

There was something familiar about her. It took Ceony only seconds to pinpoint where she'd seen this woman's face before.

The fortuity box.

Mg. Thane paled. "Lira?"

Ceony's stomach sank. That was all the response her body could manage before the woman stepped forward, a vial of dark-red liquid clutched in her hand.

It happened in a blur. Mg. Thane grabbed Ceony's arm and tried to pull her behind him, but the woman, Lira, dribbled the red liquid into her hand and flung it toward Ceony, shouting, "Blast!"

An impact like a giant fist slammed into Ceony. It knocked the air from her lungs and sent her flying into the corner of the table, hard enough that the table turned over with the impact, dumping its still-hot contents over the floor with a loud crash as ceramic plates split into hundreds of pieces across the hardwood. Ceony's backside slammed into the dining room wall, and she slumped to the floor.

Everything went black for a moment, then morphed into shadows and light. Ceony blinked several times as something else thumped against the wall nearby—she felt the vibrations through the wood. Her vision clear and her back throbbing, she lifted her head to see Mg. Thane pressed against the wall, held up by invisible hands. He struggled to speak, but something unseen held his jaw closed. The artery on the side of his neck had swollen.

Ceony looked at her hands, spotting blood on them. She panicked for a split second until she realized the blood was cold and not her own. The liquid Lira had thrown at her—blood.

Her whole body froze.

*Blood.*

*Flesh magic.*

Lira was an Excisioner. A practitioner of the forbidden craft.

Ceony looked back up to see Lira grab Mg. Thane's collar and rip it down clear to his sternum, exposing his chest. "I'm finally leaving, dearie," she whispered, "and I'm taking you with me."

She plunged her right hand into his chest. Ceony stifled a cry. A golden ring of dust sparkled about Lira's wrist as Mg. Thane screamed between clenched teeth. Lira pulled her red-stained hand back out, clasping a still-beating heart between her bloodied fingers.

Sweat beaded on Ceony's forehead and temples. Her own heart sped in her chest, making her dizzy.

*Put your head down!* she thought, skin cold. She tried to feign unconsciousness, but her body trembled and tears drizzled from her eyes. If this woman could so easily defeat Mg. Thane, then she would kill Ceony in an instant. She likely had meant to.

The heels clicked against the floor. Ceony opened her eyes, peering between toppled chairs. Lira dripped several droplets of Thane's blood into her palm, smiled, then threw the blood to the floor. She vanished in a swirl of red smoke.

Ceony cried out the moment the woman faded. Scrambling to her feet, her hips screaming with deep-set bruises, she ran to Mg. Thane. Before she reached him, the spell holding him up wore off and he slumped to the floor.

# CHAPTER 6

"No, no!" Ceony cried, tears streaming readily from her cheeks. She put an arm behind Mg. Thane's neck and laid him down, gaping at the deep, scarlet hole in his chest, still rimmed with glittering gold magic. The hole grew smaller and smaller with each of her own heartbeats.

Fennel whined beside her, an airy, paper whine. Ceony, shaking, looked to the dog, then back to Mg. Thane, his skin growing paler and paler with each passing second.

She bolted upright and ran for the study, knocking a kitchen chair out of her way as she went.

Her mind swirled, her legs felt numb, and her hands perspired as she climbed over rubble in the hallway that had once been the front door and threw herself into the study. She ran for the shelves of paper, frantically sifting through them until she found a thicker piece. Not the thickest, but she had no time to be choosy.

She ran back into the dining room and slipped on spilled blood. She stumbled onto her knees and winced, but began Folding right there, against the wooden floorboards. She didn't know the Folds—she couldn't—but she had to try.

Visions of Mg. Thane's handiwork zoomed through her mind. His Folding of the bird, the fish, the fortuity box. The paper trinkets, sculptures, and chains lying around the house. The few lessons on paper magic she had taken notes on at the school. The half-point Fold, the full-point Fold. Folds she didn't know the names of. Anything. *Just line the edges up.*

She Folded the paper in half, then in half again, working it until she had the square that started Mg. Thane's long-necked bird. From there she made up the rest, her brain summoning images from *Anatomy of the Human Body.* Her hands stilled. It looked something like a heart. Something like it . . .

She crawled to Mg. Thane, to the still-closing pit in his chest, and commanded the heart, "Breathe!"

It pumped weakly in her hands. She pushed it into the bloody cavity and withdrew her hands just before Mg. Thane's skin closed around it.

The paper magician didn't stir.

"Please," she cried, his blood on her fingers. She patted his cheeks, slapped them, pressed her ear to his chest. She could hear the paper heart pumping weakly, like the heart of an old man on his deathbed.

He didn't stir.

"You have to live!" she screamed at him, tears falling from her chin onto his chest. If magic couldn't save him . . . this was all she had!

Breaths coming in short gasps, Ceony stood, ran up the stairs, and bolted to the library. Grabbing the telegraph, she connected the wires to the one person whose route she knew—Mg. Aviosky.

Her trembling fingers punched in the code quickly. She swallowed against a dry throat.

thane hurt stop come immediately stop emergency stop excisioner stole his heart stop

She backed away from the telegraph as though it were a corpse and pressed her palm to her mouth to suppress a sob.

Fennel barked at her feet, jumping wildly on his paper legs.

As soon as Ceony glanced at the dog, Fennel darted into the hallway. Ceony ran after him, following him back down the stairs and into the dining room. She heard Thane's rasping breath just before she saw him.

"Thane!" she cried, dropping to her knees beside him.

He looked dead, his eyes merely slits and his veins showing through his white skin. He tried to lift a finger to point, but dropped it. "Window," he said, the words straining through his throat. "Second . . . chain. Get . . ."

Ceony jumped up and ran back into the study, distinctly remembering the chains hanging over the window there. She counted the second one from the left and pulled it down, a tightly knit chain made of Folded rectangles. She also grabbed the second from the right, a looping chain of ovals.

Rushing back into the dining room, she showed them to Thane. "Which one?" she asked.

He weakly jerked his chin toward the tight-knit chain made of rectangles. "Around . . . chest," he whispered.

Pinching the end of the chain, Ceony leaned over Thane and pushed it under his back, then brought it forward over his chest so that the ends overlapped.

"Ease," Thane said weakly, and the chain tightened about him at the command. Thane sucked in a deep breath of air and coughed.

Ceony lifted his head to help him. When he finished, he opened his eyes and looked at her.

She gasped. His eyes . . .

Their light had vanished.

No brightness, no emotion. Just dead, glass eyes.

Her tears started anew.

"I telegrammed Magician Aviosky," she said, every other word shuddering in her throat. "She'll be here. Someone will be here to help you."

"That was wise," he said, his weakened voice almost a monotone. "The closest doctor is . . . far."

"Oh heaven," Ceony whispered, pushing locks of hair from Mg. Thane's forehead. "What has she done to you?"

"Lira . . . took my heart," he said matter-of-factly. Like a talking textbook.

"I know," Ceony whispered. "Why?"

"To stop me."

"From what?"

But Mg. Thane didn't answer. His glassy eyes shifted slowly about their sockets, taking in the room with no expression.

Ceony kept brushing his forehead, even when she had pushed back all his black locks. "What is the chain?" she asked, wiping her cheek on her shoulder. If she could just keep him talking . . .

"A vitality chain," he said quietly, his dull eyes now focused on the ceiling above him. "It will keep this new heart beating, for a time."

"A time?"

"A paper heart will not last long, especially one crafted poorly," he said. "The chain will make it last a day, two at best."

"But you can't die!" Ceony cried, and Mg. Thane didn't so much as flinch at the volume, or at the tear that struck him on the bridge of his nose. He didn't seem aware of her at all. "You have too much to teach me! And you're too nice to die!"

He made no response.

Gently setting his head down, Ceony stood and retreated to the front room, stepping over debris and wiping away tears that refused to stop running from her eyes. She took a pillow from the couch and a blanket from a chest shoved behind it and tried to make Mg. Thane as comfortable as possible, for she dared not try to move him. Fennel sat by his side, still whining and wagging his tail anxiously behind him.

Two hours after sunset, three people climbed their way over the rubble-filled hallway and into the dining room. Ceony knew all three, if two only from memory. Mg. John Katter, a Smelter, and Mg. Alfred Hughes, the Siper, both sat on the Magicians' Cabinet—Katter for Agriculture and Hughes for Criminal Affairs. Mg. Aviosky stood among them.

Ceony, who had cried herself sore and dry, retold the story with every detail she could muster, including her reading on Mg. Thane with the fortuity box. She wondered if, perhaps, she had mistakenly willed Lira's appearance, and that this was all her fault.

"Don't be ridiculous," Mg. Aviosky assured her as Magicians Katter and Hughes studied Mg. Thane lying on the floor by the light of four candles. "The only one who can manipulate Emery Thane's future is Emery Thane himself."

Mg. Hughes hovered over Mg. Thane for some time, prodding his neck and chest with rubber gloves. Ceony knew he was a Siper, and she wondered, briefly, if the gloves were enchanted, especially since he tucked the pair into his coat pocket instead of tossing them in the trash. "It's Excision work all right," he said in low tones, "and powerful at that. I thought the wards would keep them from coming here, Lira especially."

"Wards?" Ceony asked, heart thumping. "What wards? Why would she hurt Magician Thane? Who is she?"

Mg. Hughes frowned and stroked his short, white beard. Mg. Aviosky put a hand on Ceony's shoulder and said, "Perhaps you should go to bed, Miss Twill. You've had a hard day."

"No!" Ceony cried. "You have to let me stay here with him. You have to let me help!"

Mg. Aviosky frowned, and in the dim lighting it made her look much older, and much taller. "You may no longer be a pupil at Tagis Praff, Miss Twill, but you are still under the board's jurisdiction. Go upstairs and get some rest. It is not a request. I will discuss matters further with you in the morning."

Ceony's skeleton slumped within her skin. She stepped away from Mg. Hughes so she could see Mg. Thane on the floor. His eyes were closed and his breathing sounded even, albeit faint. Mg. Katter scribbled something in a notepad beside him.

Clutching her hands over her breast, Ceony stepped past Mg. Thane, watching him, and took to the stairs. Mg. Hughes shut the door behind her, but she knew he didn't lock it, since he wouldn't have the key to do so.

Hesitating for a moment, Ceony tromped up the stairs and to her bedroom door, where she then slipped off her shoes and carefully, very carefully, snuck her way back downstairs, skipping the squeaky ninth step.

She squatted on the first stair, shying away from the thin light filtering through the door's keyhole, and listened.

". . . getting close," Mg. Hughes's voice said quietly. "Emery's the one who tipped us off for the Lillith capture, if you remember. That was less than two months ago."

"But have there been attempts on the other members?" Mg. Aviosky said, sounding very worried. More worried than Ceony had ever heard her sound.

"Magician Karl Tode was killed yesterday morning in a similar manner," Mg. Hughes replied. "A hunter, like Emery. But it wasn't Lira's handiwork. She's . . . much cleaner than her accomplices."

Mg. Katter said, "But that's it. Nothing else since they took out

Piper last year. Don't you remember what Gabon Suter said when we arrested him? Reeling around in his chair like a madman . . . 'We'll get the rest. Hunt us down like animals, but we'll turn on you . . .'"

"It could just be a personal vendetta in this case," Mg. Aviosky said. "Unless my information on their relationship isn't accurate."

"'I'm leaving,'" Mg. Hughes said, repeating the words Ceony had related to him, "'and I'm taking you with me.' That's all she said. No letters, no ceremony. I know this woman, Patrice. She wouldn't just do the deed for revenge and not make a show of it, unless she did so outside of Miss Twill's witness."

"Perhaps," Mg. Katter cut in, "she's finally gotten smart. In and out, job done."

Mg. Hughes said, "No. Not her." He paused. "She knows Emery is critical to the syndicate, they all do. He's personally invested in it. That, and she's always kept a . . . keen . . . interest in him."

*Syndicate?* Ceony thought. Her legs began to cramp, but she dared not move, not yet. Excisioners, and a syndicate?

Was Mg. Thane personally policing the dark-magic ring? And what "keen interest" did Mg. Hughes refer to?

The floorboards shifted again, and someone blocked the light coming through the keyhole. Ceony held her breath, but the door didn't open. Instead someone leaned against it, which made the talk in the dining room that much fainter.

"Sounds like she plans on leaving England," Mg. Katter said, so muffled Ceony could barely tell one word from the next. "Perhaps Europe altogether."

"So what do we do?" asked Mg. Aviosky, the one against the door.

"Document it," Mg. Hughes said slowly. "Gather what evidence we can, sketches and the like. Find any blood on the floor that Lira might have used."

"Go after her?" asked Mg. Katter.

"It has to go through the Cabinet," Mg. Hughes replied, sounding exasperated. "We have to get approval, sanction off this house, assign a force."

Ceony clutched her skirt in her fists. Approval? Lira would be long gone by then!

"She'll be out of reach by then," said Mg. Aviosky, as if she had heard Ceony's thoughts and agreed with them.

"You must understand, Patrice, that Excisioners are a tricky matter," Mg. Hughes explained. "They are wildly dangerous, and if they touch you, they can pull magic through your body. It is a killing magic. One cannot merely race in and capture them. And if she disappeared in a blood cloud as Miss Twill stated, she could be anywhere within a thirty-mile radius by now."

A moment of silence made Ceony aware of her pulse drumming in her ears. Her face felt hot, and her eyes stung. Would they really let this woman get away?

"What of Emery Thane?" Mg. Aviosky asked, almost too soft to hear.

Another long pause before Mg. Hughes said, "We make him as comfortable as we can."

*No!* Ceony's mind screamed, and she clamped both hands over her mouth to keep herself from shouting. How could they? How could they let him die?

Ceony shivered. Standing, knees creaking, she tiptoed her way up the stairs, unable to bear any more words from the Cabinet. At the top of the stairs her tears started anew, only these ones felt very cold.

He was going to die. Magician Emery Thane was going to die, and without his own heart in his chest. It seemed so very wrong.

Soft padding announced Fennel coming down the hallway. He paused and stretched as a real dog would, then scratched at the turquoise collar around his neck.

Ceony scooped him up in her arms and held him delicately to her chest, careful not to cry on him.

So very wrong.

She paused at her room, but rather than go in, she continued walking until she reached Mg. Thane's. Cradling Fennel in one arm, she pushed the door open, lit a candle on the dresser, and took a look.

It was all as she had left it, minus the laundry on the bed. Feeling a chill, Ceony hugged Fennel closer and walked past the dresser, the bookshelves, the window with its darkening light. She paused by the closet and hamper and absently sifted through Mg. Thane's clothes, some of which had been in her washbasin just days ago. In the back of the closet she found Mg. Thane's white dress uniform— white, as that was the color that represented paper. The double-breasted jacket, gold-polished buttons, and thick cuffs all looked new and neat, as though the uniform had never been worn. Ceony couldn't help but think that Mg. Thane would look rather dashing in it. A good thing he had not worn it at their meeting yesterday, or Ceony may have found herself tongue-tied and very flustered.

She frowned. A pointless thing to think.

She pulled away from the closet. Fennel wriggled in her grasp. She set him down and dug her cold hands into her skirt's pockets. Something brushed the knuckle on her right hand.

From her pocket she pulled a tiny snowflake, the one she had stowed there after her first day as a Folder. She rubbed her thumb over its tiny, delicate cuts, grateful she hadn't yet washed this particular skirt. The snowflake still felt frosty, just like real snow. Snow he had made for her. All of it had been for her in one way or another, hadn't it?

In the glow of the candlelight she said, "I have to do it. I have to save him."

For she knew no one else would.

Biting her lip, Ceony hurried from the room, protecting the light of the candle with her hand as she went, quietly calling Fennel to follow. She went across the hall to the library and set the light down on the table under the window. Sitting down, she grasped a green square of paper of medium thickness and began Folding, leaning on her memory until she made a bird. The Folds hummed beneath her fingers.

Taking a pink piece of lightweight paper, she Folded another, then another with white. She imagined Mg. Thane's hands over her own, guiding her Folds, and squinted in the candlelight to ensure all her edges aligned and all her creases were straight.

When she had six birds, she commanded them, "Breathe," feeling a confidence above her station.

Five came to life. The pink one, the second she had made, remained still and lifeless, as a folded piece of paper should be. Somewhere in the folds of its body Ceony had done something wrong, but now was not the time to determine what.

Two of the five living birds took off into flight, one began grooming itself, one watched her without eyes, and the last hopped about the table, making Fennel growl. Ceony shushed the dog and, finding a pen, pulled a white piece of paper over to her.

She began writing, the pen's ink flowing in quick strokes over the parchment. She wrote quickly, but cautiously enough not to misspell anything. She didn't know if this trick would work, but she couldn't afford to have something as simple as bad grammar mess it up.

When she had finished, she called to the birds, "Come here. Come here, please!" and whistled to them in her best birdsong.

The two escapees flew down. The others came closer. They stood in two rows before her on the table.

Taking a deep breath to keep her voice smooth and calm, Ceony read, "A woman stormed into the dining room, her dark chocolate hair nearly black and her eyes almost as dark." She pictured the scene in her mind—Lira's confident stature, the curl to her red-painted lips, the length and sharpness of her fingernails as she dipped them into her vial of blood. "She was an evil woman and wore it in her face and clothes. She had a sneer that could sober any drunkard, and her dark arts left blood on her fingertips."

The story, at least the beginning of one, formed in ethereal colors before the birds, forming the shape of Lira just as Ceony remembered her, and Ceony credited herself as having a picture-perfect memory. The dining room formed around the image of Lira, but Ceony concentrated on Lira, which made the background fade to mottled blurs while Lira's face became sharp.

"I need you to find her," Ceony said, letting the illusion slowly dissipate. "Find her and come back to me. Can you do that?"

The birds hopped in place. That was as much of an affirmative as Ceony expected to get.

Nodding, Ceony moved to the window and, with a great heave that seemed to rock half the room, opened it high enough for five paper birds to fly out. The wind felt cool, but no rain threatened the sky. At least Mother Nature was on her side tonight.

Then, with Fennel at her heels, Ceony gathered what she needed.

She took a small stack of paper from each pile in the library and set it aside, then went into Mg. Thane's bedroom for the larger pieces, which she rolled together and fastened with a hair tie. In her room, with the door closed, she retrieved her Tatham pistol and stashed it at the bottom of the bag. She barely had time to so much as look at it over the past weeks, but she had made sure to keep it clean. The heft of it in her bag felt . . . soothing. Back in the library, she found an atlas and ripped out two maps, one of England and another of the entire continent of Europe, just in case. As she shoved the maps into her knit bag, Ceony had a sinking feeling that, if it came down to using the Europe map, she would never find Lira. It was far too big . . . and Mg. Thane had only two days, at most, to live . . .

She shook her head once. "I'll find her," she said, half to herself and half to Fennel. "I've got to."

When Ceony had everything packed save the food downstairs—where she dared not go—she reluctantly turned in for bed, though sleep came only in discomforted spurts. At dawn she rose and trudged downstairs.

Only Mg. Aviosky had stayed, and she slept on the couch in the front room. Leaving her, Ceony grabbed cheese, bread, and a chunk of salami for her pack. Enough to survive two days. Then she knelt beside Mg. Thane's still body. He breathed slow, raspy breaths.

She pressed an ear to his chest, which one of the magicians had had the decency to clean up. The only telling sign of the accident now was the blood around his ripped collar.

*Pft . . . pft . . .* , the heart pattered. The second beat sounded so faintly Ceony couldn't hear it.

Looking at his pale face, a knife of fear passed through Ceony's own heart. The Excisioner, Lira, had taken Mg. Thane down so easily. What chance did Ceony have against her?

*Just don't touch her*, she thought, remembering the Cabinet's discussion the night before. Ultimately, Ceony knew her only chance would be the element of surprise.

"Please live," she whispered to Mg. Thane. "I don't mind being a paper magician if you're the one to teach me, so please live. Otherwise I'll be ornery for the rest of my life and no good to anyone."

She touched his hair, took a deep breath, and retreated back up the stairs to wait. She thumbed through the library, picking out books on Folding and flipping through their pages, pausing wherever something looked important or interesting, then staring at the pictures—or the text—until she felt the information write itself in her memory. She listened for Mg. Aviosky's stirring downstairs, hoping the woman would sleep long.

Instead, her ears picked up the faintest tapping on the library window.

She turned and saw a paper bird in the morning light, its tail bent at an awkward angle and the tips of its right wing ragged, as though it had experienced a bit of a stir. Opening the window, the green bird flapped in. It was the first of the six she had crafted.

Ceony cupped the paper creature in her hands. "Tell me you found her. Tell me you saw something, please."

The bird hopped.

"Is that a yes?"

The bird hopped.

"Could you take me there? If I mended you?"

The bird hopped.

Growing jittery, Ceony set the bird down and straightened its tail, then shuffled through Mg. Thane's things until she found some glue, which she used to seal the tiny tears on the bird's wings. It pecked at the stuff, getting glue on its paper beak.

"Stop that," Ceony said, hefting her heavy bag onto her shoulder. She scooped up the bird, stepped into the hall, and then stopped.

What would she do, hire a buggy? How would she explain? Could she even afford one? How far out was Lira? The paper bird couldn't tell her.

And what if Mg. Aviosky had woken and was waiting for her to come down? She had no time to argue her way out! She had to move swiftly, before Lira did . . .

Pausing, Ceony turned about and looked at the stairway behind her, the one that led to the mysterious third floor. The "big" spells, as Mg. Thane had put it. Even during Mg. Thane's absence, she hadn't ventured up there. Could something useful be up there?

Swallowing hard, Ceony took the stairs two at a time. The top seven all groaned in protest of her weight. She wondered if the knob would be locked, but when she reached out and clasped it, it turned with only mild resistance.

She smelled old dust and mildew, and the temperature felt decidedly cooler than downstairs. The third floor looked to be all one room with an extraordinarily high ceiling from which dangled a rope that opened a door facing the sky.

Ceony gaped at the two things the morning light streaming through dirty windows revealed to her. Fennel hopped up the stairs behind her and sniffed her shoes.

The first was a giant paper glider, the sort that boys folded at their desks and threw at girls they liked when the teacher's back was turned. The second looked very similar to the bird Ceony held in her hand, albeit unfinished.

Both were three times the size of the buggy that had dropped Ceony off at the house just weeks earlier.

"You *are* mad," she whispered, walking toward the glider. It had a thin coat of dust on the top, and two handholds near the nose. No seat to sit in, no belt to strap in.

Surely Mg. Thane hadn't flown *in* this. No one could fly! It must have been a prototype. Surely a man couldn't find groceries a bothersome chore if he could retrieve them in this!

She marveled at it, and the handholds near its nose. So it *did* fly, or was supposed to. Only something like this would enable her to catch up to Lira. Mg. Thane depended on her.

For the first time since her assignment, Ceony found herself wishing for a more boring solution.

Straightening her shoulders and balling her hands into fists, she said, "Let's go, Fennel," and walked around the glider's long wing. One hand on the green bird and the other on her bag, she stepped over the glider's nose and straddled it. The thick paper had been greatly reinforced and didn't bow under her weight.

*Thank the heavens.*

Ceony pulled the cord to the door in the ceiling. A few dead leaves fell down on top of her, carrying the scent of dew and the sound of birdsong.

Taking a deep breath, Ceony lay on her stomach and grabbed the handholds of the glider. She could only pray it worked like an animation, or else she'd never find the right spell in time.

She commanded the bird, "Take me to Lira."

The little bird flapped its wings and flew out the door.

"Breathe," Ceony told the glider.

It bucked beneath her like a wild bull. Ceony shrieked. Fennel jumped onto the glider and growled.

Ceony gripped the handholds and pulled them toward her.

The glider arched its pointed nose upward and took off through the gap in the roof.

# CHAPTER 7

CEONY *FLEW* UP FROM the yellow cottage disguised by spells and into the sky itself, gaze locking onto the little green bird that banked hard to the west.

Ceony, her knuckles white from gripping the handholds on the glider and her right elbow latched securely around Fennel's neck, attempted to follow. She leaned in with the glider and pulled the right handhold harder than the left, but she oversteered and went veering hard to the south, then hard to the north, then hard to the southwest. Trying to force herself to remain calm, even as the glider rose higher and higher into the sky, Ceony guided the massive spell back and forth until its nose pointed toward the distant speck of green that was her guide. Then she lay low—wind blowing strand after strand of orange hair from her braid—and zoomed toward it.

With the help of currents and updrafts, the glider flew faster than the bird, so Ceony had to reel it in with care every few minutes. Pulling too hard on the handholds made the glider climb, and pushing made it descend, but switching between the two and lifting her body higher off the paper seemed to slow it down fairly well.

When she finally took a moment to look around her, she gasped with surprise. One would think a girl who attended the top-ranking magic school in the country would have had some spell or another take her high enough for the view she saw now, but that was not the case. She had never seen London in such great expanse.

The city, in which Mg. Thane lived on the far, far south side, stretched before her in a motley assortment of colors that grew less and less sharp the farther she flew. It took on the shape of a triangle, and Ceony swore she could see the Masters' Tower of the Tagis Praff School for the Magically Inclined beyond a line of trees that must have been Dulwich Park. Streets like slick eels wound through the city, none of them quite straight, and many of them looking quite lost. She saw the Mill Squats where she had grown up, mostly brown buildings too close together for her to discern her house, as well as Steelworks Avenue, which led to the catering house that had employed her before her accident with one of its most prestigious customers— something that Ceony didn't regret, but didn't like to ponder.

Homes, shops, trees, even the smokestacks all grew smaller and smaller as she looked over her shoulder, sailing away on the air the way a sea captain might sail on the sea. How foolish of her to ever think Folding was pointless. Surely no Smelter would be able to fly like she did! Mg. Thane needed to patent the glider. That was, if he ever got the chance to.

The thought sobered her. Ceony faced forward, catching the green bird in her vision. Mg. Thane would have the chance. Ceony would make sure of it. However, she had to admit that once the little green bird got to where it was going, she wasn't entirely sure what to do. Fortunately the sights below—roads diverging for thick forests and country cabins, rivers weaving in and out of the trees—and the wind singing loudly in her ears made it difficult to think of the con-sequences of her rash actions.

On and on the little bird flew, its wings never tiring, though on occasion a sudden gust would send the poor thing off track, and it had to flap relentlessly to get back on course. The morning sun turned the sky light blue, then a solid cerulean as it reached and passed its peak. Fennel huffed softly under her arm, thankfully not squirming. Ceony's fingers felt ready to break from her hand, and her stomach rumbled, but she dared not release the handholds long enough to either rest her fingers or fish her lunch from the heavy bag at her hip.

They flew until Ceony smelled brine flies and seawater, and she saw the great azure expanse of the English Channel ahead of her. Judging by the coastline, the bird had directed her right to the edge of Foulness Island. Adequately named, given the circumstances.

Her stomach churned and her white grip on the glider's handles brightened as she squeezed all the harder. *Please not the ocean*, she thought. She didn't know if she could follow Lira past the coast. The ocean was so endless, so vast . . . and she couldn't swim. Ceony hadn't stepped foot in water any deeper than what a bathtub could hold since she was a little girl, and she never would, if she had any say in the matter. She could still taste the algae of the Hendersons' fishpond in her mouth, hear the silence of water in her ears.

She swallowed against a dry throat and prayed.

Thankfully the small bird began to descend, sea-spray splotch-ing its wings and slowing it down. Ceony pushed her glider faster until she came up beside it. Daring to release one handhold, she snatched the bird from the air and tried to determine how to land without breaking every bone in her body.

"Here, is it?" Ceony shouted over the whistle of the wind, her voice only cracking once. The bird pulsed beneath her.

Ceony circled the glider around a dozen times, taking each loop lower and lower, aiming for a spot well away from the water.

"I don't suppose I can command you to land, can I?" she asked the glider. "Take me to the ground, softly?"

The glider seemed to heed her as the birds had last night. It arched its wings up and dropped in altitude, making Ceony's stomach lurch, but its speed slowed and it glided *almost* smoothly onto a length of dirt patched with crabgrass.

Ceony's fingers stubbornly held to their pained, crooked positions even as she unhooked them from the handholds. The glider continued to slide along the ground, and she looked over the sides, checking for puddles to ensure her ride would stay dry. "Cease," she commanded it, and the glider drooped and teetered onto its left side. "Cease," she told the little bird, and it too went still. She tucked it into the large crease along the center of the glider's body, hoping to give it time to dry off without being blown away.

Fennel in her arms, Ceony gazed out onto the rocky coast along the sea edge made purple and orange by the lowering sun ahead of them, which cast a golden road across the seawater as it considered its set. Ceony looked about the unfamiliar place ridged with black rocks of all shapes and sizes and free of trees. No sandy beaches comprised the coast here, just steep cliffs formed by the bellies of long-dead volcanoes. One wrong step on those and she'd drown.

Ceony sucked in a long breath and pulled a piece of cheese from her bag.

"Stay quiet, Fennel," she instructed as she set the dog down on the ground. "Stay away from puddles and let me know if you smell anything sour."

Ceony nibbled on the cheese as she walked toward the rocks, searching for a safe way down. She thought Lira very smart. If Ceony were a criminal, she would try to escape England as quickly as possible after committing such a heinous deed. Straight for the coast, where a ship of her accomplices could pick her up. The only faster way out of the country seemed to be by paper glider, and Ceony greatly doubted Lira had one of those.

Ceony pulled her Tatham pistol from her bag and held its wooden and steel barrel against her breast, pointing the muzzle over her shoulder. She found a drop between two large crags that did not look too steep and carefully climbed her way down. Fennel sniffed all about it before following after, slipping only once. Down on solid rock, much closer to the water, Ceony smoothed her skirt and continued forward. She didn't need to muffle her footfalls; the crashing of waves against yet more rocks below hid her presence, even if they did make her hands shake. She stayed close to the cliffs. Her heart quickened, and while the ocean air made her skin cold, her blood pulsed hot and her insides grew taut as guitar strings.

A burst of salty wind tossed the last locks of her hair from her braid. She snatched the whipping strands from the breeze and hurriedly tied them at the nape of her neck before climbing downward once more, where droplets of water from those crashing waves pattered her cheek. She tried to stand between them and Fennel, who began to huff excitedly—perhaps he had smelled something.

A loud, uneven cry pulled her attention toward the ocean. Whirling around, she pointed the pistol not at a person, but at a squatting seagull staring at her with red-veined eyes. Half-molted feathers and stitches speckled its neck. Pieces of dried, blanched skin hung off its face and legs in strips, and the top of its beak had been broken in half.

Ceony froze, clutching the pistol in her hands. A dead bird. A *living* dead bird. The work of an Excisioner.

The gull cried once more and flew out over the ocean. Ceony's heart started beating again when it was out of sight.

Her teeth chattered. She told herself it was from the ocean's cool mist.

Could Excisioners truly reanimate the deceased? The thought made Ceony shudder inside and out. But why a bird? Was it a messenger? Ceony hadn't seen a note tied to its mangled legs . . . Perhaps it had already dropped its message off, or it was a spy of some sort. Ceony didn't know enough about Excision to know. Perhaps someone was trying to contact Lira. Someone trying to help her escape.

The cheese she had eaten grew heavy in her stomach. Ceony scooped Fennel into her arms and turned him away from the ocean, as much for her own comfort as anything.

Ceony picked her way along the rocky coast for perhaps a quarter mile before she saw a dark half oval ahead of her—a cavern of some sort. A splendid place to hide, for sure. Clutching Fennel and readying her pistol, she crept toward it.

The sun had sunk one-third of its majesty behind the horizon when she reached the cavern. There were no lanterns or torches to light, but the cavern didn't look too deep. Spying about and seeing no one, Ceony moved inside the cave, keeping her back to one of its rough walls.

Fennel squirmed. She hushed him. She didn't need a paper dog reminding her what a fool brain she had inside her skull.

Her heart thrummed as she neared the back of the cave. She spied a pair of shoes set near the opposite wall. Someone else had been here, and recently, for the shoes looked fairly new and fairly clean, albeit not the ones Lira had worn at Mg. Thane's home.

*Pumpom . . . pumpom . . .* A heartbeat. But not hers. No, this one beat much slower than her own.

Ceony inched forward, squinting in the dim light slinking in through the cavern's mouth. The base of the back wall jutted forward, making an uneven shelf about four feet high. Something glowed along its ridge.

Ceony gasped. There, in a shallow bowl amid the black rock, gleamed a pool of wine-colored blood shimmering gold about its edges. Beating calmly in its center rested Mg. Thane's heart, just as she had seen it clenched in Lira's hands.

Gooseflesh prickled her skin as Ceony approached it. Mg. Thane's heart. She had found it.

She had found it too easily.

Fennel huffed and jumped from Ceony's arms just as Ceony spun around, clutching her pistol in both hands. There, a few paces in from the mouth of the cave, stood Lira.

She looked just as she had in Mg. Thane's dining room, though her pants had been torn just above the left knee and the humidity caused her hair to hang heavier from her scalp. Her dark eyes narrowed beneath rows of long, dark eyelashes, very different from Ceony's blond. They made her look both menacing and beautiful. She could not have been any older than Mg. Thane. Not so much older than Ceony herself.

"I thought I hadn't hit you hard enough," she said, eyes dropping to the pistol for only a moment. Lira wore no guns that Ceony could see, only several vials of blood strapped to one side of a leather belt, and a long dagger strapped to the other. "But it seems my generosity in letting you live has turned against me."

She smiled as if she had told a joke.

"Lira, isn't it?" Ceony asked, leveling her pistol. She hoped the woman didn't notice how it trembled in her hands. "I'm taking this back. Don't interfere, and I won't shoot you."

Shoot her. Ceony had never shot a real person in her life, only targets.

Lira took a step forward. Ceony's palms sweat. Lira, smirking, asked, "Do you even know how to use that?"

Gritting her teeth, Ceony leveled the pistol and cocked back its hammer. She could never afford the enchanted bullets that always met their mark, but she prided herself on her aim regardless.

The Excisioner took one more step forward and paused. She

slipped a vial of blood off her belt. Ceony struggled to hold the gun steady. Mg. Thane's heart beat loudly behind her—or was that her own pulse?

"Put it down," Ceony said. Clearing her throat, she repeated, "Put it down or I'll shoot you, I swear I will. I'm taking this heart back with me."

Lira's face turned to a scowl so gradually Ceony hardly saw it change. "I'm not letting some ginger tart take what's rightfully mine."

With a thumbnail she uncorked the vial and spilled blood into her palm. She stepped forward.

Ceony stepped back. "I'll kill you!" she cried.

Lira began chanting in that mysterious tongue. Ceony didn't understand any of it—the spells were so different from the materials she had studied. Lira's hand began to glow gold. She took another step forward.

Ceony fired.

The pistol jerked back in Ceony's hands, its *boom!* filling the cavern and stinging Ceony's ears. The sharp scent of gunpowder scoured her nose and slipped into her mouth. Fennel whined at her ankles.

Lira's eyes widened as wetness, dark as dried rose petals, bloomed over her right breast. She grunted and dropped to one knee, her hand still glowing. Her lips muttered something too quiet for Ceony to hear.

Ceony lowered the pistol. Her eyes felt ready to pop from their sockets. Her mouth went dry and her hands turned cold. Thought fled her, swirled above her head, and returned just as Lira pressed her glowing palm to the wound on her chest.

The strange light spiraled under her hand for less than two seconds before flashing once and disappearing. Lira sucked in a deep breath and stood, then popped her neck once to the left and once to the right. She dropped something small and metal from her hand. It clinked against the cavern floor.

A bullet.

Ceony nearly dropped her gun. Had . . . had Lira just *healed* herself?

Her mind spun. Excision had power over flesh. Lira took a step forward, seemingly unscathed save for the stain on her dark shirt. Ceony had only one bullet. Only one, and it rested on the dark rock behind Lira.

Lira had started her healing spell before Ceony had fired. Lira had *wanted* Ceony to use up her shot. Fear had played Ceony right into the Excisioner's hands.

And now all Ceony had was a bag full of paper, the least offensive material a magician could wield. Even rubber would have suited her better here.

"No more games," Lira snarled, taking another step, then another. Ceony backtracked, her gun slipping from her clammy fingers.

Her back bumped into the rock shelf, her elbow touching Mg. Thane's heart.

The cavern twirled before her and Ceony felt herself fall, a sudden whoosh swooping around her. The sunlight at the mouth of the cave jerked from her eyes and she hit something warm and firm. A loud *PUM-Pom-poom* sounded all around her.

"Oh, the bane of the unprepared," crooned Lira's low-pitched voice around her, echoing between unseen walls.

She broke the echo with a heinous cackle that unsettled every nerve in Ceony's body. "Now I have Emery and his suckling brat."

# CHAPTER 8

A STEADY THREE-BEAT DRUM surrounded Ceony, vibrating in the very floor itself. When her eyes adjusted, she saw a crimson-cast room, its walls more bowed than straight. The one to her right appeared concave, and the one to her left looked convex. Even the floor wasn't flat. She could see via a muted light, but when she searched she found no candles, lanterns, not even a single electric wire. The room's heat pressed into her, and when she tried to stand she stumbled, the constant *PUM-Pom-poom* beat shaking her already shaky legs.

Fennel barked beside her—it seemed Lira's trap, whatever it was, had caught him up as well.

She spied a narrow river of what looked like blood flowing between the wall and floor to her right, and she gasped. She had seen something like this room before, only it had been very small and had lain out on a metal table enchanted to stay cold. She had seen it after she had removed it from a dead frog.

This was Mg. Thane's heart, and Ceony stood inside it.

*PUM-Pom-poom. PUM-Pom-poom.* Ceony couldn't tell if she heard the throbbing walls or her own chest. She breathed hard and deep and spun around, examining the strange chamber, feeling as though her body couldn't get enough air.

Something dark caught the corner of her eye and she turned to see Lira, who held the Tatham pistol in her hands like a child's toy. She slipped the trigger guard over her index finger and spun the gun around her knuckle.

Fennel growled a soft, papery growl, and Ceony scooped him into her arms, trying not to look as terrified as she felt. The muscles in her legs had turned to icicles.

Lira smiled. "Emery surrounds himself with fools. The heart trap was only a backup. Someplace I could put you where you wouldn't run away."

She stilled the pistol and clasped it in her right hand, looking as if she could crush it. "Did you really think you could beat *me* with *this?*"

Ceony gaped. She trembled. She had to get away. She couldn't face Lira, not like this. She wasn't prepared. She knew nothing of the dark arts, what to expect or how to combat them. She hadn't thought this through at all!

She took a step back, and Lira took two steps forward. Sweat beaded on Ceony's back, gluing her shirt to her skin. Ceony stepped back once more—

—and the entire chamber shifted around her.

She nearly dropped Fennel as the red, fleshy walls morphed into a blue sky speckled with wispy clouds, the bloody streams transformed into carpets of lush, green grass. The distant beat of Mg. Thane's heart dulled to a quiet echo. Ceony smelled clover and sun-heated leaves, felt a warm summer breeze on her face. A few thick-boughed, leafy trees sprang up some ways away from her, one dangling an umber birdhouse from its second-lowest branch. Numerous gray boxes occupied the space between the trees and herself. Each stood about four or five feet high and seemed to be made of shorter weathered boxes.

Ceony's gaze shifted back and forth, fear and confusion coating each other in her thoughts. She wiped her hands on her skirt.

Laughter touched her ears.

She whirled around and saw four children before her, their heads donning broad-brimmed canvas hats with tightly woven nets draping over their faces and necks, and long gloves pulled up past their elbows. Their ages looked to range from three to twelve, or so Ceony guessed.

Fennel wriggled from under her arm and jumped down on the grass, running about to join the children. He ran quickly for having legs made of cardstock.

A round honeybee buzzed by her, and by instinct Ceony swatted it away. It wasn't until that moment that she noticed the buzzing speckles surrounding each of the gray boxes, swarming and churning like humming clouds.

Ceony's lip parted in surprise. Was this a honey farm?

In the middle of Thane's heart?

A tall, thickly built man approached a buzzing box behind the children. He wore sturdy canvas over his entire body, tucked into his shoes and drawn with a string under his chin. Ceony had a difficult time seeing his face through the netted veil hanging from his hat, especially when honeybees began crawling over it.

Rubbing her eyes to ensure what she saw was real, Ceony stepped forward and called out to the canvas-clad man.

"Excuse me!" she shouted, but the man didn't turn, even when she repeated herself. The eldest boy ran an uneven circle around her, but his eyes never saw her, only peered *through* her. He didn't notice her presence at all. None of them did.

And Lira . . . where was Lira? Ceony moved around the bee boxes searching for her, the insects ignoring her as readily as the people did. She scanned beyond the trees to shallow, rolling hills, but saw no sign of the Excisioner.

She pulled a white sheet of paper from her bag and held it between both hands. It made her feel safer.

"You're it!" shouted a girl of about eight, two auburn pigtails peeking out from beneath her face net. She ran away from the eldest boy, laughing even as bees swarmed from half a dozen boxes.

"Don't touch the hives!" the adult shouted as he pawed at his bee box. He had a low, brawny voice, deep and rugged. He pulled a tray from the box's top, and Ceony marveled at the thick, amber honeycomb clinging to it. The man brought it to a wheelbarrow, bees crawling all over his protected arms, and scraped honey into a tall bucket. Ceony's mouth watered, but still she wondered, *How did I get here?*

More importantly: *Where* is *here?*

Surely Lira's spell hadn't whisked her away. Why would a practitioner of the forbidden arts ship Ceony to a remote—and rather jolly—honey farm?

Fennel stood on his hind legs as he tried to get a better look at a particularly fat bee flying about his head. Another bee buzzed about Ceony but never landed, never tried to sting her. At least, if it did, she didn't feel it.

"Emery, get me that spoon, will you?" the man shouted, pointing to a long metal spoon in the grass.

The name made Ceony's eyes dart to the second-youngest child, perhaps six years old, running between hives to the spoon. Still clutching the paper, Ceony ran to him and peered through the pale netting over his face. The child didn't notice her at all, even as she crouched in front of him. She saw uneven patches of black hair sticking out from under his hat and bright, green eyes.

"Magician Thane," she whispered. The eyes gave him away. The child phased through her like a ghost and handed the spoon to the man whom Ceony could only assume was his father. The man patted Mg. Thane's head—Emery's head—and the boy grinned a wide grin before returning to play with his siblings, darting between boxes with a precision that told Ceony he could do so blindfolded.

*Mg. Thane's family* . . . , Ceony thought. But why did she see this . . . memory? Dream?

Didn't he say he was an only child?

"Magician Thane!" she called out to him, but as she did she spied a shadow beyond the hives, where the grassy ground dipped down into a hill and a tire swing hung from a tall tree. Dark locks of hair caught on the breeze.

Lira.

Ceony's breath caught in her throat. Her fingers turned cold, but she managed to snap them and call Fennel. The dog followed her as she ran in the other direction, away from the Excisioner and the bees, and away from the young Emery Thane. All she could do now was run . . . and figure out how to defeat an Excisioner who couldn't be killed.

The view warped, darkened, and Ceony found herself assaulted by thunderous applause that nearly made her jump from her skin.

Fennel yapped at her heels as rows and rows of men and women Ceony didn't know clapped around her in the auditorium of what looked to be the Royal Albert Hall in West London. Scarlet carpet lined the tilted aisles, and chandeliers filled with candles—not electric bulbs—hung unlit overhead. Ceony spun, her eyes landing on a heavyset woman in a fur coat clapping in a nearby chair. Approaching the woman, Ceony asked "What's happening?" over the applause, but the woman didn't answer. Didn't look at her. Ceony found herself once more a ghost, though the vision unfolding around her seemed far more ghostly than she herself did.

Ceony glanced behind her, but didn't see Lira anywhere. She sucked in a deep breath of relief. The applause died down, and Ceony crouched in the aisle between seats to Fold a paper bird.

"And Magician Emery Thane, Folder, District Fourteen," boomed a voice from behind her. Ceony blinked at the brightly lit stage lined with velvet curtains. A man who looked like a younger Tagis Praff with a mustache stood stage left behind a broad podium with the Magicians' seal painted on its front. He clapped his hands loudly together, and the audience followed suit.

A row of eleven chairs lined the stage opposite the podium, all empty save for one with a young man in a white magician's dress uniform, complete with high collar and golden buttons. Ceony's hands froze mid-Fold as Magician Emery Thane, barely older than herself, crossed the stage to accept his magician's plaque—the same one that hung in his study.

She felt herself blush. He *did* look excellent in that uniform—it fit much more snugly about his shoulders than that awful indigo coat. It narrowed at his waist, and the sharp creases in the legs made him appear taller. Taller than Tagis Praff, anyway. Ceony hardly recognized Mg. Thane, especially with his hair cropped short enough to hide its wave. It was enough to make her forget Lira. For a moment, anyway.

Fennel sniffed at the half-formed bird beneath Ceony's fingers, and Ceony sat in the aisle, watching the newly appointed Mg. Thane shake gloved hands with Tagis Praff.

"I'm in his heart," she said to Fennel. "I never left it, so this must be part of it. I'm *seeing* his heart, but . . . how do I get out of it? I can't help him from in here!"

But saving the paper magician's life wasn't her only predicament. She peered over her shoulder again, but Lira hadn't followed her here. The fact didn't make her feel safer. *If I don't get out,* I'll *die, too.*

Tagis Praff began bellowing a speech over the podium, but Ceony forced herself to focus on her bird and finish Folding its head, tail, and wings. What she would use it for, she didn't know, but birds were one of the few things she knew how to make. What she wouldn't give to be a Smelter right now, to have a gun with enchanted bullets that never missed their mark. She might have a chance against Lira if she only had one of those.

Shoving the white bird into her bag, Ceony ran down the rest of the aisle to the stage. Mg. Thane began walking down the stairs beside the podium. Ceony hurried in front of the unaware spectators toward him. She had to try.

"Magician Thane!" she called, but he didn't turn. She ran up to him and grabbed his arm, but it merely passed through her, a phantom. He took a seat in the second row, alongside other materials magicians in their designated uniforms.

Ceony tried once more to grab him—his shoulder—but it did no good. "Magician Thane, can't you hear me?" she asked, waving a hand in front of his face. "How do I get out?"

The young paper magician leaned his cheek on his fist, suddenly bored with the procession in his honor.

Ceony pursed her lips somewhat in imitation of Mg. Aviosky. Then she ran up the scarlet aisle toward the doors leading out of the auditorium, Fennel at her heels.

A woman screamed at her as soon as she stepped through them.

The noise startled Ceony so much that she fell back, but no doors or auditorium walls caught her. Instead she hit old, wooden floorboards rump first, not the marble tiles of the Royal Albert Hall. A dull, boney feeling shot up her back.

"Breathe, Letta: in and out," a midwife in uniform instructed a young woman lying on the floor of a sparsely furnished room—the one who had screamed. The woman, her belly bulging with pregnancy, puffed through pursed lips. She held herself upright on her elbows. Towels surrounded her. A tin bowl of bloody water sat near her ankles. Blond hair stuck to her forehead with sweat. Outside, rain hammered onto the windows, and a flash of lightning boasted before the nearly spent candles. Thunder shook the house three seconds later, and the staccato report of raindrops hitting the roof drowned out the distant sound of the paper magician's heartbeat.

"Thane!" Ceony shouted, spying her teacher kneeling at the pregnant woman's legs, his sleeves rolled up nearly to his shoulders. He looked older, more himself. His forehead wrinkled in determination. His bright eyes shined with hope.

"That's it," he said. "Bear down. Push again!"

The woman cried out, her nails raking against the floor.

Ceony paused, ogling the woman in her labor. Was she related to Mg. Thane?

Ceony crawled to Mg. Thane's side and waved a hand in front of his face, but he too didn't see her. Even if this vision had been real, he wouldn't have seen her. His attention focused solely on the delivery at hand.

But time was ticking away.

"You have to help me!" Ceony shouted over the rain. "I'm trapped inside your heart! How do I get out?"

Like the previous two visions, he didn't hear, and neither did the woman nor the midwife.

The woman rested back on her shoulder blades for a moment, sucking in air as the midwife dabbed her forehead with a wet cloth. That's when Ceony noticed a chain around the woman's stomach identical to the one the real, present Emery Thane wore about his chest—a spell for good health. What had he called it? A vitality chain.

Fennel sat on his haunches and whined.

Crouching, Ceony pet the back of the dog's neck. Where was the doctor? Why was Mg. Thane here, delivering this baby? Folders had no expertise in childbirth! Ceony finally noticed the wetness of

Thane's shirt—not from sweat, but from rain. It dripped from his hair. The storm—Mg. Thane must have been the only one close by, save for the midwife. A doctor wouldn't be able to travel in this weather, not with rain gushing over the roads. Mg. Thane must have been the closest aid . . . and the midwife seemed to trust him.

The birthing woman gasped, and Ceony gaped as Mg. Thane pulled a tiny infant from between her legs, purple skinned and bloody. A boy, bald and writhing with deep blue eyes. The babe cried a healthy cry and kicked weakly at the umbilical cord that still connected him to his mother.

Mg. Thane laughed, cradling the babe in his arms as the midwife hurried over with scissors and a wet sponge. "It's a boy, Mrs. Tork. It's a boy. Congratulations."

The woman, face streaked with tears and sweat, laughed and held out her arms. The midwife cut and tied the babe's umbilical cord, then carefully laid the infant onto its mother's breast.

Mg. Thane's shoulders slumped, and he pressed his soiled hands onto the floor to hold himself upright. He looked tired and weathered, but he laughed, his eyes gleaming with happiness. Ceony marveled at him.

"Are these your achievements?" Ceony asked the deaf magician, who was nothing more than a replaying memory. "Your happy moments? Your good deeds?"

Ceony backed away from him and shook herself to the present—her present, at least—and pressed her palm to her own heart, feeling its quickened rhythm. She wanted to know—wanted to connect the little pieces that created the mosaic of the man she knew—but she had to focus on getting *out*. But where did the visions end?

Lightning flashed, and Ceony spied Lira's silhouette outside the window. Fear like a cold lance pierced through her middle. Had Lira followed her through the graduation ceremony after all?

Forcing her rigid muscles to move, she and Fennel ran to the closest door. Ceony grabbed the worn brass handle and turned it hard.

She stumbled through, a tornado of charcoal and navy swirling through her vision. Fennel barked. Ceony tottered with the dizzying effect of the whirling colors, which darkened and settled onto a new vision of Thane in an office that did not match the study in his cottage on the outskirts of London. He sat at a desk with a stack of papers in his hand. He looked similar to the Emery Thane who had delivered a baby just moments before. Evening sun and the light from a single kerosene lamp highlighted his features.

"It's finished," he said with a sigh. Not to Ceony, of course, but to himself. Ceony had heard the paper magician mumble to himself before, usually behind the closed door of his office.

She spied over his shoulder to see *A Reverse Perception of Paper Animation* scrawled across the front sheet of paper. A book. Mg. Thane had written a book! And an absurdly thick one as well . . . She wondered why he hadn't assigned her to read it yet.

"All of these are the same," she said to him, though she knew the image of her teacher wouldn't turn at her voice. "They're all good things, good memories, happy times. I'm in the warmest part of your heart, aren't I?"

Ceony's mind shot back to her secondary school's biology class taught under Mr. Cooper, the same class where she had dissected that poor frog. The homework assignment she had turned in on the eleventh of February surfaced in her mind as fresh as if she had completed it yesterday.

"Four chambers," she whispered. Hadn't the anatomy book said something similar? "The heart has four chambers. Could it be that I'm in your first?"

Mg. Thane stretched in his chair with his arms over his head, his back popping twice and his neck popping thrice. Standing, he hefted his manuscript and phased through her on his way to the door.

"Is that it?" Ceony shouted after him, pulling out another piece of paper and Folding a yellow fish. A fish had fewer Folds than a bird, and she completed it in half the time. Fennel pressed his paws against the side of the desk and sniffed at it. "Is that the answer? If I get to the end of your heart, will I find the way out?"

She added the fish to her arsenal and followed Thane's footsteps through the door.

She found herself on a knoll covered in golden grass and wild-flowers—the same blossoms Ceony had found pressed in Thane's room. A warm wind rustled through them, carrying in it the taste of honeysuckle and sweet pea. The smells of summer. A large, molten sun sunk slowly into its bed in the west over a horizon speckled with dark trees. It cast a magenta and violet light through the sky and over a woodland canopy at the base of a ridge ahead of her—the North Downs, almost a day's journey south of London. She had hiked the area with her father a few years ago, but had never seen this hill before. She would have remembered a place so . . . reverent. So beautiful.

She turned, taking the view in, and found Thane just above her. He rested beneath an old plum tree with wide boughs and deep-maroon leaves. He lay on his side on a blue and yellow patchwork quilt, talking quietly to a woman beside him.

Ceony yelped at the sight of Lira, but something looked different about her. She was younger—they both were—and her hair looked lighter, not as long. She wore part of it pinned back in a silver clip, and the rest curled freely about her shoulders. Instead of black pants, she wore a modest white sundress that fell to her ankles and had no sleeves. A long golden locket hung about her neck. Its chain appeared so delicate Ceony feared the very breeze would snap its links.

Like Thane before, this Lira didn't seem to notice her.

Ceony stared at them, something cold and itchy pricking her heart. She reminded herself that this was another memory, another piece of goodness nestled in the first chamber of Thane's heart.

"Lira," she whispered. She treaded up the hill until she could get a clear shot of Thane's face, his bright eyes that looked almost hazel in the plum tree's shade. Those eyes—Ceony saw love in those eyes. Adoration. Bliss. Serenity.

He loved her.

Fennel pawed at Ceony's leg, but Ceony didn't move.

Mg. Thane . . . in love with *Lira*?

Her stomach soured, and she rubbed it with the palm of her hand. Visions or no, it was too stuffy between this heart's walls. She was starting to feel ill.

Ceony studied the magician, trying to guess his age. Perhaps twenty-four or twenty-five. Several years ago, at least. That made her feel somewhat better, but the longer she watched the happy couple, the sicker she felt. Like her body wilted on her bones.

Shaking her head, Ceony tore her eyes away and rubbed her temples, trying to get some sense into her brain. She needed to focus. Be objective.

She let out a long breath. "All right. Why would a woman Thane loves leave him to die?" she wondered aloud. "If she already has Thane's heart, why would she need to steal it?"

As she stepped away from the happy couple, her footsteps turned from grass-muted to hollow. Backtracking, she spied hinges among the wildflowers, as well as an old brass handle tarnished in the middle. Reaching for the handle, Ceony pulled the small door open.

The colors of the sunset, the wildflowers, and the plum tree swirled around her as the old office had, making her woozy. The sensation subsided quickly, and Ceony found herself looking straight up into Thane's eyes. They bore that same, adoring expression, and he wore his white magician's uniform, newly pressed, with a pink rose pinned to his left breast.

Ceony flushed deeply enough that her cheeks stung. She blinked and found herself standing elsewhere in the same vision, to the side of the chairs set up near a stream and a bridge in a park filled with cherry trees, their ruddy blossoms catching on the wind and filling the air like blushing snow. Crickets chirped softly in patches of long grass the groundskeeper had missed shearing. Swathes of white and yellow gossamer lined the aisles between chairs and a broad, wooden arch shading Mg. Thane, a man in a tawny robe, and Lira.

Lira now stood where Ceony had been, garbed in a white beaded dress with a long train, a short veil pinned into her lovely hair with a golden comb studded with pearls. The wedding dress had short, sheer sleeves and a neckline that revealed an ample chest—much larger than Ceony's own, she noted with some chagrin.

Ceony's heart thudded almost painfully against her ribs as a minister read from a leather-bound text to perform the ceremony. So Lira had been his wife.

*Had* been. That hymnal in his room made sense now.

Ceony rubbed the back of her neck, trying to stifle the heat creeping along it. The way Thane had looked at her in that moment before the switch . . .

Ceony's pulse drummed in her ears.

But it hadn't been her. It had been Lira. A younger Lira. A different Lira.

Ceony whirled around, half-expecting the Excisioner—Thane's wife—to appear behind her at any moment, but she saw only happy wedding guests, including that same beekeeper and his wife. Men and women Ceony didn't know. The memories moved so quickly—perhaps Lira wasn't able to keep up. Perhaps she didn't *want* to be here. Ceony didn't, either.

Ceony pinched herself. She needed to stay alert. Mg. Hughes had said an Excisioner could pull magic through another's body with just one touch, which meant it wouldn't take much time for Lira to destroy her, should the crazed woman catch up to Ceony. Touch was one advantage Ceony didn't want to give the psychotic woman chasing her through a stolen heart.

She had to find the next chamber.

She ran from the wedding with Fennel at her side, not bothering to give the ceremony a second glance. Something about it . . . bothered her. Pink cherry blossoms blew across her path, lacing the air with their subtle, lustful scent. The song of crickets muted to her ears.

The cherry trees grew thicker until Ceony found herself facing a copse of them, too thick to pass through save for a wrought-iron fence wedged between two of the smaller ones. She pushed open its narrow gate and ran until the sod turned firm and a book-lined wall stopped her from running any farther. A dead end.

Ceony found herself in the midst of a library.

It was similar to the one Mg. Thane had now, albeit smaller and with more windows and a second table, over which stooped a younger Emery Thane than the one who had been getting married. He wore his dark hair short and had rolled his white shirtsleeves up to his elbows.

Paper covered the tabletop in neat piles, all white and off-white, all varying thicknesses. A pile of half-Folded, half-crumpled papers formed a sizeable pile on the floor, and beside them stood a second-hand dressmaker's dummy tacked about with dozens of papers rolled and Folded to form a rib cage around the torso, a collar across the shoulders, and a spine along the back. Ceony recognized the structure as Jonto's—this must have been his creation, or part of it.

"Here's the paperboard," said an unfamiliar voice from the hallway. "That was just the carrier dropping it off."

Ceony shifted her attention from Thane and his skeletal project to the man entering the library. He carried two giant cardboard totes of paper that looked heavy enough that Ceony doubted she could even lift one without pulling a muscle.

Yet the totes seemed almost tiny in this man's arms, a man whose boyish face put him only a few years Ceony's senior. He had to be six and a half feet tall and looked wide enough that Ceony felt sure she could fit inside him at least three times. Everything about the man was simply . . . big. Big shoulders, big stomach, big hands. Each of his calves looked like a feast day ham.

"Excellent, Langston," Thane said, glancing up from his work for only half a second. Ceony couldn't tell what he was working on—it looked almost like a bent-up crescent roll roughly the length of his hand. Fortunately, Thane's next words answered the unspoken question: "I want to try integrating thick and thin together for this one—thick at the jaw's joints and at the chin, thin in between. Maybe *that* will work."

"Maybe," Langston replied with a slowness and drawl that had Ceony suspecting he hadn't grown up in England. "I'm sure you'll figure it out soon, Magician Thane. My ma always said the word *damn* came from beavers who gave up on their houses one stick short."

"Your mother says many things," Thane replied offhandedly. "See if you can't duplicate that hip, hm?"

Ceony marveled as Langston pulled out a chair nearly too small for him and took a seat across the table from Thane. He hardly had space to set down his giant elbows.

"Is this your apprentice?" Ceony asked, not expecting an answer. Judging by Thane's age, Langston had to be the first . . . though he could have been the "half." Ceony could understand firing an apprentice like Langston. Those monstrous hands could never form the minute and intricate Folds required by intermediate and advanced Folding.

Yet Ceony found her own jaw dropping as Langston picked up Jonto's right hip with a fairylike touch and turned it over in his hands, examining its components. Setting it down, he picked up a square parchment of medium thickness and, with his tongue pinched in the corner of his mouth, began carefully Folding it to reflect the hip's smallest part.

"Astonishing," Ceony commented as the two worked. "I wouldn't mind having a fellow his size with me right now."

Rubbing a chill from her arms, she murmured, "I wouldn't mind either fellow with me right now."

Fennel pawed at her leg. Ceony absently reached down to pet his head.

Surely Langston had been certified as a Folder by now. She wondered how long his apprenticeship had taken. She wondered if he had been happy to arrive at Mg. Thane's abode. If he had been polite upon meeting his teacher. If he had been grateful, as she should have been.

"We need to go," she said to Fennel, tearing herself from her ruminations. She gave a last fleeting look to Jonto—and to Thane—and hurried for the library's unpainted door. She had to throw her shoulder into it to nudge past a half-rusted lock—

Ceony found herself stumbling over lush beige carpeting. The sun had vanished, replaced by the lights of hundreds of electric bulbs centered between violet-painted alcoves studded with thick gold tiles, enchanted by Gaffers—glass magicians—to spread light outward in nearly prismatic rays. Soft music from multiple instruments touched her ears, alongside the clinking of wine glasses and unintelligible murmurs of too many people idly chatting.

Ceony paused, taking in her new surroundings. Fennel ran a few yards more before skidding to a halt.

Ceony knew this place—she had catered multiple dinners here with her old employer. This was Drapers' Hall on Throgmorton

Avenue, the finest hall in London, if not in all of England. At least, the finest Ceony had ever visited.

She stood on the balcony between wide gold-leafed pillars, their chapiters carved in tiers. Beyond them a great mural of wingless angels surrounded by flora painted the ceiling. She ran a hand over the balcony's gold-leaf railing. Though this was only a vision, little more than a dream, this one *felt* as though it were real.

She peered to the floor below. Round, white-clothed tables filled it in neat rows, while men and women in black carried silver trays and glass pitchers to and from the kitchen tucked away in the northeast corner. A string quartet played soft melodies in the southwest corner. Ceony recognized all of it, though her memory had a more up-front view. She had donned that same black dress and frilly apron before.

No . . . *she* had catered this event.

Pulling away from the railing, she looked about the balcony. Small tables, none large enough to fit more than four people, lined either edge of the mezzanine where it followed the curve of the wall. About a quarter of the tables were unoccupied, but Ceony walked briskly and searched them first, for if the heart had spit her out here, she knew Thane couldn't be far.

And she was right. She spied Thane looking no different than she knew him now—save for the lack of that indigo coat—sitting at a small, square table with a balding man Ceony had never before met.

Thane leaned his chin into his palm, much the same way he had at his titling ceremony when he became a magician, looking every bit the part of bored. His companion must not have noticed, for the balding man prattled without the slightest hitch or hesitation, gesturing every now and then with a flick of his butter knife or a tip of his head.

". . . and she insisted that all proper ladies needed satin scarves, and said that Mary Belle had three satin scarves all in shades of blue, so of course I had to allot her the money," the stranger said, pausing only to take a sip of his drink—mulberry wine, and from a very expensive year, if Ceony remembered correctly. Yes, she remembered the wine served at this event *very* well. "With her coming-out party in May, I certainly can't have her go without a satin scarf. I try very hard to keep in tune with women's fashion, what with her mother away to Crafton and all."

Mg. Thane tapped the nail of his middle finger against the edge of his plate, his food only half-eaten. He'd already drained his wine glass, and with most of the servers on the main floor, no one had come by to refill it. His eyes looked glazed—not from alcohol, but from tedium. Couldn't this bald man see that?

"What do you think, Emery?"

Thane blinked, and Ceony caught the brief reigniting of his irises. "Oh yes. The neck, of course, is crucial for a proper coming out. The irony in covering it, of course, clashes with the event, but you can't have your youngest colder than the other girls at the party."

Ceony smiled at that, though the balding man only nodded and said, "Exactly. She'll stand apart in all the wrong ways."

Ceony laughed. Were Thane and this man even having the same conversation?

Thane's gaze drifted back to the ballroom floor. Stepping beside him, Ceony tried to follow his line of sight, knowing it wasn't worth trying to get his attention. She guessed he peered at the grandfather clock against the north wall, likely hoping for an escape of some sort.

*Escape* . . .

Stepping around her teacher, Ceony leaned over the balcony in search of Lira—if she could find the Excisioner first, perhaps she could form some sort of upper hand—but instead spied a familiar braid of orange hair waiting tables below. That was *her*!

She remembered this event, though she didn't recall Mg. Thane being at it. She would have remembered his face. Then again, at this event—a fund-raiser for some school board—she had only served on the floor, not in the balconies. The date was July 29, 1901. Just a week before the school year began at Tagis Praff.

It also happened to be her last day of work.

She squinted, watching herself fill wine glasses. She looked awful in that dress. It accentuated all the wrong places. Thank goodness she hadn't known Thane then. Her ears burned at the thought.

Ceony recognized one man in particular at the table her younger self served. Though he was a few years short of middle-aged, he had gray hair with a receding hairline and a long gray mustache that framed the sides of his mouth. He boasted broad shoulders and a well-tailored suit—perhaps the best-tailored in the entire ballroom, with three real-gold buttons and a red-pleated cummerbund. Oh yes, she remembered him. Him and his foul talk about the Mill Squats where she had grown up, blathering nonsense about its education and a nonexistent prostitute program just because the district was a poor one. Ceony remembered this night distinctly. She had hated that man, and she had done a good job of keeping her temper controlled, until—

She held her breath and watched, waiting for that moment. Waiting . . .

There it was. Ceony—younger Ceony—reached over to fill the man's wine glass, and his ungloved hand swooped right under her skirt. She still remembered his clammy fingers against her thigh.

Younger Ceony jumped back, scowled, and dumped the rest of that expensive mulberry wine right onto the man's lap. The man yelped and leapt up so quickly his chair fell backward and clamored against the marble floor. The sound—both the chair and the man's curse—echoed through the entire ballroom.

Beside her, Thane burst into laughter.

It startled Ceony. She glanced to Thane, ogling him, then realized he had been watching as well. He had seen Ceony dump half a pitcher of vintage wine onto the best-dressed man in the establishment, embarrassing the both of them in front of England's finest.

And Thane *laughed.*

"What's gotten into you?" the balding man across from Thane asked, oblivious.

"One of the waitresses just dumped a pitcher onto Sinad Mueller's lap," he chortled, picking up a sage-green cloth napkin to dab at his eyes.

Ceony paled. Had he said . . . Sinad Mueller?

Time seemed to freeze as that name processed in Ceony's mind. Sinad Mueller. *The Mueller Academic scholarship.* The scholarship Ceony should have been first pick for, but had lost last minute, crushing her dreams of pursuing magic. The scholarship that—once lost—resigned her to a life of housework just to earn enough for school to become a half-decent chef. It all made sense now.

Ceony stared as she watched her younger self storm back into the kitchen—where she would promptly be fired—as Sinad Mueller continued shouting expletives. Two of his colleagues darted from their chairs with napkins ready to make a futile attempt at cleaning the man up.

She released the rail and took a step back. All her muscles went lax.

That was why Ceony had lost the scholarship. She had dumped a pitcher of wine onto the very man who would have awarded it to her.

"He deserved it."

Ceony turned to see a second Mg. Thane standing over the one sitting down. This one wore a long indigo coat and his arms folded across his chest.

Ceony's eyes darted between the two Thanes, nearly identical, and gasped. "Thane?"

But the second Thane didn't look at her, only at the scene unfolding below. He appeared almost as unaware as his counterpart. And yet, when he spoke, it seemed as if he spoke *to* her.

"Sinad Mueller is a vile man behind closed doors," he said. "You can hear it in his voice, the way he talks, the way he looks at women—even young men. He hoards his money and doles it out publicly to only the best specimens, and he makes sure half the country knows of his 'generosity.' He plays the school board like a fiddle, and I for one believe he cheated on his exit exams. He enchants rubber about as well as a tire salesman."

Ceony clutched the strap of her bag and felt Fennel circle her legs. "He knew who I was."

"I found out who you were," Thane said, and Ceony wasn't sure if it was in response to her statement or merely the next line of his monologue. "He revoked your scholarship, so I stepped in." He chuckled to himself and rubbed his chin with his thumb. "I wanted to see the look on his face when that 'petulant, fiery girl,' as he put it, waltzed into Tagis Praff and stuffed his manner and his foul money right back into his coat pocket."

Ceony glimpsed the ballroom floor, but Sinad Mueller had already left the room. "You gave it to me to spite him?" she asked. "Fifteen thousand pounds just to spite someone you didn't like . . . not that I'm ungrateful. You have no idea how much it means to me—"

She turned back only to see the second Thane vanish. She darted from the railing, searching for him, but he had disappeared as easily as the moon on a cloudy night. If only she could put into words how much that scholarship meant to her, regardless of why she received it. The thank-you letter in Mg. Thane's office couldn't even come close to covering it. One more reason she couldn't let him die.

Ceony's gaze dropped to the ballroom and locked onto Lira, who appeared to be searching for her as well, near the string quartet. She held a small pool of blood in her palm and shook it slightly. A divining spell?

Ceony backed away from Lira's view, slipping her hand into her bag and counting her thin arsenal. She had something, at least, but what real good would paper animals do against a practiced Excisioner? Folding had never been meant for combat! "I have to get out of here," she whispered, picking Fennel up beneath his front legs. "I have to get out. Thane, where are you?"

But he didn't answer. Whatever method he had used to speak to her earlier had been lost.

Swallowing and clutching Fennel to her chest, Ceony hurried across the balcony. Where could she hide? What sort of damage could she do with a mere stack of paper? There was a reason she never wanted to be a Folder!

*I need to get out!* her mind screamed.

She slowed at the end of the balcony, then stopped altogether. Before her stood a door that she knew wasn't part of the ballroom—a white door rimmed with scarlet, without knob or handle. Glancing behind her, she saw Lira's head crowning the top of the stairs that led to the balcony.

Ceony pushed her way through the door and staggered through a puddle of blood.

She gasped and bit her lip to stifle a scream as the door behind her vanished. She had reentered the fleshy chamber of Thane's heart and stepped right into a river of blood that flowed steadily past her ankles. The loud pulsing of Thane's heartbeat reverberated through the chamber's walls: *PUM-Pom-poom.*

Trying to steady her breathing, Ceony followed the river's current, her knuckles straining with the closed fists at her sides. The blood flowed higher and higher up her leg until she waded with it above her knees. Almost too deep. She gritted her teeth and tried not to think of being pulled beneath its surface.

She saw another door, but this one made of flesh and veins, pulsing in rhythm with the rest of the room. One with no windows or knobs, no locks or hinges. Just flesh pressed tightly against flesh, like a long, swollen cut that wasn't meant to heal.

Somehow, Ceony knew she needed to get through it.

Lira's voice sounded softly above her, no doubt carried on the particles of a spell, for the woman lingered nowhere in sight. *Caught up in a vision, somewhere*, Ceony hoped. "Not that I'm discontented to leave you trapped in here, dearie," the voice said, "but I don't want you stinking up the place. Let's get this over with, shall we? Swift and quick. I'll even leave your body in one piece. Maybe two."

Despite the wet heat of the chamber, gooseflesh pimpled Ceony's arms. She clutched the strap of her bag and forced air into her lungs, though a flutter broke her breath here and there. She couldn't fight Lira, not yet. Her best option was to keep going—find the end of Thane's heart and, hopefully, its exit.

"I need you to fold up, Fennel," she told the dog, her words nearly inaudible. "Fold yourself up and get into my bag, where it's safe. Just for a little while."

The dog quirked its head to one side.

"Go on," she said, and the dog tucked its head down and its legs in. Ceony pressed against Fennel's sides gently with her hands until he formed a thick, lopsided pentagon. She carefully wedged the creature into her bag, between sheets of paper.

Taking a deep breath and holding it in her throat, Ceony pushed herself between the fleshy walls of Emery Thane's heart into the second chamber.

# CHAPTER 9

THE WALLS OF THANE's heart pressed against her on all sides, pulsing with their loud *PUM-Pom-poom* and drowning out the unnatural light. They squeezed against her, tight and tighter, as if she were being run over by an empty buggy with more and more passengers climbing inside it, making its wheels crush her. It felt like drowning.

Her own muscles tightened as adrenaline surged through her body. She couldn't breathe. Heat from the walls seeped past her clothes and into her skin, making her too warm, too hot. One would think a heart disconnected from its person as long as this one had been would feel cold, but not Emery Thane's heart. Emery Thane's heart defied the physics of everything Ceony had come to know over her nearly two decades of life. Though unless she found a way out, she wouldn't see her twentieth year!

A tear squeezed through clenched eyelids. She clawed at the walls, trying to shove past them, gasping for air but finding none. She tasted blood on her lips—blood that wasn't hers. She inched forward, pushing back against the flesh that pushed against her and tugged at her bag. Her head began to pound, her vision blurred—

A surge of blood from the river at her feet pushed against her rump, shoving her through the valve. Her hand touched open air. Digging her heel into flesh, Ceony pulled herself into the second chamber of Thane's heart, gasping and choking, spitting and wheezing.

She bit down hard on her own teeth, sucking in mouthfuls of hot air, trying to calm her own trembling. Trying to prevent a sob. *It's over, it's over,* she told herself, and it helped somewhat. *I chose to do this. I can do this.*

*I* have *to do this.*

She had barely caught her breath when she heard a suctioning sound from the valve behind her.

Ceony looked over her shoulder. The river that had pushed her out of the valve—and into a chamber almost identical to the first—continued to flow after her, filling the gutters around the edges of the heart and beyond. Flooding them . . .

"No, no," Ceony said, shooting up with a renewed vigor. Her clothes, sticky from the bloody valve, clung to her clammy skin. "Stop, stop. Please stop."

But the blood—thin blood, watery blood—continued to gush from the valve and overflow the rivers, inching closer and closer to Ceony's feet.

Ceony backstepped to the center of the chamber, the highest ground. The first tides of blood touched her shoe.

Her skin turned to ice. Her lips numbed. "Thane!" she shouted, hugging her bag tightly to her. "Let me out of here!"

She took another step, the blood up to her ankles. At this rate it would fill the entire chamber in minutes. Ceony couldn't swim. She had nowhere to go.

She really was going to drown.

"Thane!" she screamed, trembling from chin to ankle. Even her cry shook.

*Anything but this. Anything but drowning.*

The blood continued to flow, the heart's thumping deafening. She squeezed her eyes shut, released her bag, and pressed her palms to her ears. Too much.

"Please, please, please . . ."

The lapping blood around her feet vanished, leaving her socks dry, albeit stiff. Biting her lip, Ceony opened her eyes to shelves of familiar books and a ray of dust-filled light. She released a long breath and offered a silent thanks to both God and the paper magician.

Images flickered around her: Thane in a gray coat instead of indigo, Folding on the floor, a blond man she didn't know studying at the desk, another Thane in scarlet thumbing through books. The people flashed for half a second, sometimes a whole second, and then dissolved. Someone or something had pulled Ceony from the flooding chamber and stuck her here, but the heart itself seemed unsure as to what to show her.

She spied over her shoulder, but the tight valve she had just passed through no longer throbbed behind her. It had been replaced by a tall shelf of books, all as they had been in Thane's true library, though she noted these had been arranged by color across the entire wall, from shelf start to shelf end. She gaped at them. Red books, dark and light, lined the left shelf closest to the door, and following them sat a few orange books, then tawny and yellow books, and then white. On the right shelf the colors continued—green, blue, violet, gray, and black. Incredibly aesthetic, but entirely absurd. Thane's library didn't look like this at all. Was this a past arrangement, or a future one?

Quick to her feet—which still wavered just a bit from her unpleasant traveling between chambers—Ceony took a moment to unfold and reanimate Fennel before picking through the titles, searching for something that might help her should Lira catch up to her. Something to fight with, to defend herself with. Even a heavy book for melee would do her better than nothing.

Her index finger passed over *Mating Habits of Crocodiles*, *A Living Paper Garden*, and *Frankenstein*.

"Ah," she said, her hand pausing on a short, fawn-colored volume where the orange covers shifted to the yellow spectrum: *Basic Chain Spells*. To her relief, the book felt solid beneath her fingers. Perhaps in a heart, knowledge was more stable than memory or thought. Judging by the window in his office, it was clear Thane knew paper chains well.

She opened *Basic Chain Spells* to the table of contents, the constant *PUM-Pom-poom* in the distance reminding her of the need for swiftness. Lira could have warped out of Thane's heart and be throwing it into the ocean right now for all Ceony knew, and Thane's time was ticking away besides.

Skipping the table of contents, Ceony began thumbing through pages illustrated with black-and-white diagrams of different chains from basic to complex. She spied the vitality chain Thane had used on both the birthing woman and himself, but kept turning the pages.

The word *shield* popped out at her, and she paused just past the book's midway point. She read quickly.

The three-fold shield chain is the most basic of the defense chains. The breadth of its links does not matter, so long as their length is enough to circumvent the item one wishes to protect.

A link is created by taking a standard 8" x 11" sheet and slicing it in half longways, as seen in Figure 1—

Ceony's eyes scanned the figures and their captions, then she turned the page and scanned them again, committing them to memory. Setting the book down, she pulled sheets of paper out of her bag until she found pieces already cut as the diagram showed.

She began Folding, her hands unsteady, but not shaking quite as badly as they had when she formed Thane's pathetic heart. She prayed it still beat. If he died . . .

Ceony didn't want to think too hard on the idea.

She matched up the edges and creased them. Another flash of Thane appeared behind her with his Folding board, this one in the correct shade of indigo. He phased in and out, Folding different things with his hands, his voice pealing and cutting short. Ceony could barely make out a word he said, but she thought she heard her name.

She saw a flash of herself in her apprentice's uniform before both apparitions vanished.

Ceony refocused on her chain. "Do you want to keep teaching me?" she asked as she started her second link, working a little faster now that her fingers knew the Folds. The faint tingling sensation she felt when Folding now had almost become natural to her. "I don't mind, if you do."

Ceony listened to the steady, distant beats of Thane's heart as her fingers pressed paper and her nails set the Folds' creases. When her chain reached just long enough, she hooked its ends together diagonally over her breast and pulled out another sheet of square paper, Folding something Thane had given her several days to practice—a paper fan.

*"Made well, it can give gusts that would embarrass a thunderstorm,"* Thane had said. She had yet to test the spell's true power, but she hoped the paper magician hadn't been exaggerating.

The library began to waver about her as she finished—her small sanctuary had begun to collapse. She'd change scenes any moment now.

Stuffing her untested fan into her bag, she ran for the library door. Fennel loped behind her.

Ceony passed through the library door and, for the second time since meeting Mg. Thane, stepped into a room thundering with applause.

The Royal Albert Hall. She recognized the auditorium and the chandeliers, only these boasted electric bulbs. A spotlight blinded her, forcing her to shield her eyes with one hand. Unlike last time, she didn't stand in the aisle, but on the stage.

Fennel panted at the sight of so many people. Ceony felt faint.

The glare of the spotlight diminished enough for her to take in her surroundings, the pale stain of the wooden stage, an older Tagis Praff standing at the podium stage left. Looking down, she saw herself dressed in a magician's uniform, all its seams perfectly pressed. The white fabric fit her better than any clothes she had ever worn, and she noted she wore slacks, not a skirt. Didn't all female magicians wear skirts with their uniforms?

"Ceony Twill," Tagis Praff said, and the audience continued to clap. Ceony spied Thane in the front row, donning his own uniform. Watching her with smiling, proud eyes. She drank that expression in, storing it in the deep wells of her memory.

Tagis Praff waved for her. Fennel trotted up to the podium, and Ceony, hesitantly, followed suit. She reached out to accept the magician's hand.

The applause died and the spotlight vanished. Her sticky dress replaced the crisp white uniform of her dreams. The temperature dropped and Tagis Praff's hand vanished, replaced by a long, stone hallway.

Ceony blinked twice and realized she was in a prison.

She gasped, having not expected a place so dreary to be within Thane's heart. She stood at the end of the hallway, which was lined on either side by broad metal doors that bore the sheen of enchantment. Ceony had never been inside a real prison, but she had read books concerning them. And just like in those books, all the doors had locks, and the hallway had a gray, prestorm cast to it, made by thin trickles of sunlight that came through narrow windows between each cell. Windows that even a toddler could barely fit a hand through.

Ceony snapped her fingers to beckon Fennel to follow her, as her voice had been startled from her throat and floated somewhere between her lungs and her stomach. She took a step forward, her skirt swishing about her calves, the fabric cold after its dampening in the tight, suffocating passageway that had led her to this chamber. She hoped she wouldn't have to pass through another. The thought gave her goose bumps, but the prison gave her chills.

A guard came around the corner, a brawny man with a mustache and a neck so muscled it looked as if he bore steel cords beneath the skin. He wore a pistol at one hip and a club at the other, and his face settled into the sort of look that guaranteed no criminal would dare *sneeze* on his watch, let alone escape. Ceony froze under that stare until she validated that, as with all the previous visions, this man could not see her. She waved a hand in front of his face as he passed to be sure. She didn't play a role in this vision, then.

"Sit up for breakfast!" the guard shouted, pulling his club from his belt and beating it along each prison door, lifting a small metal flap that revealed wrought-iron bars just wide enough to let a plate of food slip past. "Sit up or don't get fed, your choice!"

Ceony winced at the loud clamor of the club on iron, then dared to peek into one of the cells.

She stumbled back from its bars until her shoulders touched the opposite stone wall.

*Lira.*

Lira lay in that cell, her hair long and frayed at the ends, her body draped in a brown prisoner's uniform, her eyes downcast. She sat up before the guard's club reached her cell, but that didn't stop him from rattling her door all the same.

Lira in prison. If only.

Ceony tiptoed away from her and peered into the next cell, seeing a lanky, dark-skinned man with a long scar across his nose. She didn't recognize him, but the face in the next cell sparked a memory—the thick chin, small eyes, and crinkled forehead looked just as they had on the WANTED poster she had spied at the post office two years ago:

WANTED

GRATH COBALT

FOR CRIMES AGAINST THE STATE

Ceony stepped back from the bars. She remembered what the poster had said. Remembered the way it had made her scalp itch. Excision. Grath Cobalt was an Excisioner—and the most dangerous Excisioner in all of Europe, so rumor told.

Ceony's back hit the cool stone behind her once more as she watched the powerful man now in chains and behind bars, jarring ever so slightly as the guard's club passed over his door. Now that she studied him, she noticed he had lost weight from what the poster had depicted of him. Lost muscle. He looked . . . docile.

"These are your hopes," she whispered as another strong guard pushing a wheel-cart of food came down the forlorn hallway. "These are your hopes, aren't they, Thane? You hope I'll continue to learn paper magic, that I'll study it like you have. You hope these Excisioners—the people you've been hunting down—will finally be arrested and pulled from society."

"But it won't happen," said a sickly sweet voice down the corridor.

Ceony whirled around. Lira—the real Lira—stood at the end of the hallway clad in black, her long dagger cradled in her right hand. A heavy leather sack hung off her left shoulder. The vision of the prison began to shift and blur around them, as though Lira's presence made the dream harder for Thane's heart to grasp. Like a sleeper being woken from a dream.

Ceony's spine went rigid and she stepped back, ready to call for the bulky guard—but he had vanished. Both guards had, and the cells around her stood empty, leaving Ceony alone in the midst of a dripping, warping prison with only Lira and Fennel as company.

Fennel growled, his paper lips almost rippling with the sound.

"What do you want?" Ceony asked, her voice quivering almost as much as the rest of her did. She touched her shield chain, then reached shaking fingers into her bag.

"Me?" Lira asked with a red-painted mouth, taking a broad, strong step forward, then another. The bag on her shoulder swayed stiffly with the movements. "I want Emery's whore dead. I don't like sharing."

"I'm not . . . his *whore*," Ceony said, stepping back once, twice, three times. Gritting her teeth, she forced herself to hold her ground. She had come here knowing she'd have to face Lira. That, and Ceony would rather go down fighting than be crushed like a cockroach backed into a corner.

Lira quirked a brow at Ceony's stance—perhaps she was impressed. Or amused. Thane's wife—hopefully *ex*-wife—wasn't as easy to read as Thane himself.

"I don't care what you are," Lira said, the words so light they chimed like laughter. "But Emery's heart is mine—it always has been, my dear. Even if the rest of him defies everything I believe in . . ." She lifted a long-nailed hand and squeezed it into a fist. "His heart is still worth something to me. A heart that's known love is stronger than one that hasn't, did you know that?"

Lira took another step forward, and her dark eyes dropped to Ceony's chest. "You'd make an interesting pet. Have you known love? Hate? I wonder how strong *your* heart is. Why don't we find out?"

"No!" Ceony shouted, fingers clutching the first Folds they felt in her bag. At the same moment, Lira dropped the leather bag from her shoulder and, with a quick command, half a dozen severed hands rose from its mouth, bloodied and raw at the wrist, their fingers pale and violet, their nails jagged and blue. They floated on invisible wings, their stiff, foul fingers wriggling and reaching.

Lira swiped her own hand forward, and her army of extremities sailed down the hallway toward Ceony like a wave of hornets.

Ceony threw out her own spells and shouted, "Breathe!"

The yellow fish and white bird she had Folded earlier sprang to life before her, the fish swimming through air as though it were water, the bird flapping its stiff wings and charging right for the palm of the darkest hand shooting toward her.

But Lira had six hands, and Ceony only had two animals— paper animals. Two of the hands crushed Ceony's delicate paper creations in their palms and dropped to the floor. The other four rushed for her.

"*Thane!*" Ceony screamed, turning around and running down the hallway. She reached the door at its end, but its handle stuck. Locked.

Ceony held her breath and fished into her bag for something, anything. She felt sheet after sheet of paper until she touched something Folded: the paper fan. She whirled around and raised it.

The lead severed hand grabbed her by the throat just as she flapped the fan across her body.

A gust of wind burst from the fan and filled the corridor, striking the remaining three hands just before they reached Ceony. The wind pushed them back, sending them spiraling through the air.

The gale didn't reach the hand around Ceony's neck. It squeezed, cutting off her air. She choked, but flapped the fan again and again.

New gusts pushed the hands farther back and lifted the fallen ones off the floor, the crumpled bodies of her bird and fish flying with them. The hands, paper, and gales collided into Lira—one hand knocked the dagger from her grasp. The second gust knocked her off her feet, and the third made her skid across the stone floor to the opposite wall.

The prison walls began to melt as the vision held by Thane's heart broke. Ceony dropped to her knees, red-faced, clawing at the fingers digging into her neck, gasping for air that wouldn't come. Her face grew hot. Her eyes bulged. She pried off one finger, two—

Fennel launched himself at the hand's thumb and chomped down on it as hard as a paper jaw could chomp, and with a hard jerk he pulled the hand away from Ceony's neck. Hot air carrying the scent of iron and rot rushed down Ceony's throat. She coughed so hard she thought she would wretch, especially with the bloodied appendage flopping on the dissipating stone floor before her.

Staggering to her feet, Ceony stomped her shoe down on the hand twice before it stopped moving. She stomped it twice more for insurance.

Sinking to her knees, Ceony rasped, "Good boy. Good . . . good boy."

Her hand clutched the paper chain that wrapped around her chest and over one shoulder. The shield. She had Folded it wrong. Gotten overconfident.

But Lira—Lira was gone, for now. The pain in Ceony's neck lessened as the Excisioner's absence dawned on her. Lira had bested even Ceony's pistol, but Ceony had won this round. Barely, but she had won. Thane would be proud of that.

Ceony leaned against the heavy door behind her, cracking it open. Fennel's paper tail wagged wildly behind him as wildflowers in fuchsia, marigold, and amethyst grew beneath his feet. The gray hues of the prison lightened to deep orange highlighted by salmon, and a warm summer breeze tousled Ceony's hair.

Slipping the fan—her fantastic, wonderful fan—back into her bag, Ceony rubbed her neck and stood once more.

The same scenery from the flower-covered knoll in the first chamber surrounded her—the hill looked over a thick tree line at sunset, and the broad plum tree reached skyward just ahead of her. Thane lay beneath it, but he looked as she knew him, not younger, and the woman beside him wasn't Lira.

She closed her eyes for a moment, inhaling the sweet flavors of honeysuckle and earth, expanding her lungs and giving her heart a chance to calm down. She rubbed the lingering sensation of cold fingerprints from her neck before opening her eyes to the beauty once more and approaching the plum tree.

Her heart twitched in her chest as she neared, and while she wanted to believe it twitched from her nearly fatal run-in with Lira, she knew that wasn't the case. However, the more she tried to focus on this new woman beside Thane, the more her image blurred.

Ceony paused just at the edge of the blanket. The woman . . . she wasn't a woman, not really. She had no face, only the start of one, and her hair seemed to have no definite length or color. The lines of her body curved enough to show her womanhood, but not enough to define weight, height, or shape. Beside Thane—who watched the setting sun with such peace, with such light in his eyes—the "woman" seemed imaginary.

*Because she is*, Ceony realized, a second breeze tickling her skirt and blowing loose flower petals across her vision. *These are the things Thane—Emery—hopes for.*

She studied him, his peace and his contentment, the eyes that seemed to radiate life. She studied the shadowy woman beside him from head to foot. *He wants to fall in love again.*

Though she knew he would not see her, Ceony waved her hand before Emery Thane's face, hoping he would blink and look up at her, wanting those eyes to notice her the way they had noticed Lira amidst cherry trees and gossamer. Because she needed his help. She needed Thane's help to escape him, for if she didn't escape him, she'd never save him, and Ceony felt she'd be doing both herself and the rest of the world a great disservice to let such a life-filling gaze vanish from existence.

And if Emery Thane died, some other poor chap with dreams of bespelling metal would be assigned to paper out of necessity, and Ceony certainly couldn't let that fate fall onto anyone else's shoulders.

She twisted her messy braid around her index finger. Hope. She wondered what her hopes looked like now.

She stepped onto the blanket, just at its edge, and knelt down, massaging her throat. She'd have bruises, surely, but nothing worse than that. Nothing she couldn't manage. *I've managed worse.*

The warm breeze twirled about her shoulders before scooping up the seeds of an aged dandelion and tossing them into the plum tree's dark leaves. The wind reminded her of the stickiness of her hair and stiffness of her clothes, the aftermath of pushing through the valve between chambers.

Taking a deep breath in an attempt to encourage herself, she slipped the paper chain over her head and studied it. Though she knew the version of Emery Thane beside her was not the real one, she felt safe in his presence. Safe as she could feel, sharing his heart with a practiced Excisioner, who could be anywhere . . .

A quick survey of the scene showed that Lira was nowhere to be found, so she turned her attention back to the Folded paper she held. Ceony passed the links of the chain slowly through her hands, studying each until she found one just a bit wider than the others—that must have been the error. Pulling a half sheet of paper from her bag, she began to create a replacement.

Laughter touched her ears, but not cold laughter. Not Lira's. She heard a child's laughter, light and happy. Fennel barked in response.

Ceony turned and saw a shapeless child that matched the woman beside her—a child no older than three, but without a definite face or solid coloring. *A boy,* Ceony thought. He ran through the wildflowers with his small, nondescript hands stretched high over his head. A moment later a second child joined him, a little taller. A girl. They laughed and twirled about one another, parading up and down the hill in their own little game. Their play woke an orange butterfly from the grass at their feet. Its wings looked like fire in the setting sunlight.

Ceony couldn't help but smile to herself as she finished Folding the link. "So you want a family," she whispered. "I do, too. Someday."

She replaced the bad link in her chain and stowed it under the blanket, where Lira—should the woman be tracking her—wouldn't find it. This time, when Ceony placed the chain around her, it stiffened and tightened like a belt. Hopefully that meant she had done the spell correctly.

As Ceony stood, she realized she didn't want to leave this vision. This hope buried deep in Emery's heart, so crisp and real that she could smell the sugar welling deep within the flowers' stems and feel the lingering heat of the sun that seemed frozen in its descent. It was such a peaceful hope. Ceony wondered if her own heart could create something even half as stunning as this.

She touched Emery's hand where it rested on the blanket, and found that, for once, she didn't immediately phase through it.

Instead, it felt like touching glass. "I'll take care of you," she said. "You'll have this day. I promise."

She and Fennel stepped off the blanket and back to the grassy door Ceony had stumbled upon on the last flowery knoll. She pulled the brass handle, and the sunset melted away into stone and wood.

Ceony stood in the middle of Parliament Square.

# CHAPTER 10

THE SLOPE OF WILDFLOWERS changed instantly into cobblestone in all shades of gray—charcoal, ash, slate, and steel. Big Ben—the bell in the tall, pointed clock tower to the north—rang out nine o'clock. The great statue of Sir Ryan Walters gripping the reins of his frenzied warhorse stood proudly in the center of the square. Its detail was so infinitesimal that the statue looked ready to come alive on all sides, but of course it never did. Sir Ryan Walters and his steed had been carved in stone, and since man had not created stone, no magician could enchant it.

People milled about Ceony on all sides of Parliament Square, seeming to give her a great deal of space without actually noticing her presence. They passed by numerous shops that all had doors facing the statue, and a few shuffled in and out of a six-story apartment building wedged between a dumpling shop and a post office, with narrow alleys on each side. Ceony had never been inside the building, but she imagined seeing the bill for one room's rent would hurt her eyes for all the digits it would have.

Many of the square's shops had CLOSED signs over the doors—Wickers, the candle shop; Her Ladyship's Arms, a custom firearms dealer where she could have been contracted had her path to magic gone differently; and St. Alban's Salmon Bistro included. Ale for You, the liquor store, and Fine Seams, the tailor Ceony had patronized a few times, still boasted OPEN signs on their shops. It must have been a Sunday. Most businesses closed on Sundays.

Ceony loved Sundays. They were her favorite time of the week—the only break the Tagis Praff School for the Magically Inclined allotted its students, outside of feast days and Parliament Day. Sunday was the one day when, if Ceony did not have homework to catch up on, she could go into the city and enjoy herself. Indulge in a nice walk, soak in the sounds of life, savor a simple sandwich, or read by the three-tiered water fountains opposite Big Ben in Parliament Square. Those fountains *did* have an enchantment, for when they had been constructed, a Polymaker—a plastics magician—had designed a special lining for each tier that made the falling water cascade in different patterns every five minutes. There were a few months of Ceony's life when she considered becoming a Polymaker, if only to create something similar to that fountain.

She idly wondered if Emery—Mg. Thane, that is—enjoyed Sundays as well.

Skimming her surroundings, Ceony found an odd archway ten paces to her right, wooden and painted red. She neared it, touched its side—

Ceony blinked and found herself standing in a different spot on Parliament Square, the far-east side, her nose only inches from an old wooden door bound with ironwork rusted along its edges. A particularly long splinter pointed at her right between the eyes.

She took a step back as a bell pealed through the air—not Big Ben, but the brass bell that hung somewhere within the building before her. This place was a church—the faded sign above the door read "Collegiate Church of St. Peter at Westminster." She vaguely remembered the building from her passes through the real Parliament Square. Fennel scratched the bottom of the door with his paw.

Though a thorough scan of the crowd brought no signs of Lira, Ceony Folded a paper jay and commanded it, "Breathe." Holding one wing so the creature couldn't flit away, she added, "Keep an eye out for a woman in black, with long hair and bloody nails. Peck at the windows if you spot her."

The bird hopped in Ceony's palm and she released it, letting it fly high over the square.

Ceony grabbed the church door's thick iron handle and heaved the door open. She stepped into a dim hallway. On her third step she felt herself whisked away once more, and on her fourth she appeared on a narrow balcony in the back of a wide congregation hall, sandwiched between two circle-top windows trimmed with stained glass. Two rows of white Y-shaped pillars stretched before her, between which rested two rows of brown-lacquered pews. More circle-top windows let in sunlight, and three-tiered chandeliers with looping arms provided more light yet. At the front of the chapel the largest window took up almost the entire wall and had such minute stenciling in its stained glass that, from where she stood, Ceony couldn't decipher the images. She did, however, have a good view of the church's attendees.

They filled about half of the pews. A man dressed in a white robe and a long, dark stole over his shoulders stood at the front of the congregation holding a heavy-looking and worn Bible in his hand, but what he read Ceony couldn't hear.

"I envy them," said a familiar baritone beside her.

Ceony jumped. Emery Thane stood beside her, not quite touching the balcony railing, his arms folded across his chest. He looked as he did when he appeared at the banquet where Ceony had lost both her scholarship and her job. His dark brows pulled together just slightly, but not enough for true consternation, anger, or whatever he might have been feeling. The rest of his face and posture remained calm. Ceony couldn't see enough of his eyes to read them, as they were downcast and watching the minister below.

Tingles like the trails of soft feathers coursed down her neck. If he looked the same, would she be able to talk to him?

"Thane!" she exclaimed. "I need your help!"

But the paper magician didn't respond, only held his gaze. Ceony chewed on her lips before trying something else.

"Envy who?" she asked, stepping closer to him.

"Them," he answered with a slight jerk of his chin, directed to the faithful audience in the pews. It relieved Ceony that he replied to her at all. It seemed this Emery Thane, while outside the vision, was only a sliver of his true self—a sliver that existed in the second chamber of his heart. "All of them, really. I envy their faith."

Ceony glanced to the men and women in the church. "You want to be Anglican?"

Her friend Anise Hatter had belonged to the Church of England, one of the sects that embraced the use of material magics. Ceony had only been to the Church's Mass once.

"I think life would be much . . . simpler . . . if a man could believe in one solid thing," he answered, still not looking at her. "Bits and pieces here and there do no good for a man's soul. Thinking all of it is right or all of it is wrong does no good, either. Just as a magician cannot work all materials. He must choose one. But how does he know? How do these people believe in this faith, but not the others? Yet they are happy."

Ceony touched his elbow, finding it solid—more proof that this Emery Thane stood separate from the vision. "You just have to learn, I suppose," she said. "Explore until you know which one's right for you."

He glanced at her, his green eyes deep in thought and wondering in a subdued sort of way. "Do you believe in one thing, Ceony?"

Her heart sped as he said her name.

She considered the question. "I've never given it a great deal of thought. I suppose I don't. I think I understand what you mean, about there being good in all faiths. In all gods, in all beliefs. When I think about it . . . I guess I've just taken what bits and pieces I felt were right for me and made my own faith with them. Faith is a very personal thing, really. Just because you don't meet with a group of people once a week who believe everything exactly the way you do doesn't mean you don't believe in *something*."

He nodded, but his expression didn't waiver.

Ceony studied him, the set of his jaw and the lines of his profile. She would never have guessed that a paper magician such as Emery Thane would have hoped for a faith. She had fit him into a one-dimensional mold during their first meeting, and had done so with ease. Langston, too. How many others had she judged and set aside like that, thinking them no more than a one-sided piece of paper?

In the lull of their conversation Ceony heard the distant *PUM-Pom-poom* of Emery's heart, but it sounded . . . tired. A shiver coursed down her back. She scooped Fennel up in her arms and turned away from the balcony. She had to keep moving, keep progressing. She had to reach the *real* Mg. Thane before either of his hearts gave out.

She found the stairs that led off the balcony and took them quickly. They wound round and round, far longer than they should have been to reach the main floor only a story below. After what felt like four stories, Ceony spied a shimmering door at the stairs' end—a white door rimmed with scarlet, without knob or handle.

Holding Fennel tightly to her chest, Ceony reached one hand forward and pushed it open.

The church vanished around her, and with it Parliament Square. Ceony once more stood in a tall, fleshy chamber lined with blue veins and pulsing arteries, the constant *PUM-Pom-poom* that echoed throughout Emery's visions drumming in her ears and vibrating through the floor, a little slower than she remembered it.

Not ten paces from her she found another shallow river of blood and a valve—a different valve than the one she had come through. It led to the third chamber of Thane's heart. It had to.

The hairs on Ceony's arms stood on end and she whisked around, searching for Lira's dark hair, half expecting more severed hands to rise from the floor and seize her. Her heart beat just as loud as Emery's, thinking of the Excisioner. How long did she have before Lira caught up to her? Unless the woman waited in the next chamber . . .

She swallowed hard. Fennel licked her chin with a dry paper tongue.

"Fold up, boy," she whispered, trying hard not to tremble. She'd never trembled so much in life as she had in the last twenty-four hours! Curse Emery Thane for being such a difficult man to rescue!

Fennel did as told and folded up into his lopsided pentagon, and Ceony gingerly placed him between paper stacks in her bag. She eyed the valve and cursed again. She still remembered *exactly* how it felt to pass through those suffocating walls, unable to breathe and barely able to move. Too hot, too dark. Bitter fear on the back of her tongue tasted like unripe radishes. What if she didn't make it through *this* valve? What if it caught her up between its tight walls and . . .

She swallowed the fear and it formed a noxious lump in her throat. Still, it tasted better than failure. If Ceony lost Emery now, she'd never forgive herself. She had invested in this too deeply to go back.

Grinding her teeth, Ceony approached the tight valve sideways, pushing one arm between its thick walls, clutching her bag to her hip with another. She counted to three in her head.

On count two, she shouted, "I *deserve* a stipend after this!" The words echoed offbeat with the pulsing walls.

On count three she sucked in a deep breath and pushed herself between the walls.

The shield chain around her torso hugged her, and the hot walls of the valve pulled a few inches away from her, allotting her space to breathe. She sighed in relief, until she realized what an open valve would do to the rest of the heart.

Blood flooded around her feet, reaching clear to her thighs. The *PUM* of every *PUM-Pom-poom* shook her, freezing her every first beat of three. Her hair looped around her neck like a noose. Her own blood danced on her tongue from where she had bitten it.

She couldn't breathe. *She couldn't breathe.*

She forced her feet forward, her guiding hand searching for something to grasp. She squeezed her eyes shut as sweat from her forehead trickled into them.

Ceony felt empty space on the other side of the valve just as her lungs threatened to burst. She clutched the edge of the valve and pulled herself into a dark chamber, sputtering and gasping for air. Wiping her face on her dirty sleeve, she lifted her head and looked around. She stood in some sort of dark office. The only light came through a two-paned square window about three feet across, without blinds or curtains. Outside, a few stars glimmered in a deep-blue night. Was this the same office where Emery had finished his book? Wondering, Ceony pulled Fennel, still folded, from her bag.

Shuffling feet drew her attention away from the window. She scoured the room, searching for its source, but the shadows hid the perpetrator.

She clutched the folded Fennel to her breast. "Who's there?" she asked.

The shadows moved, and someone flew at her, ramming into her like a train. Ceony sailed backward into a wall, her head slamming against the boards, her newly found air expelling from her lungs. Her attacker pinned her with a forearm across her collar. For a second the dark room spun. *Lira!*

But as Ceony's eyes adjusted to the dark, she realized it wasn't Lira who had thrown her back. It wasn't Lira who scowled at her with bright emerald eyes.

It was Emery Thane.

# CHAPTER 11

EVEN IN THE DARKNESS she could see the anger blazing in those eyes, feel them pierce her like two jagged shards of glass. Emery's forearm pressed even harder into her collar with an almost painful strength. Black hair like shadows drooped over his forehead. The shield chain must not have recognized the pressure, for it did nothing to help her.

And suddenly Ceony stood on the other side of the office, Emery's arm gone from her chest. She gripped the side of a long desk for support. She had moved, but Emery remained where he had been, only instead of Ceony pinned against the wall, it was Lira—a younger Lira, her dark hair in loose ringlets over her shoulders, but her face still held a touch of familiar hardness.

"How dare you!" Emery seethed, almost shouting. The venom in his words hit Ceony's ears like hammers and shook her bones. It jarred her to hear such harshness from the paper magician's lips. "Do you even understand what all this means?"

"Get off of me!" Lira shouted back.

Emery conceded only a few inches of space. Still clutching the folded Fennel in her hands, Ceony edged toward them.

"Three days with no word. No word!" Emery hissed, his hands flying through the air like striking cobras. His shoulders tensed and made his neck look shorter. "And now you're a suspect in the Fräulein's disappearance!"

Lira's eyes widened.

Emery grabbed fistfuls of his hair and looked away for a moment—those boiling eyes passed over Ceony, but didn't see her. Unlike the Emery Thane in the Anglican church, this one was fully incorporated into the vision, unaware of Ceony's presence. Spinning back on Lira, Emery said, "And you don't even know. How have you not heard, Lira? Where have you been?"

"Does it matter?" she asked, her voice just as sharp as his, but her words touched the air with frost, not fire. "I'm not your dog, Emery!"

"Do you think it's not my business when my wife vanishes without a trace?" Emery asked, flabbergasted. A loud crash made Ceony jump, and it wasn't until she squinted that she saw Emery's fist against the wall, the paint cracked around his knuckles.

"Emery," Ceony whispered.

He pulled his hand back, wincing, and turned to Lira. "It's Grath Cobalt, isn't it?" he asked, half angry and half hurt. The emotions rolled over him like thunder, the lightning flashing behind those fierce eyes. He rubbed his sore knuckles like they were his own heart.

"Leave him out of it," Lira snapped.

Emery grabbed Lira's shoulders and shook her. "This is Excision you're dabbling in, Lira! Damn it, it's Excision! What excuses could you possibly assign it? Have you turned your back on everything good and right in the world already?"

The room heaved as Lira's hand sailed across Emery's face. Ceony's shoulder hit the office door—she had retreated from them and had run out of space, gaping as silvery light from the office's one window highlighted their persons. This wasn't the Emery Thane Ceony knew—his motions so sharp, his voice so commanding and hard. It scared her.

She fumbled for the doorknob behind her with a clammy hand, turned it, and fell onto her back.

She landed on cool, wet grass, a murky, overcast sky spread in even swathes above her. Soft half droplets of rain pelted her face and she quickly rolled over, protecting Fennel from the moisture. Cold air made her skin prickle and sent chills through her upper arms. Tucking Fennel beneath her shirt, Ceony pushed herself onto her knees, swiped a mess of rain- and sweat-dampened hair from her forehead, and took in her surroundings.

A flat lawn with no trees or gardens greeted her. A redbrick building that almost looked like a schoolhouse without a bell loomed far in the distance. No path led to it, but Ceony spied a cobbled road winding through the landscape far to her right. To her left stood several gray slate buildings with gabled roofs and no windows or chimneys. Too small to be homes. They looked like sepulchers, the homes of the dead.

Ceony found her legs and stood, her bag tugging at her shoulder. She switched it to the other side.

Standing gave her enough height for her eyes to find rows of neatly spaced indentations in the ground, each with its own cement plaque engraved with names and dates. Some had soggy or dead bouquets of flowers resting upon them. One had a small stuffed lamb, no larger than Ceony's hand, soaked through with rain.

Ceony did not frequent cemeteries. They were such sad places. Even the heavens thought so, for they wept steadily above her.

Nearly five years had passed since Ceony last trod among graves.

Ceony reached back for the office door, despite knowing it wouldn't be there. A chill in her arms drilled into her breast and stomach. "Not here," she whispered, shivering. She hugged herself. "I don't want to know what's here, Emery. Please."

But the scene didn't warp or shift. The cemetery awaited her, quiet as snowfall, the accompanying drizzle soaking through her blouse.

Chewing on her bottom lip, Ceony trekked to the cobbled road and followed it up a shallow hill. Fatigue finally dragged at her legs. What time was it? How long had she been inside Emery's heart? How long did she have left? She had no pocket watch, nothing to answer her questions. She imagined, by her weariness, that it had grown late . . . though her run-in with Lira and her scramble between chambers would be enough to tire anyone.

She pulled some cheese from her bag and ate it slowly, her stomach too tight for anything more. In the back of her mind she heard Emery's voice looping like a disc stuck in a phonograph, betrayal and anger lacing his words. If this chamber turned out to be what she thought it was, Ceony wanted to leave as soon as possible.

The cobbled road stretched up and over a small hill, and off to its left side Ceony spied a small gathering of people dressed all in black—two men in black suits, a preacher with a white-and-black collar, and four women in long black dresses, three of whom wore broad hats and netted veils over their faces. She approached them slowly, sore legs trudging up the wet slope. One of the men turned to a woman and whispered something in her ear. Ceony knew the man—the beekeeper—though he looked different. Perhaps it was merely the sorrow lining his features that changed him, but he looked drawn. Tired. The beekeeper. Emery's father. A jolt of panic shot through Ceony's torso.

Finding a new store of energy, Ceony jogged the rest of the way to the gravesite. Surely this wasn't Emery's grave! No person's heart could know the future, could it?

She froze mid-stride, only a few paces from the gravesite. *Unless this isn't the future*, she thought. What if she was too late? What if Emery had already . . .

Biting her lower lip, Ceony phased through the women, none of them sensing her presence, and faced two clean graves above two fresh mounds of dirt.

Between them stood a little boy no older than three holding a tiny bowler hat to his stomach. Rain weighed on his loose black curls and plastered the strands to his forehead, temples, and ears. He stared forward with little thought or expression, save for the pucker of his tiny mouth.

Ceony knelt beside him and tried to brush wet hair from his eyes, but of course her hand passed through him. Then she read the tombstones: "HENRY THANE, 1839–1874" and "MELODY VLADARA THANE, 1841–1874." Both had doves in mid-flight carved beneath the names, along with the image of two overlapping wedding rings.

Ceony pressed both hands to her chest.

"These are your parents," she whispered, glancing to the little boy, then to the beekeeper behind her. He had to be an uncle, judging by the family resemblance, slight as it was.

Anger. Infidelity. Death. Dark times—that's what these memories were. Ceony had passed through Emery's goodness and his hopes; it made sense to see his darkness, too. To see his hurts and his vices. To see the shadows cast behind those bright eyes.

The rain in the grass seeped into her skirt where her knees pressed the fabric to the ground. The little boy looked through her to an unmarked spot between the tombstones, the lids over his large eyes drooping. Raindrops clung to his dark eyelashes and pattered against his round cheeks.

"Please let me," Ceony whispered. "I know you're somewhere in here, Emery. Let me help him."

Ceony tried to push soggy hair back from the boy's face once more, and this time her fingers felt a glassy solid. Not skin and hair, but at least she could touch him.

She wrapped her arms around the little boy's shoulders and hugged him to her. "It will be okay, I promise," she murmured. "I've seen your future, and you accomplish a lot. Your parents would have been proud. It will get better. You'll be happy again." *I'll make sure of it.*

She kissed Emery on his forehead and pulled his hat from his fingers so she could set it on his head. The storm had already drenched him, but at least the hat would keep the water from his eyes. Standing, she searched for something dry to wipe her face with, but she had few options. She needed to get away from the rain—if she soaked through, so would Fennel, and she didn't think she'd make it much farther without him. Not in this dark place.

Reverently stepping over the graves, Ceony slid between the beekeeper and the priest and moved away from the funeral service and the path altogether, rubbing chills from her shoulders and neck. The cemetery seemed to stretch on forever, past all horizons, until the very sky seemed filled with graves.

Onward she trudged.

She reached a stone wall only as high as her knees and stepped over a portion that had weathered and crumbled. The grass grew shorter and harder beneath her feet until her shoes clacked on wide black and white tiles. An arching ceiling nearly three stories above her head replaced the clouds and rain. Ceony's hair and clothes instantly dried, and the air warmed to room temperature.

She took several seconds to absorb the massive atrium—no, a hallway—into her brain. Copper-colored columns lined the walls to her left and right, and between them pear-shaped alcoves showcased different treasures: painted vases, old and yellowed documents framed in thick glass, portraits of the queen or busts of queens past. One bust, oddly enough, looked especially worn on the nose.

Long rows of square windows let in sunlight through the ceiling itself. Something about the place seemed familiar to Ceony, but she couldn't pinpoint what. She had never been in this particular spot before. Or, perhaps, just not seen it from this angle.

She retrieved Fennel from the confines of her blouse. If the rain from the cemetery had gotten to him, then the change of scenery had dried that as well.

She unfolded the dog, who immediately popped to life and began scratching behind his paper ears with his back leg. Ceony laughed and rubbed his chin. "Stay close, boy."

She began walking, her footsteps sounding particularly loud, Fennel's especially quiet. The dog trotted off to a fern against one of the columns, sniffing the edge of its ceramic pot.

Faint whispers brushed Ceony's ears. She paused, listening. They came from ahead and around the corner. Given her recent interaction with the characters of Emery's heart, she approached the whispers with caution.

She recognized both voices—the first was Emery's. The second, which she strained to hear, belonged to Mg. Hughes.

She spied around the corner to see them both leaning against a wall outside a room with double doors. Those doors jogged Ceony's memory; this was Parliament. She had toured it once many years ago, back when her father still worked as a chauffeur.

". . . don't think it will work out," Emery whispered. He stood with his hands clasped over his elbows and his eyes cast to the opposite wall. He wore a sage-green coat similar to his indigo one, but with more buttons. "I've neglected him. He's only brought it up once, but at this point I'm delaying his certification. Edward is a bright young man. He deserves better, and I'll hardly make him defer."

"No, not defer," Mg. Hughes agreed, rubbing his short white beard with his index finger and thumb. "But they'll avoid transferring.

It hurts the method of the thing, takes time to switch over lesson plans and readjust. You both would need to make a good case."

"My marriage is falling apart, Alfred," Emery said. He let out a long breath and slid his hands into his pockets. His voice carried such weight that Ceony withered against the wall.

Mg. Hughes rested a hand on Emery's shoulder. "I'm sorry. On my third, myself. It's a hard thing, but surely given a bit of time —"

"I think she's an Excisioner," Emery interjected.

The words were barely audible, but they rang like cymbals in the empty corridor.

Mg. Hughes mumbled something on a dry tongue before sputtering, "You . . . you can't be serious."

"I prefer not to be, in most cases," he replied, "but I've seen the signs." He hesitated. "Then again, I haven't even *seen* her in four months."

The two men quieted for a long minute. As Ceony turned to leave, Mg. Hughes said, "What you *do* know, Emery, could be of use. I know some people—not the police, per se—who work tirelessly to extinguish the dark magics from her ladyship's domain. If you're willing, I could introduce you . . ."

Mg. Hughes's lips continued to move, but no voice filled the words, leaving him little more than a mime. Ceony's eyes darted between him and Thane, waiting for more information to pass between them . . . but they had become two marionettes, and Ceony was a poor lip-reader. Groaning, she resisted the urge to stamp her foot.

Fennel huffed behind her, and Ceony blinked, eyes burning from staring. As she moved away from Thane and Hughes and under a granite archway, however, she found not Parliament, but crowded hallways and stairs beneath a pebbled ceiling. A shrill bell rang over her head.

She stood at the end of the main hallway of Granger Academy, her secondary school.

The hallways were filled with young people chatting, walking, and eating lunch. One particularly frisky couple kissed by the tennis trophy case—which had far fewer trophies than Ceony recalled it holding—until a man in a sweater vest smacked a ruler along the boy's backside and told the couple to get moving. Behind her a trio of girls with high hairstyles and brightly painted lips whispered to each other with hands shielding their mouths. The shortest of the group laughed so hard she snorted, which caused her companions to snicker in turn. The trio shifted as a narrow-bodied woman holding a clipboard walked down the staircase behind them, a pair of spectacles balanced on the edge of her nose. The woman didn't look up at anyone as she passed by, including Ceony.

Ceony pulled her eyes from the people and refocused her attention on the building itself. She recognized Granger Academy, though the school looked a little different than she remembered it—some sort of linoleum tiles comprised the floor instead of the stiff maroon carpet she had tramped between classes for four years. The stair railings were pine with faded stain instead of oak. Other than that, the building looked the same. Granger Academy had been Emery's secondary school as well—perhaps this was what it looked like when he attended.

Thoughts of Anise Hatter surfaced in her mind. She pushed them away. Today she walked Emery's heart, not her own.

A flicker of black hair made Ceony jump, but it was only another girl not much younger than herself, a young woman who looked similar to Lira but with a broader face and stronger nose. Still, Ceony grit her teeth and said, "Who knows what we'll encounter here, Fennel."

She had to admit that the casual nostalgia of the school didn't quite match the mood the previous visions of the chamber had born.

Still, she would stay on alert, and hopefully Fennel would catch anything unusual that she missed.

Ceony touched the shield chain around her chest. If the water and blood had damaged it, the shift to Parliament, and now the school, had restored it. Good. She thought to take the time to Fold more birds against the hard school floor, but decided against it. The feeble paper heart she'd given Thane only allocated her so much time. She would have to trust her shielding spell and the fan to protect her.

She picked her way through the hallway lined with coat hooks and cubbies stuffed with books, crumpled homework, and lunch boxes. Class—or perhaps lunch—must have recently ended, for the hall filled with bodies. Ceony tried to evade them at first, but there were too many. They simply phased through her when she held her ground, reminding Ceony once more that she was the anomaly in this place. She and Fennel both.

The bulk of the students passed, followed by Mrs. Goodweather, Ceony's algebra teacher, looking plumper and a bit younger than Ceony's memory of her. Mrs. Goodweather swished by quickly in her tight purple skirt, and in her wake Ceony spied a group of boys, three standing and one on the floor with a book in his lap. He held a folded paper in his hands. The sight of his black hair made Ceony run to him.

"Em—" she began, but the chap on the floor was not Emery Thane in the slightest. He had shaggy black hair, yes, but his acne-pocked skin was too pale, his nose too pointed, and he wore a pair of finely wired glasses. Freckles like Ceony's own speckled his hands, and his eyes were a light brown, not green.

Still, she recognized the half-folded item in his hands—a fortuity box. Or the beginning of one.

"Guess paper's the only thing that'll let you put your hands on it, eh?" asked one of the standing boys, and his companions sniggered. "Don't you have anything better to do than take up space, Prit?"

Ceony rounded on the boys—she couldn't *stand* bullies—ready to give them a piece of her mind in hopes that the vision would allow her to interact with them. As she opened her mouth for a retort, however, her words caught somewhere between palate and tongue and dribbled over her lips incoherently.

The boy doing the jibing had short ebony hair and bright green eyes.

*Emery.*

He looked different—much younger, and lankier as well. He must have come into his height at an early age, for he stood half a head taller than his comrades and could not have been a day older than seventeen. His face looked thinner, his jaw slacker, and Ceony spotted a distinct lack of maturity around his eyes. Eyes that held no sympathy. Eyes just "having fun," as adolescent boys were bound to do.

"You deaf?" one of Emery's friends asked, the one on the left with a square face and broad build. He nudged Prit with his foot. "Don't you have anything better to do? We need this space for walking."

Prit frowned, his eyes downcast. He tried to smooth the fortuity box against his book—an astronomy textbook—to make the next fold, but Emery wedged his toe between Prit's legs and the book's cover, then flipped the book over. It tumbled off Prit's knee and onto the floor, closing on top of the fortuity box, ruining it. Not that it would have worked without the bonding, but still.

Emery and his companions laughed as Prit quietly gathered his book and stood. He turned his back on Emery just as the bullied had always been taught to do. *Just ignore them,* Ceony's mother had always advised, but Ceony knew from experience that ignoring didn't make pigs go away. The image of Mickel Philsdon surfaced in her mind, a broad-shouldered and stout boy who had called Ceony a walrus in the seventh grade, before Ceony had grown into her teeth. She had ignored him for two years, but the relentless torture had only gotten worse. It wasn't until the first day of secondary school when Ceony rounded on Mickel and cut him a steaming piece of her mind that he stopped his torment. As far as Ceony was concerned, the only thing bullies understood was bullying, plain and simple. Mickel had avoided her after that.

"Stick up for yourself," she found herself saying to Prit, who didn't respond.

Emery shoved Prit in the shoulder, making the boy stumble. "A little faster, paper boy?"

Prit picked up his pace and disappeared into the crowded hallway.

Frowning, Ceony turned to Emery and said, "You used to be a real jerk, you know that?"

Emery reached down to where Prit had been sitting and snatched up a paper sack—Prit had left his lunch behind. He rifled through it, the friend on his right trying to peer around his arm to see what was inside.

"Dibs on the cookie," Emery's flunky said.

Emery grabbed a red apple and tossed the bag to his companion, then slid down to the floor, stretching his skinny legs in front of him. Rubbing the apple on his sleeve, Emery took a bite.

Leaning to one side, Emery reached beneath him and pulled a folded frog out from under his backside—more of Prit's handiwork. He chuckled around a mouthful of apple and crumpled the frog in his hand. "What a barmpot," he said, throwing the paper wad at a dark-skinned girl passing by. The girl gave him a sour look, but continued on her way without retaliation.

"Come on, Fennel," Ceony commanded. As she lost sight of the paper magician, she took a deep breath. This was the past, after all. No use getting upset over it. "Still," she said aloud, "I'll have to ask you what changed your mind about Folding. And I hope you apologized to him."

Students filtered from the halls into their respective classrooms, thinning out the population enough for Ceony to find a set of double doors that appeared to lead outside. She assumed those doors would either reveal to her another shade of Emery Thane's heart, or warp her back to the third chamber itself, which she had yet to physically see. She hoped for the latter—she needed to escape Lira's trap quickly, and the only plausible way out seemed to be at the heart's end—she had to reach it, just as she had to play out each of these stories, one by one, to get there.

She opened the door and found herself in a familiar office—the first she had entered in this chamber, albeit lit with dim evening sunlight filtering through that square window and candles set on the desk and surrounding shelves. Ceony hesitated at the doorway to the office, the too-recent memory of it raking her brain with needles.

Emery sat at his desk, poring over a thin stack of papers, though not the Folding kind. He held a pen in one hand and tangled the other in his hair, worn shorter than in present day.

Fennel sniffed around the mauve rug strewn over floorboards stained with age. Ceony let the door shut behind her.

Everything in the office—smaller than the study at the yellow-brick house on the outskirts of London—spoke of Emery. Shelves, trunks, and furniture pressed against all four walls of the room, each set in an almost symmetrical order without allowing the tiniest bit of space to go unused. A fine-looking shelf of cherrywood held stacks upon stacks of paper in eggshell, chartreuse, and rose, all cut into different-sized rectangles and squares. Another shelf held together with metal clamps bore endless volumes of very old books, some of which Ceony recognized from a different shelf in Emery's present bedroom. Atop that shelf rested an assortment of glass bottles filled with bright colors of sand layered on top of each other, and beside those, an empty picture frame. Ceony wondered if it had ever held a photo. She didn't recognize it from the yellow-brick house.

A glass half-filled with some sort of tea sat at the end of Emery's desk. Ceony touched it—cold. A sniff caught a hint of peppermint. Now that she thought of it, she hadn't seen any coffee in Emery's kitchen—perhaps he didn't like the flavor. Or perhaps it made him jittery, and Ceony imagined "jittery" would not complement the list of Emery's personality traits.

Carefully placed clutter littered the desk everywhere except a perfect rectangle where Emery read those papers—a jar filled with writing utensils and a compass, a short calendar depicting a different species of tree for each day of the year, a bottle of blotting sand. More papers, folders, and small racks holding more papers and folders. Her inspection hesitated on a model of the Surrey Theatre entirely crafted from paper, from the columns standing guard at the front entrance to the English flag that flew from the spire protruding from the top of the theatre's dome. Ceony marveled at it for a few long seconds, wondering how much time and precision must have gone into such a detailed piece. Phasing or no, she dared not touch it, though the front doors *did* look like they were meant to open via the mouselike hinges that held them to the building's foremost wall.

She glanced to Emery. He created such beautiful things.

Emery flipped one of his pages over and began to write along the bottom of the next. Ceony finally settled her attention on the documents—thick legal jargon in small print crammed between one-inch margins on all sides. Each paragraph had its own number, and some sentences had been typed in all caps and separated with bold lines. Across the bottom Emery scrawled his signature—he had stunning handwriting, his lowercase letters all the same width and the capital E and T of his name drawn with minimal flourish. Part of Ceony wanted to trace those letters just so she could learn to scrawl half as well.

He turned that page and began to scour the next, his lips in a frown, his eyes set in concentration and wrinkled at the outside corners. Ceony read the header at the top of the page: "BERKSHIRE COUNTY CLERK | DECLARATION OF DIVORCE."

The light in the office dimmed as the sun finally dropped behind the world. Ceony spied the date he penned alongside his second signature. Exactly two years and five months had passed since this memory. Had he been living alone all this time?

Something clacked elsewhere in the house. Ceony stiffened and reached into her bag for her fan. But Emery had stiffened as well. He had heard it, too, which meant it couldn't be Lira. The images of Emery's heart reacted to Lira's presence just as they reacted to Ceony's—not at all. Whatever had made the noise had a place in this vision, though a prickling sensation still churned beneath Ceony's skin.

Emery stood from his chair, its legs scraping against the old wooden floorboards as it slid away from the desk. His jaw set above the high collar of his shirt. Stepping around the desk, he phased through Ceony as he approached the door.

A moment passed before he folded his arms and said, "I didn't expect to see you again."

Silence answered him.

A long sigh passed over Emery's lips. Ceony reached for his hand, but stopped herself. He said, "I have wards set up."

Another moment passed before the door opened past its crack. Ceony squeezed her fan as Lira appeared, to remind herself this wasn't the real Lira, the present Lira. Her hair was too short, and the malice in her face was less . . . prominent. In fact, she looked at Emery with the eyes of a lost hound dog and chewed on her lip like a scolded child. She wore a slim dress with a slimmer belt accenting her waist. The dress's collar had been unlaced halfway down, revealing the soft curves of her breasts.

Fennel barked and Ceony seethed inside, despite knowing all that she did. She forced her grip around the fan to relax, lest she wrinkle it and destroy its enchantment. Lira's tormented disposition was an act—that much was plain. Ceony didn't buy it for a second.

And neither did Emery. His expression remained perfectly schooled, like that of a frustrated parent.

"I need help," Lira whispered.

"Give me one reason why I shouldn't march to the telegraph right now and report you," he said, his voice stony. Ceony made a guess that Lira had been in more than one skirmish with the law since the last vision in this office. Ceony wondered if she'd bonded flesh yet, then cringed as the thought of *how* crossed her mind. She had no idea how one became an Excisioner, and she didn't want anyone to enlighten her.

Tears—real tears—brimmed on Lira's dark eyelashes. The woman had some talent. "Just one night, please, Emery," she pleaded. "I'll be gone in the morning. I just need someplace to stay."

"I know a few good prison cells that might do the trick."

"I'm innocent!" she said, and Emery only responded with an incredulous raising of one eyebrow. Lira's cheeks flushed and hard lines ridged her forehead. "Think of all I've given you, Emery! Don't you know what they'll do to me? I'm innocent!"

Emery scoffed and threw his hands out to his sides. Ceony winced at how the gesture exposed his heart. She pushed down the vivid memories of Lira's sharp fingernails digging into his chest as he hung against the dining room wall, Ceony helpless to stop it.

"I know what you are, Lira!" he exclaimed. "Everyone does! You think you can play on your innocence now?"

"You weren't there," she cried. Ceony stepped closer to her, studying her face, trying to find her secrets. Ceony wanted to push Lira away from Emery, but her hand passed through the woman's torso as if she were an illusion read from a storybook. No, Ceony wouldn't be allowed to interrupt this memory.

"You don't understand." Lira wept.

"I've tried to," Emery countered, sitting against the edge of his desk and grabbing it with stiff fingers. "Heaven knows I've tried to, Lira. Just . . . just go."

"I can't," she whispered. "They've tracked me here."

"And the others?" Emery asked. "Grath? Menion? Saraj?"

Lira shook her head, looking desperate. "I came alone. I want to get away from it all, Emery, you have to believe me! But how can I clear my name when Grath and his gofers have slandered it so? How can I start a new life when every cop in a blue hat is trying to fit a noose around my neck?"

Emery shook his head and rubbed his temples. "Criminals have gotten worse for less, Lira. Or have you forgotten—"

"I'm innocent!" she cried, stepping forward and grabbing Emery's sleeve. "I've been nothing but a mascot for them, a scapegoat! I know I'm a fool, but everyone deserves a chance to recover from their mistakes! And oh . . . my mistakes . . ."

Ceony frowned. "She's toying with you," she said. "Look at her eyes—it's an act. I took theatre in secondary—I know."

But this was the past; Ceony couldn't change it. Couldn't prevent the heartache this woman piled on top of Emery. Couldn't stop her from ripping his heart *out*.

But she wanted to.

She looked at Emery, whose eyes had begun to soften.

"Don't believe her!" Ceony shouted, and Fennel barked his agreement from behind her. A paper dog had more sense than this man! "You know what kind of person she is! What kind of person she'll become!"

"The worst of it is you," Lira whispered, batting those thick eyelashes. She sunk against Emery like a half-filled sandbag. "You are my everything, Emery, and I've ruined all of it. I let them get into my head . . . I thought you . . ."

She paused dramatically, pulled away from him. "But that doesn't matter anymore. You don't believe me."

"Lira—"

"Can't we go back to how it was?" she asked, eyes wide and wet. "Can't we just run away and shed all of this skin?"

A bad metaphor. Emery began to harden again.

"You know I'm one of them," he said. "I've helped them track you before."

"I know," she said. Ceony stared hard at her face, but this time she couldn't read Lira at all. Curse the woman and her perfect porcelain features. "I know, and I deserve your scorn. I know I've lost you . . ." Lira looked deep into Emery's eyes, and Ceony could see that they had indeed softened, and she began to doubt her own assessment of the Excisioner. "Or have I?"

*I should leave. I have to leave,* Ceony thought, the sourness still churning. She had a feeling she didn't want to see where this vision led. She reached for the door behind Lira, but when it opened, she saw only the hallway outside, the hallway and the rest of the house. No new images, no fleshy chamber walls. The distant *PUM-Pompoom* still echoed somewhere beyond her reach. She hoped its faintness was only a side effect of her being caught in a memory.

She turned back to Lira and Emery. Something else clacked in the house. Moments later a solid knock came at a door—two slow beats, two quick. The furrow in Emery's brow told Ceony he recognized the knocker.

Emery's lips pressed into a thin line. Lira clung to his shirt.

"Please," she whispered. "Please believe me. You know me better than anyone, Emery. You must listen to me."

Emery hesitated for a moment before grasping Lira's wrists and pulling her fingers from his clothes. He moved into the hallway— passing through Ceony—toward the front door. The house silently built itself around Emery as he walked, as though his presence allowed Ceony to see what lay in the dark beyond the vision.

She followed him down the hallway. Though the front door had a narrow glass window in it, it was too dark to see anything but yellow light beyond it.

Emery opened the door to two policemen, each holding a lantern.

"What's wrong?" Emery asked.

"Sorry to bother you so late, Master Thane," the taller policeman said, "but we believe Lira Hoppson to be in the city."

"Lira?"

"No," Ceony murmured behind him. "No, Emery, don't lie to them. Don't protect her."

The policeman nodded. "We thought she might try to contact you, or her mother. Have you . . . ?"

Several stiff seconds passed. Ceony held her breath.

"I'm sorry," Emery said. "But thank you for the warning. I'll ward the house."

"Perhaps you should stay elsewhere until we've tracked her," the second policeman said. "If you hear anything . . ."

"I'll tell you," Emery said with a nod. "Of course. Thank you."

The policemen bowed their heads and stepped off the porch. Ceony felt her own heart drip cold drops into her stomach, making her nauseated.

She leaned against a wall for support, only to hear the creaking of hinges near her ear. The dark colors of the house swam around her, but she didn't shift to another vision. Instead she appeared back in the office with Fennel and Lira as Emery closed the door behind him.

"Thank you," Lira whispered.

"It is more than you deserve," Emery replied, eyes cast to the floor.

Lira stepped up to him, hesitant, and wrapped her arms around his waist. She buried her face into his collar and repeated, "Thank you."

Ceony bit her lips until she tasted blood. She felt immobile. How would the future be different had Mg. Thane turned Lira over when he had the chance? Ceony was trapped inside his heart trying to save his life, all because he couldn't deny this horrible woman a prison cell!

Her face grew hot and she felt tears sting the back of her eyes. She stepped toward the far wall. *Let me go*, she pleaded. *Let me go somewhere else. Anywhere else.*

Emery said something quietly—Ceony didn't catch it.

Lira pressed herself against him in such a way Ceony flushed all the hotter. Lira murmured, "I love you, Emery. You know I love you. Surely you know."

"Lira . . ."

"You wouldn't have sent them away if you didn't know it," she whispered. "If you didn't still love me."

Her long fingers crept behind his neck like spider legs, each step sticking him with venom. Lira pulled his mouth to hers. He resisted at first, but like a bitten insect he stopped fighting and let Lira pull him into her web.

A tear escaped Ceony's eye. She had to get out, but they blocked the door—they—

She backed into the wall and pounded the side of her fist on it. Nothing changed. Before a second tear could fall, she scooped Fennel off the floor and screamed "Let me out!" so loudly that her own eardrums rattled. "Emery Thane, let me go!"

The office faded into shadow, then into nothingness. The sleepy thrum of *PUM-Pom-poom* beat against her at all sides, a pale imitation of her own heart's frantic rhythm. *One more chamber*, she thought, grasping onto the shreds of calm that came with the words. *One more chamber left.*

But the darkness of the third chamber hadn't finished with Ceony yet. Instead of the red walls, the river of blood, and the tight valve that would take her to the fourth chamber, Ceony found herself in an unfamiliar city, the twilight sky overcast, and shrill police whistles sounding all around her.

# CHAPTER 12

CEONY HAD NEVER SEEN this city before.

A narrow street of wet cobblestone stretched before her, its gutters packed with hard snow several days old and mottled with mud. The overcast sky made everything blue and gray—it seemed to be evening, near twilight, but the cloud cover hid the sun so completely Ceony couldn't be sure. A breath fogged before her mouth. Fennel backed up and sandwiched himself between Ceony's legs as blood pulsed up and down her neck. Brick walls, dark brick walls, loomed two stories up on either side of her. One broke into an archway, unlike any architecture Ceony had even seen in London. The narrow road ended behind her in a set of cement stairs that led around some sort of office building. The other side ended in another brick wall where one building had backed too far into its neighbors.

Police whistles buzzed like banshees around her, shrill and high, bouncing off the bricks. Ceony covered her ears and closed her eyes. She didn't want to be here. *Let me go, let me go, let me go.*

But she couldn't will the scene away. Its chill looped under her fingers and snuck up her clothes, burned the inside of her nose. The whistles grew louder, followed by the heavy stampede of standard-regulation military boots.

Ceony ran.

She ran with Fennel yapping behind her, and she stopped only long enough to scoop up the dog to protect his paper feet from the wet ground. She dodged through the brick arch to another street, its cobbles split and sparse. Her foot came down in a murky puddle that splashed ice water up her skirt, soaking her stockings. The whistles multiplied between buildings—a bank with dark windows, a restaurant with shutters drawn—and attacked her from all directions. They drowned out the quiet *PUM-Pom-poom* that should have filled the silence between her misty breaths.

Taking a sharp turn at the next intersection, Ceony ran into two police officers and phased through them. She stumbled on the slick stone and fell, twisting midair to keep Fennel from the wet street—an action that slammed her hip into the road and sent a crunching pain through her tailbone and leg. Ceony yelped.

Fennel squirmed in her arms and whined a papery whine, then chomped onto some of Ceony's matted hair and tugged on it like he would a rope toy.

Ceony winced, but picked herself up, swiping away mud that clung to her side. She ground her teeth and blinked in an effort not to cry. More policemen—and now two soldiers from the army—ran down the road toward her. She closed her eyes and squeezed Fennel in her arms as they phased through her.

None of this was real. Not real to *her*. But she didn't feel it that way. No matter how much she reminded herself that these were Thane's memories, she couldn't feel the unrealness of any of it.

Blowing hair from her face, Ceony watched the policemen run up the street, shouting to one another in incoherent words, blowing their whistles with pursed lips and puffed cheeks. Hounds chasing down a fox. But who was the fox?

"Emery," she whispered. She broke into a run, her right hip protesting with every other step. It promised her a good bruise in the morning, if it wasn't morning already.

Her bag tugged on her, seeming to weigh five times what it should. She switched shoulders awkwardly as she ran, still balancing Fennel in her arms. Her legs moved swifter than they would have if this were the real world. Dark buildings, sleeping beggars, and half-melted snow piles passed her in blurs of dull colors.

She reached the policemen as their chief—a man with a thick mustache—directed them with sweeping motions of his arm. The band split into three and took different paths deeper into the city.

A small paper glider, similar in style to the one Ceony had ridden to the coast on, sailed through the air, passed her nose, and prodded the police chief once in the arm before flopping to the ground.

Ceony stared at it wide-eyed and reached for it, but the chief snatched it first. Standing on her toes, she read it over his shoulder, instantly recognizing the perfectly spaced letters of Emery's hand-writing, though his name didn't sign the page.

*They're hiding in the packing warehouse. Send your men around to the north. I'll meet you there.*

"This is what you did. What you do," Ceony said, looking up at the police chief's haggard face, though she didn't address the words to him. He looked scared, confirming what Ceony had deducted. "You're hunting them down. The Excisioners. Lira. But when? When is this? When am I?" *Are you safe?*

The police chief blew his whistle, making Ceony's ears ring. He ran northeast, two new officers joining him at the next crossroads.

Ceony took a step forward, then stopped, turning to the path the glider had taken to reach them. Emery would be in that direction.

Body hurting and lungs dry, Ceony sprinted.

She didn't know where the factory was, but she didn't need to—the city unfolded itself before her just as every other vision had, directing her toward Emery Thane, for she ran through the secrets of *his* heart. She passed over the bridge of a sluggish canal with olive-colored water, around a bakery with a faded sign and boards nailed over the windows. She climbed another snowbank where the road narrowed, adjusting Fennel carefully in the crook of her elbow as she went. Above her, over an apartment building and a tavern, she saw the expanse of a large square building with a flat roof and a single cylinder chimney. It was a tan-brick warehouse with dark broken windows. An abandoned bird's nest hung off its southern ledge.

She saw him before a heavy sliding door rusted on its handle and around its edges—he wore all gray that matched the city and sky. Dirt smudged his face and he looked haggard, his hair longer and more unkempt than in past visions. Ceony saw him, but only for a moment before he, armed with a strangely complex paper sphere and a belt filled with tightly Folded paper stars, pulled open the heavy, creaking door and vanished into the shadows within.

She realized the police bells had ceased. But not just the bells—everything around her had fallen into silence. No footsteps, no birds, no chatter or buggies or wind. Fennel felt heavy in her arms. Her bag felt heavy on her shoulder.

Ceony didn't call Emery's name or run after him. It seemed somehow wrong to break the perfect hush that enveloped her. Instead she walked, each short step especially deliberate and soundless against the wet cobblestone. The rusted door seemed too far away, and yet impossibly close. When she reached it, the door opened of its own accord.

The smell of sodden meat—fresh and spoiled—wafted like a cold song over her. She shivered, the warehouse temperature even cooler than the wintry outside. Her feet crunched on rock salt spilled across the cement floor. Setting Fennel down, Ceony whispered "Stay close" between chattering teeth.

Dull, slate-colored light filtered through high windows, many cracked and patched with cardboard or wooden slabs. They illuminated metal walkways protruding from the walls overhead. Ceony gripped her paper fan in her right hand and the strap of her bag in her left. This place would be a perfect setting for Lira—the real Lira—to exact her revenge. Ceony only hoped that she would not be added to the odor of meat that grew more pungent the deeper into the warehouse she traversed.

She stepped into a second, larger room, the metal walkways winding above her. Here the dimming light illuminated dozens of steel racks bearing meat hooks. Every third hook held half a pig's carcass or the long side of a cow. The bodies hardly looked like animals anymore, save for an occasional snout or de-hoofed foot. The white- and scarlet-marbled hunks of muscle dangled over foul-smelling grates and drains in the floor.

Fennel sniffed about the carcasses with a wagging tail. A rat scurried past. Ceony hissed at him and waved her hand to draw the dog's attention back to her. Unfortunately, she did so with her right hand, which still clutched the paper fan. A gust of stale, stinking wind burst from the fan's tips, moaning as it sailed over Fennel's head and filled the room. Ceony closed the fan quickly in her left palm and bit down on a shriek as a slab of beef nudged her in the back, creaking as it swayed on its hook.

All the meat swung now, back and forth, squeaking on the metal beams that suspended them. The movement made them look alive. Forlorn.

Blowing out a foggy breath, Ceony moved forward, squinting into the darkness until she spotted a door left ajar across the massive room, just past the hanging loops of entrails and sausages. She hurried for it, the steps of her shoes horribly loud. Dusky taupe light filled the small room the door had guarded—a storage room—and Ceony found Emery turned away from her. His drooping shoulders heaved with every breath. The police chief stood beside him, rubbing his mustache and grimacing. Like a switch flicked on, the warehouse behind Ceony filled with officers carrying lanterns, as though Emery's heart had waited for this specific moment to include them in the vision. None blew whistles—none even spoke. They walked around, investigating, some seeming unsure what to do with themselves.

Fennel growled with his head between Emery's legs. Stepping around the chief and the paper magician, Ceony looked out onto the scene.

Her body tensed all at once, and so much bile filled her throat she couldn't keep it down. She barely managed to turn her head before vomiting over the cement floor. It stung her throat and sinuses. Her stomach pressed in and up, in and up, over and over until not a single drop more could be squeezed from it.

Even if the others had been able to see her, her retching wasn't enough to get their attention away from what lay before them:

Bodies.

Pieces and halves of bodies, *human* bodies, just like the pieces and halves of the animals in the next room. Ceony couldn't look twice, but her memory—*curse* her memory!—had seen enough. To know that image . . . the image of headless men, women sawed in half, and children missing their hearts, their chests filled with maggots . . . to know that image would never, *never* leave her mind . . . Ceony would have wept had she not felt so dry, sore, and sandy inside.

They smelled no different. They smelled no different than the animals, and Ceony found herself grateful to have the scent of her own sickness on her tongue instead of tasting those poor, dead, and ruined people in her mouth.

"So close," the police chief murmured. "So close. They're gone now. This one's fresh, and this one. So close."

Shuddering, Ceony looked up to Emery's face, his eyes wide and sunken, his skin pale, his chapped lips parted. Though he did not speak, she could hear his thoughts. *Because of me*, they said. *Because I let her go. They died because my heart was too weak.*

She could see it ripping him from the inside: the creased layers in his forehead, the tautness of his neck, the wet gloss of his eyes. She breathed, spat, wiped her mouth. Emery's guilt pressed into her like the hot throbbing walls of the valves, suffocating her. It made the air thick and tart, and she knew that this room was something he still carried with him. Even without a perfect memory, no one could forget this. No one could ever forget how this *felt*.

Steam billowed in the corners of Ceony's vision and the damp smell of iron clung to her sinuses. Despite the horror before her and Thane's obvious pain, this caught her attention.

Streams of crimson whipped around her, bubbling and broiling. They sailed for her like snakes before taking sharp turns in their paths, instead colliding into the carnage of the storage room. They evaporated the corpses, the shelves, and the boxes—everything but the walls, the police chief, and Emery himself, who still gaped at where the bodies had been, his eyes wide and sunken, his dry lips parted in disbelief and self-hate. He didn't see Ceony, nor did he see Lira—the true, present, and very *real* Lira—who approached Ceony with wild eyes from the room's only door, bubbling blood dripping from her fingers. The very reincarnation of the devil from hell, the villain of every fairy tale cut into pieces and sewn into a patchwork that had once been beautiful.

Ceony paled at the sight of Lira's dripping hands, at the thought of just *how* Lira's magic worked, at what sort of horrid thing—like ripping the heart from a child—an Excisioner would have to do to make blood boil. Blood that hadn't touched Ceony, despite it being aimed at her.

Ceony touched the paper shield chain around her and staggered to her feet, backing away from the raven-haired woman who seemed more than a touch upset that her spell hadn't taken effect.

But Lira hadn't touched *her*. Thank God, she hadn't touched her. Not yet. Ceony didn't want to think—

Lira pulled that same dagger from her belt and raked it across her palm, spilling her own dark blood into her hands. She mumbled something hard and foul and shot the droplets forward. Each crimson bead steamed and warped with invisible fire, but before they struck Ceony, the paper chain crossing her chest pulsed, deflecting them into the surrounding walls. The blood dulled the details of the vision, sucking mortar from between bricks and specks of color from the cement floor. Emery began to fade.

A door appeared to Ceony's right, beside the dissipating paper magician. Not a white door rimmed with scarlet, but a red door edged with shadow.

"*No!*" Lira shouted, blood raining onto the floor. She ran for Ceony, red hands outstretched.

Ceony bolted through the door before Lira could grab her, Fennel at her ankles. But instead of the red walls of Emery's heart, she found herself once more in the dark office lit with a single starry window. Back to where she had started. Shadows moved before her, predatory. Ceony's own heart ebbed within her chest.

She had been trapped.

# CHAPTER 13

EMERY RUSHED HER, HIS forearm across her collar, and shoved her into the wall where the red door had just been. She squeezed her eyes shut, waiting for herself to phase, for the scene to replay itself, but it didn't. Emery's forearm pressed down onto her, and when she dared to look, Emery's eyes flared with green fire.

Cold sweat kissed her skin. Fennel barked his whispery bark beside Ceony, biting at Emery's leg with paper teeth. Ceony struggled, but the paper magician didn't move.

"You have no business here," he hissed, his voice too low, too rough. Not like Emery Thane at all. Even the Emery Thane from this very scene, enraptured in rage and heartbreak, hadn't sounded so cold. Ceony would have trembled had she not been pinned so securely against the wall.

"I'm sorry," she cried. "I didn't mean—"

Shadow-Emery pulled back far enough to grab her shoulder. With little effort, Shadow-Emery hurled Ceony into a stack of boxes and books meticulously piled in the corner. Cardboard corners dug into her ribs and spine; paperback novels rained onto her head

"I'm trying to save you!" she shouted.

Shadow-Emery laughed—cackled—a noise like broken organ pipes that sent cold chills up Ceony's arms. "No one can save me. You've swum into dangerous waters, Miss Twill."

Fennel hunched on his legs and barked wildly, but Shadow-Emery didn't see him, didn't hear him. His molten eyes fixated on Ceony, an owl watching the desperate run of a mouse before swooping down and nabbing it in thin-tipped talons.

Ceony tried to steady her voice, but it quivered in her throat. "Please, just let me go. I can help you if you let me go."

"Help me?" Shadow-Emery repeated with a sneer, as if the words on his tongue were laced with vinegar. "And who will help *them?*"

The vision faded by half, leaving the dark wooden walls of the office in place, but the furniture, shelves, and floor disappeared, replaced with the floor of the warehouse storage room and the ripped and torn bodies strewn across it.

Ceony averted her eyes and pressed a hand to her mouth, willing her stomach to stay calm. "I don't need to see it again!" she shouted between fingers.

"Don't you?" Shadow-Emery asked with a raised voice. "How good *is* your memory, Ceony Twill? You seem to have forgotten about them already. I killed them."

"No!" Ceony yelled, tears wetting her eyelashes. Still, she did not look. "The Excisioners killed them, not you!"

"But I didn't stop them."

"You tried to, didn't you?" Ceony asked, almost more to herself than to him. "I saw you try. I saw you try to save them."

"Not save *them,*" Shadow-Emery said as the vision of death faded back into the office, to the silhouette of a littered desk and the dark splotches of literary debris across the floor. "Save myself. I was only after the Excisioners."

She looked up at him, the spilled boxes and books still hugging her. "You didn't know about them, did you? Not personally. They were victims, but not yours. Did you even know their names?"

Shadow-Emery looked away.

"That's why, don't you see?" she pleaded. "You hunt the Excisioners because they hurt people, even people you don't know. How is that evil?"

Shadow-Emery laughed. "I'm just like her. Just like Lira."

Ceony flew to her feet. "She manipulated you, Emery Thane. You loved her once. I saw that you loved her." She folded her arms and rubbed their skin, fighting off a chill creeping into the vision. "I've never loved like you have, so I know I don't understand completely, but if I were in love and there was a chance I could save it, I would take it."

*Just like I'm trying to save you . . .*

Shadow-Emery faded and reappeared behind her, grabbing a fistful of her hair. Ceony gasped as he wrenched her head to one side.

"There is no love here," Shadow-Emery growled.

"Maybe not here," Ceony whispered, "not in this room, but this is only one part of you, isn't it? Just one piece of the whole—"

Shadow-Emery released her, vanishing and reappearing again several paces away. Fennel yapped loudly, jumping on all four legs. Scowling, Shadow-Emery snatched Fennel up, crushed the dog's paper skull in his hands, and tore the creature in half.

Ceony screamed and lunged for Fennel, but the spell on the dog's carefully crafted body had already been destroyed. The paper pieces that had comprised her companion pattered softly against the floorboards as Emery released them.

Ceony stared in shock. She dropped to her knees. Tears streamed down her face.

Emery had *made* Fennel for her. Because she missed Bizzy. Because he cared. Fennel, her only real tie to the world outside Emery's heart. Her one companion in this dark place, her one constant in a world that wouldn't stop changing.

She touched the broken paper pieces, feeling as crumpled as Fennel's lifeless, misshapen head.

"This isn't you," Ceony whispered, pulling a cold finger back from her dog's lifeless form. "This isn't who you are!"

"Ha!" Shadow-Emery barked. "Do you even know who *I* am?"

His fingers seized her hair once more and hauled her to her feet. "Dark and dangerous waters . . . ," he repeated.

A new laughter—Lira's laughter—filled the room, and Ceony felt herself crack like a hot glass pan set in snow. She didn't see the woman, however, and Shadow-Emery didn't seem to hear her. At least, he didn't react.

"Didn't you know, little girl?" Lira's distant voice echoed through the dark office, as if her larynx had been embedded into the very walls. "The rules of Excision are very clear cut, especially for the heart."

"I d-don't understand," Ceony said with a dry tongue, her eyes locked on Shadow-Emery's, her fingers clutching his to keep him from pulling her hair from her scalp.

Lira laughed again, the sound somewhat fainter. "No man can harm his true love within his own heart. Don't you see what that means?

"He doesn't love you, you beef-witted girl."

She laughed again, thinking the situation truly wholesome and fun, and then the noise faded. Where she went, Ceony didn't know—the laughter died out like a fire caught in the rain. With Ceony so thoroughly trapped, Lira must have abandoned the heart to finish whatever it was she had planned. Another gruesome spell. Escape across the ocean, with Emery's heart in tow.

Emery would die if she did.

More tears trickled down Ceony's face, and she squeezed Shadow-Emery's wrist. "I know," she whispered. *I know you don't love me. Not yet.*

And it was that last thought that drove her.

"Do you think you're the only one who's done something wrong?" she asked. "Do you really think no one in this world has made a mistake but you? Are you so *blind* that you can't see beyond this room?"

Shadow-Emery snarled, but Ceony didn't flinch. She dug her nails into his wrist until he released her hair; then she pushed him back. She would not be the mouse in this. She *would not.*

"What about Lira?" she asked, gesturing to the door as though the Excisioner stood behind it. "What about what she's done?"

Shadow-Emery's glower only darkened.

"What about me?" Ceony asked, fainter, pressing both palms to her own heart. "What about my mistakes? I think about them, too, but where would I be if I thought of nothing else? What sort of person would I be if I drowned in them?

"What about the time I was supposed to pick up my baby sister from school because my mom was having surgery on her foot?" she asked. "It was the middle of January, but I didn't go because I had a diorama I was supposed to present in English the next day and I wanted to get it done. It took me three hours, Emery! Three hours my sister stood in the cold, waiting for me. She got pneumonia and almost *died* because my homework was more important than her!

"And I've stolen before," she continued, taking a small step forward. "I saw an old man drop six quid on the side of the street and I pocketed it. Took the long way home so he wouldn't notice."

Shadow-Emery cackled once more. "You think those are comparable to these blackened halls? You think your cold sister and sticky fingers tip the scales?"

"Who gave you the right to judge my mistakes against your own?" Ceony shot back. Her heart wrenched with guilt, twisting as her own memories bubbled up. "Do you want to know why I lived in the Mill Squats for so long? My dad had a good job as a chauffeur for the prime minister's family, but when I was twelve I stole the buggy and crashed it into the queen's wall. My dad lost his job and all our savings went to pay for that automobile. We had no money left, so we had to move to the gloomy side of town, all because of me. All because I wanted to drive a buggy and didn't listen when my parents told me no.

"And what about Anise? Hm?" she asked, more tears sliding down her face. "Do you know about Anise Hatter? Do you?!"

Shadow-Emery didn't answer.

"She was my best friend!" Ceony cried. "She was my best friend, and our first year of secondary school was hard on her. I don't know why, because I never asked. She just waned, withdrew into herself, became sickly. And one day before winter break she asked me to come by and see her. Said she wanted to talk. I was late. It doesn't matter why, but I was late. And when I got there I found her in her bathtub with her wrists slit up to her elbows."

Ceony covered her mouth with her hand, stifling a sob. How vivid that memory was, even with the years masking it from the rest of the world. How many nights after that incident had Ceony lain awake, wondering what would have happened had she arrived just a half hour earlier? For someone else, they would have blurred together, become a mass of days full of grief and tears.

But Ceony's memory was *perfect*, and she had counted those nights. Seventeen. She remembered every hour spent crying, every nightmare of Anise's white face and her bloodied arms, her glass eyes staring into nothing. She remembered every counseling session and every bad grade that followed.

The worst part was knowing everything—remembering everything. Everything but the reason why. Anise hadn't even left a note. Even her own parents had been speechless at the funeral.

"Was it my fault?" Ceony asked, almost whispering. "Was it my fault she killed herself?" She didn't wait for him to answer. "Was it your fault Lira and the others killed that family?"

She sucked in a long breath, swallowed, and murmured, "I forgive you."

Shadow-Emery twitched.

"I forgive you, Emery," Ceony repeated. "I've seen all of it, and I'm sorry. I didn't mean to. I didn't intend any of this to happen." She blinked away tears and stifled a sob lurking deep in her throat. "But I forgive you. It's okay now."

He shifted. Warm hope sparked in Ceony's chest. Something she had said had hit him. She took one step toward him.

He growled and seized her by her upper arm, flinging her back to the floor.

"You don't have the power to forgive," that low, unnatural voice spat.

"Then forgive yourself!" she shouted, pushing herself back up. She pressed her palm against the wall for support. "Everyone has a dark side! But it's their choice whether or not they cultivate it. Don't you understand? Lira's exploited hers, but not you. Not you, Emery Thane.

"You're a good person!" she exclaimed, her own voice ricocheting off the walls as Lira's had moments before. "I've only known you less than a month and even I can see what a good person you are!"

Shadow-Emery retreated into the shadows.

"So let go," she begged. "Let go of the hate, the anger, the sadness. And let go of me. I can't help you if you don't let go!"

The office around her flashed red and peach. A laborious *PUM-Pom-poom* filled the air, which became hotter, moister. Ceony blinked and found herself once more in the literal chamber of Emery's heart, silent save for its waning beat. Empty, save for herself and the broken pieces of Fennel at her feet.

Dropping to her knees, Ceony collected the pieces of her paper companion with reverence, smoothing crumpled corners and folding them carefully along their original creases.

"You're a good boy," she whispered as she stacked the pieces one on top of another, filling her lungs to their limit with every breath to keep from crying. She was tired of crying, and like her mother had always said, crying solved nothing.

After setting Fennel into her bag, she pulled free a piece of bread and swallowed it half-chewed, enough to alleviate the hunger cramping her belly.

She eyed the valve across the carpet of skin and veins.

"One more," she promised herself. "One more until the end. And even if there's no door to freedom, at least you know you tried. One more, Ceony."

# CHAPTER 14

SHE PASSED THROUGH BLINDLY, pushing her tired limbs through the tunnel that constricted around her like the big snakes at the London Zoo. But as Ceony had decided with Shadow-Emery, she would not be the mouse. With a grunt and an extra shove with her left leg, she reached the other side of the valve.

Just like chamber three, the fourth chamber opened up already playing a vision, though this vision seemed . . . different. Ceony did not find herself in a room, garden, or city. She had a feeling that this place was not a memory, either. She had never seen this landscape before, and she had a distinct feeling that, outside of Emery's heart, it didn't exist.

Before her stretched miles and miles of dry ground—not quite desert, but not quite anything else, either. Just tired, bronze ground stretching in all directions, unbroken by mountains or rivers or forests. Not a single weed or mound marred its surface. It stretched forever until it met a gray-blue sky lined with pale cerise, a sky perpetually caught in the moments before sunrise. Nothing broke the sky, not a single cloud or strip of color, no birds or seedlings caught upon the wind. There was no wind.

Ceony smelled nothing, not even the scent of dust and earth, and she heard nothing outside of herself—no crawling creatures, no whistles, thunder, moans, threats. No weeping, no rain. No *heartbeat.* Silence surrounded her. Endless silence on an endless plane.

Only one thing disturbed the endlessness of the place. One thing, one very large thing that no heart-traveler could ever miss in her adventure.

A canyon. A giant crack zigzagged over the dry, bland ground far to her left. The . . . north, she supposed. It was as good a direction as any. No bridges spanned it; no rivers filled it.

Ceony approached the canyon carefully, testing the solidity of the ground around it as she neared. Bronze sand, the same color as the earth, filled its deepness. A deepness that Ceony could tell had once been much deeper than it was. As she thought it, she saw a handful of sand drop from midair and rain onto the canyon floor.

Crouching, Ceony felt the edge of the giant crack. None of it came away in her fingers, even when she scratched it with her nails. The rock stayed hard and firm. Another handful of sand dropped to the canyon floor, seeming to make no difference in the canyon's depth whatsoever. But Ceony knew that enough handfuls would fill it, eventually. After all, it took time to mend one's heart. Enough time could heal a heart as broken as this one. It was half-healed already.

"I'm dying, aren't I?"

Ceony turned around to see Emery Thane standing before her in his indigo coat, looking just as he had at the banquet and the church, though more . . . tired. His shoulders slouched, and dark circles lined his eyes. He was a tad translucent, but Ceony didn't point it out to him.

A sliver of the real Emery Thane. One she could interact with. She answered, "Yes."

He nodded once, solemn.

"But if you help me get out, I think I can save you," she added, standing. "I've come all this way hoping there'd be a way out, at the end."

Emery's eyes scanned the expanse. "She's too strong. I'll never be able to stop her, or the others."

"We can stop her if we work together," Ceony assured him, and as she did, a realization struck her. *Doubts*, she thought. This chamber must be his doubts and regrets, just as the second chamber was his hopes. The heart had the dark to balance out the light, the uncertainty to balance the dreams. All carefully balanced, but with her caught in the middle. "But I need your help, Emery. I'm only an apprentice, and I haven't been an apprentice for very long."

"Hmmm," he hummed, neither in agreement nor disagreement. His gaze fell to her bag. "May I see him?"

It took a moment of processing before Ceony understood the request. She carefully lifted Fennel from her bag and handed his broken body to Emery.

Emery examined the pieces, a slight frown touching his lips. He held out a hand. It took her a moment to understand what he wanted. Ceony reached into her bag and handed him paper, relishing the tingle it sent through her fingers.

He worked deftly, unsnapping the turquoise collar from about the crushed Folds and re-Folding, reconnecting pieces of paper. Ceony handed him a second and third piece of paper, watching with her hands clasped to her breast as Emery remade Fennel's head, a perfect replica of what it had been before.

He handed the paper dog back to Ceony, who whispered, "Breathe."

Fennel shook his head and squirmed in Ceony's grasp, wanting to be put down. Ceony laughed and hugged the dog to her chest. Fennel licked her cheek twice before resuming his insistent squirming.

Ceony set him down, and he ran in circles beside her, stretching out his legs.

"Thank you," she said, grinning and wiping her eyes. "Thank you."

He nodded, a slim acknowledgment of gratitude, and gazed over the expanse once more, toward the pink horizon. He didn't seem to notice the canyon beside them.

"You might not live through this," he said. "It will be my fault if you don't."

"Last I checked," Ceony began, "I volunteered of my own volition to rescue you."

"Yet you're caught in your own curse," he replied, gesturing to the nothingness before them.

Ceony pondered that for a moment before saying, "Emery."

He glanced at her.

"I think you can break the spell holding me here," she said, albeit with some hesitation. "After all, it's *your* heart, isn't it? You have more claim to it than anyone, especially Lira. How else could you be speaking with me if it weren't true?"

She caught the slightest quirk to his lips—almost a smile, but the doubt that weighted the air prevented it from forming.

He didn't reply, so Ceony asked, "Can you . . . see it? The spell? How it works?"

"No," he answered. "But I can feel it. I suppose I could break it, though it will make me . . . tired."

"Tired?" Ceony asked, the word reminding her of her own fatigue. "Will it . . . hurt you?"

Again, an almost-smile. This version of Emery Thane was more similar to the real one than the others, notwithstanding his pessimism. He said, "I think I'll manage."

Ceony beckoned Fennel to her. She felt light, invigorated, as if the last chamber hadn't happened at all. As if her own chamber of hope had added this moment to its foundation. She could do this.

"I need you to teach me some new spells," she said. "Anything that can help but won't take much time. You taught me so much, but . . ."

"But it's not much use against an Excisioner." He nodded. "I know."

Emery considered for a moment, a crooked finger tucked under his chin. "How much paper do you have left?"

She pulled the diminished stack from her bag and presented it to him.

He examined the paper, his eyes bobbing as he counted the pieces, and sighed, shoulders slumping. "I'm going to teach you something I really shouldn't be teaching you."

"But given the circumstances," she urged.

He nodded. His lip quirked. "Given the circumstances. Just pretend to forget it once this is over . . . if either of us makes it past this."

"We will," Ceony assured him with a grin. "I know we will. I have some ideas of my own, but I'm not sure they will work."

She knelt down, tucking her soiled skirt under her knees, and set the stack of paper on the hard earth beside her. Dirty paper should work just as well as clean, and she didn't exactly have a table at her disposal.

Emery watched her for a moment, his eyes lacking their normal luster. Despite that, his expression still proved easy to read—curious. Doubtful, but curious. Finally he asked, "Why are you doing all of this?"

Ceony paused, one hand on the stack of paper. Fennel nuzzled her elbow. "Doing what?"

He gestured to the empty expanse surrounding them. "This. All of this. Why have you come so far to help me?"

She felt her cheeks grow warm and she looked away, stroking Fennel to occupy her hands. She supposed it wouldn't hurt to tell this sliver of Emery Thane. She could never utter the words to the magician himself, but knowing the man she spoke to was only a figment pieced together by a suffering heart lent her courage.

"Because I think I'm falling in love with you," she admitted, feeling her cheeks redden like the cerise sunrise. "I know I haven't known you long, but after all this . . ." She lifted her eyes to the horizon where earth met sky. "I feel like I've known you forever. I don't know how many women can claim to have walked a man's heart, but I've walked yours, Emery Thane. And I like the dog."

His expression didn't change save for the tilt of his lips, which very nearly formed a smile before tuckering out and returning to their flat, doubtful line.

"Very well," Emery said, kneeling across from her and pulling up his long, baggy sleeves. Not exactly the response she was hoping for, but a start. He continued, "I'll start with the most complicated first, the one I shouldn't be teaching you."

Ceony nodded as he reached for a sheet of sea-green paper.

His eyes met hers. "Do you know what happens when paper vibrates very, very fast?"

"Something I'm not supposed to know," she guessed.

"Correct," he replied. "But allow me to explain . . ."

# CHAPTER 15

CEONY FINALLY TUCKED HER last paper spell into her bag, careful not to disrupt the organized chaos within. Organized chaos—many necessary things all needing careful placement. Ceony understood Emery's method of interior decorating just a little better now. She and Emery had not used every piece of paper, just most of them, and their many intricate Folds made the bag bulge at Ceony's hip.

Her fingers fluttered over the shield chain around her torso, pinching each link to test its security. After checking the entire chain twice, she called Fennel with a whistle and a snap.

Emery stepped aside to let the paper dog pass. Fennel's expertly crafted paws left four-toe prints in the thin layer of dust covering the dry, flat earth, but the prints vanished nearly as quickly as they appeared.

"I need you to fold up, Fennel," Ceony said. Fennel whined and she added, "I don't want you to get hurt again, and it's wet outside. Just for a little while."

"Will it be?" Emery asked, once more scanning the expanse. "Just a little while?"

Ceony gave him a soft smile before commanding Fennel, "Cease."

Fennel stilled in her arms, and she folded him softly in her freckled hands. "Your doubtful side isn't very strong," she remarked. "You must be sure about a great many things."

Emery didn't answer.

Tucking Fennel far down into her bag, she said, "I think mine would look much different. More cliffs and surging rivers, or lots of roads with unexpected turns. Maybe even some lions. I've been doubtful about a lot of things in life." *Including you.*

"But no cracks," Emery commented.

Ceony glanced over her shoulder to the chasm rupturing the land, wondering for a moment how much more sand had fallen into it since her hurried paper lessons. "Plenty of cracks, but no canyons. Not yet," she affirmed. *I guess it all depends on how this goes.*

She stood, brushed off her skirt—for what good it did her— tested the shield chain for the third time, and checked the stitches of her bag's strap. She had memorized the location and number of all the spells within the bag already, should she need to retrieve them quickly.

"Good luck," Emery said.

"Thank you," she replied. "But how will you—"

Ceony turned to him, but met only the stretch of empty, pre-dawn space beyond the canyon. The paper magician—at least this version of him—had disappeared.

She barely had time to recognize Emery's absence before the ground began to quake. Ceony reached out for something to steady herself with, but of course she found nothing amidst her barren surroundings.

The land shook in broader and broader patterns, bucking back and forth like a rodeo bull. Ceony took two steps away from the chasm before she stumbled to one knee and skinned her palm on the hard earth, which had begun to fade, revealing deep red flesh beneath it.

The vision slowly collapsed. The sky broke like shards of glass. The heart's *PUM-Pom-poom* drummed so loudly Ceony felt it in her lungs. The pulse accelerated and the last of the vision faltered.

The walls of Emery's heart throbbed and rippled. The beat grew uneven, and Ceony's breath quickened. It didn't sound right; it didn't feel right. If Emery's heart destroyed itself trying to free her . . .

Her hands turned cold. A world without Emery Thane. Her entire world up until a month ago had existed without him, but to go back to it now . . . The thought made Ceony sick. It crushed her.

The rivers of blood lining the perimeter of the chamber engorged and rose. The air grew thicker and hotter, as if she hung over a pot of boiling water, ready for cooking. The heart wrenched one way, then another, and Ceony felt herself fall.

She landed on her side, her left cheek pressed to wet, rough rock. Damp, cool air encircled her, clinging to her clothes and skin. Tasting of salt. She heard the sounds of swishing and spurting nearby—waves crashing against rocks.

Pale sunlight filtered through the mouth of the black cave. The sharp cry of a gull startled her to alertness.

She was free.

"You did it," Ceony whispered, pushing herself to her feet and spinning to the rocky shelf that still held Emery's beating heart in its pool of enchanted blood. Still beating, but even weaker than before. She could still save him, if she hurried.

She hoped.

Her eyes shot back to the cave's mouth. Morning. Early morning. But had it been one night, or two? Exhaustion pinched the center of Ceony's muscles and the edges of her brain, but it could not tell her how many hours had accumulated.

Ceony swallowed, realizing for the first time just how thirsty she was.

She approached the heart like a priestess to an altar. Would it need its pool of gold-rimmed blood to survive the trip back to London? It had beat in Lira's hand after she had pulled it from Emery's chest without a spell—at least, without any Ceony could see. Then again, she knew little of the working of magicians' hearts, and almost nothing of Excision.

She needed something safe to carry the heart in, but as she considered her options the salty air began to burn her nose, and the blond hairs on her arms stood on end. Licking her lips, Ceony turned around to face Lira, whose dark hair fell in perfect, lush waves over her narrow shoulders, whose dark eyes narrowed to lightless almonds, and whose red lips curled into a sneer.

Setting her jaw, Ceony stepped away from the heart. She would allow no spell of Lira's to miss her and strike it. She would keep Emery's heart safe, especially from the woman who had treated it so very poorly.

If the Excisioner was surprised to see Ceony, she didn't show it. Her pale skin flushed almost prettily with anger, or perhaps hate. Ceony couldn't be sure—such loathing had never been directed at her before. Not to this magnitude.

Ceony took the first words for herself.

"Stand down, Lira," she said, straightening as tall as her five-foot-three frame could straighten. "You want to escape? Then go while you have the chance."

Lira smiled, looking distinctly like a cat gone half-feral. "Not when I have two hearts to take with me. Grath will find them such a handsome prize, even if I only let him keep yours."

She lifted a bloody hand—her blood or another's, Ceony couldn't be sure—and with it rose from the ground three pairs of severed, undead hands that Ceony had failed to spot, as the uneven rock of the cave floor had concealed them.

Ceony's windpipe constricted, reminding her of the bruises dotting her neck such hands had given her before. For a split second she felt herself paralyzed, but the whispered beating of Emery's heart regrounded her. Forced her to move.

Her hands shot to her bag as Lira's shot forward, sprinkling droplets of cold blood throughout the cave. The undead hands—fingers pudgy and swollen—rose like birds into the air and shot toward her on invisible wings.

Wings.

*Birds.*

Ceony grasped her paper birds in her fingers and yanked their Folded bodies from her bag. "Breathe!" she gasped as the hands charged her. "Attack them!"

Two birds fell crumpled to the cavern floor, crushed from where Ceony had landed on her bag after escaping the heart. She stiffened, but seven square-bodied cranes heeded her command and sprung to life in front of her—orange, yellow, maroon, white, white, white, and gray. Their quick flapping hummed through the cavern. Their long necks stretched forward as they sailed for Lira's bodiless army, and Ceony could almost hear them caw a selfless battle cry just before striking their targets.

One bird collided with each hand, save for two who struck a half-rotten hand at the same time, one at the thumb, the other at the ring finger. The hands closed around the birds not four paces from Ceony and, as in the prison, fell to the ground.

Ceony's mind spun. Adrenaline coursed up her neck and down into her legs, making her skittish. She had to get out of the cave—Emery's heart rested too close to the battle. Lira blocked the entrance, conjuring her next spell.

Ceony already had hers set.

*"Focus on your target,"* Emery's voice spoke in her memory as he had during his quick lesson in the new spell. *"Feel it in your mind like your story illusions. If you do, the stars will hit their mark."*

Reaching into her bag, Ceony pulled free five tightly Folded, four-cornered paper stars, just like the ones Emery had worn going into that awful warehouse. She and Emery had Folded them so tightly they hadn't been affected by the crushed bag. She locked her eyes on Lira's muttering lips and bloodied hands, threw the stars, and ran for the cave mouth.

The stars spun through the air like pinwheels caught in a summer storm. Ceony didn't watch to see them meet their target. Lira's frustrated scream told her enough.

The morning sunlight, white behind thready clouds, burned her dry eyes and sizzled against the ocean that stirred about the black-rock coast below her. So deep, so hungry.

The water sprayed cool mist over Ceony as she darted over the uneven shore. A whip of amber kelp looped around her foot and fell away again, perhaps sensing Ceony's urgency and deciding not to take part in it.

She didn't get far before a crackling ribbon of gore circled around her. The shield chain encompassing her torso stiffened. The bubbling blood warped away from her body and crashed into the wet rocks, staining them in patterns like spiderwebs. The spell's residue left a metallic taste in the back of Ceony's throat.

Lira scowled and pulled a small vial of blood from the tight waistband of her slacks. It looked like her supply was getting low. "A parlor trick," she said with a grin that was almost a grimace. "Do you really think a little paper sash can stop me?"

She advanced one step, uncorking the vial with a long thumbnail and dumping it into her hands. The blood coursed over her palm and dripped into the small, swirling streams of saltwater between jagged rocks under her feet.

"It has three times already," Ceony countered, taking one step back for Lira's every step forward. "So I'll say yes."

Lira smiled sweetly, and for a moment Ceony could see why Emery had been drawn to her, so many years ago. But the expression soured as Lira's brows drew together, her forehead creased, and her nostrils flared. She said something in a bizarre tongue and waved her bloody hand as if she were throwing a cricket ball.

Ceony's hand thrust into her bag. She braced herself for Lira's attack.

It struck from behind.

The red-veined waves crashed into her like a blizzard wind, cold and blinding, nearly knocking her to the uneven ground. A jolt of alarm—as if she had been burned—shot from navel to crown. She ran from the wave so as not to be pulled into the ocean, but it had already done its damage, soaking her to her skin.

She felt the power drain from her shield chain. Two links between her shoulder blades gave out, and the chain flopped down to her ankles, nothing more than soggy pulp.

Ceony felt as though her own blood had been drained away with the wave. She searched her bag with white, shivering fingers, pulling out spell after ruined spell. Her paper fish, the elaborate confusion sphere Emery had Folded himself while she had made the stars. It had been meant as a distraction for . . .

Her hand touched the symmetrical rhombus beside Fennel. Dry, protected by the bodies of the crushed spells, as were Fennel and her binding chain. They all buzzed softly beneath her touch. The thin stack of unused papers had protected them, thank God.

Lira closed the gap between them, a cat stalking a grasshopper, as Ceony dropped wet spells at her feet. Ceony stumbled backward, trying to keep the Excisioner and her bloody hands at bay. Her heart hammered holes into her chest. Her skin itched. She swallowed against a dry throat.

She'd rather face Emery's shadows again than be here, so unarmed. But she couldn't run, not from this. Not back to Emery, cold and heartless.

"You're weak, just like him," Lira said with a sneer. "Worthless. All Folders are. Emery never had any real power, and neither do you."

Ceony stopped retreating. She would not be a mouse, nor would she be a grasshopper. She dug her heels into the black rock. She had no confusion sphere, but she had other ways of distracting Lira.

"He signed the divorce papers the night he hid you," she said, letting her face relax into the sort of smugness she couldn't stand in other people. The sort of smugness Lira would have worn, had her anger not boiled so close to the surface of her skin. "You weren't as in control of the situation as you think."

Lira's countenance didn't alter, save for the slightest quirk of her left eyebrow, but Ceony noticed. Lira continued to advance. Ceony held her ground, trying to ignore the cold sweat beading down her spine.

"You weren't in his heart, either," she added. "Not how you are now. Not outside of a prison cell, at least. Or didn't you notice?"

Lira paused eight or nine paces from Ceony, her eyes narrowed to slits. She looked like a snake—a coiled viper ready to spring. Ceony had insulted the flesh magician's vanity . . . or perhaps, deep inside the dark, hollow chambers of her heart, Lira still cared for Emery.

No. Not cared for. One didn't rip out the heart of a man because she *cared* for him. No, to Lira, Emery's heart was a souvenir, a trophy. Something to be owned. A sick sort of revenge for hunting Lira and her kind down. Emery may have been Lira's lover once, but he had become her bane. Her nemesis. Her scourge.

And she hated it.

Swift as a falcon Lira drew her long dagger from her belt, her enthusiasm knocking its sheath askew. She held the knife out to her side like a broken wing and rushed Ceony. A distraction—Lira didn't attack with the dagger, but with her crimson-stained hand.

*"You must understand, Patrice, that Excisioners are a tricky matter,"* Mg. Hughes had said. *"They are wildly dangerous, and if they touch you, they can pull magic through your body. It is a killing magic."*

Ceony dashed to the side. Her right foot caught between two rocks, causing her to pitch forward. Lira's outstretched hand swiped the air where Ceony's head had been. Struggling, Ceony jerked her foot free, leaving her shoe wedged in its place. Jagged rock bit into her sole through her soaked and soiled stocking, but Lira didn't allow her any time to dwell on it.

Lira spun, dagger windmilling through the air. Ceony leapt back, barely avoiding the tip of the blade as it whistled past her breast. Darting into a few inches of water between teethlike stones, Ceony yanked a paper glider from her bag.

The Folds fell apart in her hands. Too much water damage.

Lira charged. Ceony shrieked and scrambled to higher ground, dodging the hand that sought to enchant her own skin. Ceony rifled through the bag until she found a spell she could use.

"Breathe!" she commanded the paper bat, who took to the air with a two-sheet wingspan. It needed no more instruction than that, perhaps sensing its surroundings the same way Fennel did. The bat flew straight for Lira's nose.

Ceony's fingers grasped the binding chain, a chain woven with tight double rows of V-shaped links. The second spell Emery Thane had taught her in the chamber of doubt.

Ceony whirled around, hair fanning around her neck.

Lira snatched the bat from the air and crumpled its right wing.

"Bind!" Ceony ordered the chain.

Like a shark in deep waters, the chain darted from her hands toward Lira—

—who cut it into two uneven fragments with a broad sweep of her dagger. The binding chain's pieces flopped to the rocks like fish out of water.

"As I said," Lira spoke, only somewhat breathless, "no power at all." Advancing, she took the last vial of blood from her waist and threw it at her feet. A cyclone of scarlet smoke enveloped her—the same spell she had used to escape the dining room after stealing Emery's heart.

Only instead of fleeing, Lira reappeared a foot in front of Ceony.

Ceony's exhaling breath dug claws into the soft flesh of her throat. Her hand shot into her bag for the rhombus, her last spell—

Lira grabbed her elbow—skin on skin—and held the dagger's edge just below Ceony's chin.

Lira grinned.

Ignoring the blade, Ceony shoved Lira away with all the strength her fatigued arms could muster and yanked the simple diamond-Folded paper from her sack.

*"Do you know what happens when paper vibrates very, very fast?"*

Lira growled and rammed into Ceony, shunting her into an eroded rock shelf opposite the ocean. Lira's hand clutched Ceony's neck. The point of the dagger pressed into her ribs. Lira smelled like blood and old, rusted coins.

Lira began to chant, and Ceony felt warm. Eerily warm. Too warm. Lira's ancient spell seemed to coax Ceony's very spirit from her bones.

She couldn't get away. She clutched Emery's spell in her hand, but she couldn't get away.

She had to use it. Here. Now.

"Burst," Ceony whispered, releasing the paper.

The rhombus began to quiver, faster and faster, buzzing like a hornet as it slowly, leisurely fell toward the ground. The buzz grew louder, higher, louder, higher . . .

The diamond-Folded paper exploded in a burst of fireworks and flame, blasting outward like a pistol with a blocked barrel.

The explosion flung Ceony sideways against the cliff. The ragged rocks cut through the fibers of her blouse and into her skin. She fell onto her elbow and hip, the taste of ash filling her mouth.

For several heartbeats everything looked white and bright, like the morning sun itself. As color, shape, and shadow gradually returned to her eyes, a high-pitched note rang in her ears, a tuning fork struck and never stilled.

She pushed herself up, arm aching, hip stiff. The rocky beach swished back and forth. Her temples throbbed with her pulse: *PUM-Pom-poom.*

Emery.

Across the rocks, nearly to where the ocean lapped at the shore, Lira sputtered and weakly tried to push herself onto all fours. Ebony drapes of damp hair hung over her cheeks.

Ceony forced herself up, clinging to the rock shelf. The morning spun and tilted. That constant note—perhaps a high B-flat—continued to ring inside her skull.

She had to act. Lira had touched her—all it would take was a quick recovery to recast whatever heinous spell the burst had interrupted.

Bits of half-soaked papers lay scattered over the ground, fallen from Ceony's bag. Lira's dagger lay on its side halfway between them, its hilt resting in a patch of lichen. Several gulls cried as they flew over the ocean, abandoning the site of the explosion.

Though the ocean still swayed in her vision, Ceony ran for the blade. Lira, peering up through her hair, staggered to her feet and sprinted for it as well.

Both their hands lunged for the knife.

Ceony's fingers grasped it first.

Hefting the surprisingly heavy blade, Ceony shouted an unintelligible cry and arched the blade up and over her in an imperfect crescent. She felt something tug back on her swing, but not hard enough to stop it. The sharp blade pulled clean through.

Lira screamed.

Blood rained over the shore. Lira stumbled back, both hands rushing to her face to stanch the steady flow of red water pouring from a split cheek and gouged eye.

Ceony dropped the dagger, feeling her stomach flip inside out. Lira cried again and lashed out, backhanding Ceony across the jaw.

Ceony fell, catching herself on raw palms. Lira dropped to her knees, gasping and cursing, blood pouring between her fingers. She tried to chant her healing spell but choked on every other word. Her blood had spilled everywhere—it dyed the tiny pools and streams of high tidewater, stained the lichen, painted crimson streaks across rocks and paper.

Paper. Crumpled, damp, and torn paper, wet with blood.

Numb, Ceony reached for a drier piece singed about the edges. Lira's blood sluggishly soaked through its fibers.

Her mind felt detached, her thoughts vacant as she touched the blood—the body's ink—with an index finger. Her mind didn't really process the idea; it merely materialized behind her eyes like a thread of nostalgia, as though it had always been there. It and nothing else.

She wrote nine letters and, with a shaky but strong voice, read them aloud.

"Lira froze."

And she did.

Ceony stared at the still image of Lira hunched over and cradling her ruined face, tendrils of ice climbing up her legs and hunched back. Her grunts and gasps vanished, her lips parted midbreath. Strands of wild hair hung in the air free from gravity's hold, as though someone had molded them in place with glue.

Ceony gaped. She had read the paper like an illusion. Like *Pip's Daring Escape*. But this wasn't a story. Or, rather, it was *her* story. Not an illusion at all

She stared at her bloody finger, but her thoughts—her ability to process—remained far from her. She returned to the page, wrote, and read, ". . . and never moved again."

The statue of Lira remained unchanged.

Ceony stood, letting the bloody paper fall to the rocks. A small whirlpool of hungry saltwater lapped up the words, sucking them back into the ocean. She backed seven steps away from Lira before a spot of brown on the ocean drew her eyes, close enough that she didn't need to squint to make out its shape.

A boat. It held two men, their features too distant to be distinct. One rowed, oars flapping in sync on either side of the boat. The other knelt at the boat's helm, peering toward the coast.

Ceony thought of the morbid seagull she had seen upon her arrival and tensed. The creature had been sent by someone, why not these two? Only the boat's nearness pushed her legs to move.

She turned back for the cave. Her soul yearned to run, but her body refused. It wasn't broken, only felt broken. Exhausted. Distant.

She stumbled into the cave, followed its wall with one hand until she reached the bowled shelf that held Emery's heart, still beating strong.

She checked her bag, empty save for Fennel. She spoke to the dog silently in thought, thanking him, promising to restore him as soon as she was able. Then she picked a few pieces of him apart, careful not to damage the greater part of his body, and tiredly Folded the links for a vitality chain, just large enough to encircle a grown man's heart.

Ceony fled the cave and climbed up the rocks before the boat reached the shore. She didn't look back.

She found the enormous glider where she had left it and flew to London, carrying Emery's heart next to her own.

# CHAPTER 16

As WIND RUSHED OVER her aching body and numb hands, Ceony's mind drifted back to Emery's home. Her home. What if he had passed on while she had been away? What if she had been too slow? Could an animated heart revive an inanimate body?

His heart fluttered weakly against hers, having lost much of its lingering strength since she lifted it from the enchanted pool.

But she still had time. Surely she still had time. Stories like this one weren't meant to end badly.

Magicians Aviosky, Hughes, and Katter would have noted her absence by now, but she found herself not caring for whatever repercussions they could offer her. She didn't regret her decision, even if her clumsy paper heart didn't pull Emery through this. She prayed her Folding had held up.

The magicians had, at least, left the giant door in Emery's roof open. The glider swooped up and landed gracefully, even without her directing it. It knew its master's house.

Ceony pulled stiff fingers from its handles, massaging them against her hip to coax movement back into the knuckles. Her head felt full of clouds, but not in the dreamy sense. Just the empty one.

The floorboards creaked under her feet. Her bag swung at her side like a broken pendulum from a derelict grandfather clock, and she felt as if she were made of paper herself. She leaned on the stairwell wall as she descended down to the second floor, holding Emery's heart to her breast, its small vitality chain soaked red. She had left her shoe wedged between the rocks of the island shore, not wanting to stay any longer than was absolutely necessary. Her sore, socked foot muffled every other step.

She passed Emery's room, the door ajar, the bed empty. They must not have moved him. He was downstairs, still alive. Waiting for her. They wouldn't have buried him without her. She hadn't been gone that long.

Had she?

Past the library, the lavatory, her bedroom. She leaned on the wall as she took the stairs to the first floor.

Mg. Aviosky opened the door, eight steps below her.

"Ceony Twill!" she exclaimed with all the anxiety of a worried mother, the sternness of an academy principal, and the relief of a farmer feeling spring's first rain on his skin. Her eyes widened round as dinner chargers. Ceony must have been a sight to see.

Mg. Aviosky's face paled and she started up the steps, but Ceony's words made her pause. "I'm not hurt," she said. And she wasn't, not really. The blood running down her blouse wasn't hers.

She gently pulled Emery's heart from beneath her collar. Mg. Aviosky pressed a hand to her mouth.

"That isn't . . . ," she whispered through her fingers.

Ceony took the last eight steps down, pushing past Mg. Aviosky, who didn't stop her. Ceony didn't have the energy for an argument, not right now. She saw no trace of Magicians Hughes and Katter.

Her own heart quickened at the sight of Emery, the real Emery, lying in his makeshift bed on the dining room floor just as she had left him. His skin almost held the pallor of death. His lips were almost violet. His eyes were almost sunken.

Almost, but not quite. Her paper heart still beat within his chest.

Mg. Aviosky closed the stairway door and asked the question surfacing in Ceony's own mind. "Will it work?"

"I don't know," Ceony whispered. It scared her that a magician as experienced as Aviosky would ask that. What if it didn't?

She walked around to Emery's left side and knelt beside him. She held his heart in one hand and reopened his shirt with the other. His flesh felt cool, but not cold.

"There's still magic left in it," she said. She knew only because no heart could beat on its own without its body, not without a spell, and Lira's magic had been strong. Hopefully it would be enough.

She placed the heart upon his chest. His skin glimmered with the gold residue of Lira's spell, and the cavity opened. The sight of an open chest would have terrified Ceony had she not just lived in one, more or less.

"How long was I gone?" she asked as her paper heart greeted her with a feeble, soggy pulse.

"One night," Mg. Aviosky answered, barely audible.

Ceony nodded. Reaching into Emery's still-warm chest, she pulled out her paper heart and pressed his own back into place.

Emery's back arched and he sucked in a rush of air. The cavity closed so suddenly Ceony barely had time to pull her fingers free. The golden glimmer vanished.

Ceony held her breath. Emery remained still, asleep.

Pressing her ear to his chest, she listened for the heartbeat. It met her with a drowsy but steady *PUM-Pom-poom*.

She smiled. She didn't have the strength to do anything more.

"He'll be all right, but call a doctor," she said, her voice light and airy. She thought she sounded like a child. She smoothed Emery's hair back from his forehead and, though Mg. Aviosky watched from the foot of the bed, leaned down to kiss him on the cheek.

"Miss Twill—" Aviosky began as Ceony stood, but the woman didn't finish her sentence, whatever it may have been. Perhaps because Ceony looked so terrible. Perhaps because Mg. Aviosky saw this as a good deed. Perhaps it was the way Ceony's legs shook as though they had aged one hundred years in the space of one night.

Mg. Aviosky's gaze prickled Ceony's back as Ceony stepped away from Magician Emery Thane, pulled herself up the stairs, and collapsed into her own bed.

———

Ceony awoke with lead bones and a mild headache in the center of her forehead. Soreness had settled into her muscles—her legs and forearms especially—warning her of further soreness on the morrow. She felt her pulse tickling hot spots on her back where she had skidded across the rock shelf along the Foulness coast. Her stomach, though it felt quite small, chortled in protest for food, and she had hardly enough saliva in her mouth to swallow.

Someone handed her a glass of water.

She didn't recognize the man kneeling at her bedside, but Mg. Aviosky stood behind him and helped Ceony prop herself up on a pillow. Ceony drained the cup in four and a half gulps and thirsted for more.

She noticed the conical stethoscope around the stranger's neck—he looked about fifty, with thorough hair loss and round-lensed spectacles—and concluded he was the doctor she had asked Mg. Aviosky to retrieve. She hadn't intended the doctor for her own use.

Morning light in the window told her she'd been asleep for some time.

"Dehydration," the doctor said, pressing his finger into Ceony's wrist, then watching to see how long his white print took to recolor. "And quite scratched. And in need of a bath. But you'll certainly survive, Miss Twill."

Ceony cleared her throat. "Emer—Thane—Magician Thane," she stuttered, feeling her cheeks heat under Mg. Aviosky's scrutiny. "Is he all right?"

Mg. Aviosky said, "As you predetermined, Miss Twill, he will be healthy after a few days' rest. Dr. Newbold has affirmed it."

Releasing a long breath of relief, Ceony sunk down into her pillow. Dr. Newbold leaned forward and touched his stethoscope to her chest with no formality, but doctors tended to be quite familiar. Nodding his head once, he said, "Liquids and soft foods for twenty-four hours. If you have to chew it, don't eat it, unless you want to cramp."

He rifled through a short-handled bag on the floor, one that had been patched several times, for Ceony noticed the stitchings along its seams were three distinctly different shades of black. From the bag Dr. Newbold pulled a shallow jar of green gel. It looked like the aloe cream the nurse at Tagis Praff always kept on the third shelf of the medicine cabinet between beds one and two.

"This will help your abrasions heal more swiftly," he explained. "Twice a day, or whenever they sting."

"And Em—Magician Thane?" she asked.

"No abrasions on him," Dr. Newbold answered. "Magic wounds are a strange sort. Tricky. If he acts oddly after he wakes, call me back." He held up a finger as a warning. "And let him wake on his own. The body often knows what it needs without our meddling."

"But how will I know if he's acting strange?" Ceony asked. "He's strange already."

Mg. Aviosky clucked her tongue, and Ceony felt herself smiling. When Mg. Aviosky clucked again, Ceony wiped the grin from her face and managed to force a flush down into her chest, where the magician wouldn't see it.

To the doctor, Mg. Aviosky said, "Will you return tonight to check on his progress?"

Dr. Newbold shook his head in the negative. "No, no, I don't believe it's necessary. He seems stable to me, especially now that he's in his own bed. I don't like patients lying on the floor unless they absolutely must."

"I can tend to him," Ceony said, sitting up. Her back ached as she did. "I don't mind, and it's just watching to make sure nothing seems amiss, right?" she asked, glancing from the doctor to Mg. Aviosky. "I'm his apprentice and I'm all right. And I know you're busy, Magician Aviosky."

Mg. Aviosky pursed her lips into a thin line, but Ceony wasn't sure if it was in regard to her statement or not. Mg. Aviosky always looked pursed.

"Things have gone from very hectic to very calm very quickly," the magician said. "It disconcerts me. But if you believe it is well, Dr. Newbold, I suppose I'll be wont to agree with you."

"It is well," the doctor said, closing his bag and standing with a grunt. His right knee popped as he did so. "But telegram if anything does go amiss."

"Me as well," Mg. Aviosky said to Ceony, clasping her hands behind her back. She still wore the same clothes she had donned when first responding to Ceony's call, and Ceony found herself grateful not only for the woman's quick response, but also that she had stayed beside Emery when the others had left him for dead.

Ceony smiled. "Of course. I'll let you know any and every change, Magician Aviosky. I promise it."

Mg. Aviosky smiled as much as her stern countenance would allow. "I am glad to hear it. I apologize for this incident disrupting your learning." She looked at Ceony with a critical eye. "I admit I'm not a fan of mixed genders in apprenticeships, and our only other Folders are likewise male, but I'm willing to consider reassignment."

Ceony bit down on her tongue to keep from blurting an adamant "No!" at the very idea. Instead she calmly, politely, said, "Magician Thane has been a good teacher thus far, and very patient with me. I'd like to continue apprenticing under him as far as the situation allows."

Mg. Aviosky nodded, a fraction of skepticism marring her otherwise poised visage, but she said nothing. "Dr. Newbold," she said, turning to the man who stood at eye level with her. "Thank you for your time. I'll send your bill through the Cabinet. If you would excuse us."

Ceony chewed on her lip as the doctor nodded and left. She had assumed Mg. Aviosky would go with him. What more was there to say?

Once Dr. Newbold had departed, Mg. Aviosky sat straight-backed on the edge of Ceony's narrow bed and said, "Tell me precisely what happened."

Ceony curled in on herself. "I'm rather hungry, Magician—"

"Is it so long a story?" Mg. Aviosky interrupted. "You fled the premises against instruction to pursue an Excisioner!" She gasped at the very idea. "And yet you not only survived, but rescued the heart of perhaps the most talented Folder in England. I deserve the details, Miss Twill."

"You didn't 'instruct' me to stay," Ceony countered. "Just to leave the dining room. Which I did."

Mg. Aviosky rubbed the bridge of her nose under her glasses. "This feels very much like detention again, Ceony."

"It's just . . . private, I guess," she replied.

"Private?" the magician repeated, obviously surprised at Ceony's choice of adjective. "How so? What is so private that you can't tell me?" She paled. "You didn't bargain—"

"No, no," Ceony said, glancing down to her hands. To the blood underneath her nails. In her mind's eye she saw Lira's frozen form, hands clutching her bleeding eye. *Blood magic*, Ceony thought. *Does that make me an Excisioner, too?*

It was the thought Ceony hadn't dared consider until now. What would Mg. Aviosky—and the Magicians' Cabinet—do if they knew *how* Ceony had defeated Lira?

Looking away from Mg. Aviosky's eyes, Ceony said, "I took Magician Thane's glider—it's in the attic—and used a bird scout— a paper bird, that is—to follow Lira. She must have seen the glider and gotten scared and fled. I chased her to the coast, where she had taken camp. I tracked her to the water. I think she escaped. I . . . I saw a boat in the water. It might have been for her."

Mg. Aviosky raised one brow. "And she left the heart behind?" Ceony nodded.

"Foolish to come all this way and leave the very objective of her attack in a camp," Mg. Aviosky said. "I'll trace your coordinates and send some detectives in."

Ceony's breath caught at that. She hoped Mg. Aviosky didn't notice.

"I think I'd like to rest now," Ceony managed. She was unsure of what anyone would find on that beach—had the men taken Lira or left her? "And eat. I can look at a map and guess where the camp was . . . telegram you the location tonight, perhaps." Buy some time.

Mg. Aviosky appeared suspicious, but she receded. Ceony was, after all, one of her best students, detention or no. Another purse of the lips and Mg. Aviosky stood and said, "I want them by tonight, unless you want the Cabinet hounding you. Magician Hughes is a very impatient man and keen on details." She adjusted her glasses. "I'll leave the buggy running, just in case," she said, and took her leave.

Leaning against the warm glass of the window, Ceony waited until Mg. Aviosky passed through the paper charms disguising the cottage's appearance before she rose from bed and padded lightly to Emery's room.

The door creaked loudly as she opened it. Emery lay still atop his bed, two blankets covering him. Curtains drawn.

She opened them halfway to give him some sunlight. He looked healthier, ruddier.

"I'm not sure what to do," she admitted, watching his chest rise and fall with every steady breath. "I have to tell Magician Aviosky where. I don't want to talk to the Cabinet. But . . . I left her there on the rocks. I didn't know if writing it would work, but the blood made some sort of connection, and it did," she said, rubbing her left arm absently. "But I'm not like her. Please don't think I'm like her."

Moving to his bedside, she squeezed his warm hand briefly before making her way to the lavatory to clean up. She never wanted to look at another's blood again, if she could help it.

Before she went to bed she pulled an old-edition atlas from one of Mg. Thane's many bookshelves and telegrammed a rough span of coordinates to Mg. Aviosky.

She had a hard time sleeping after that.

# CHAPTER 17

THE NEXT DAY CEONY rose early, started a fire in the front room's hearth, and rested her curling iron beside the coals.

Mg. Aviosky had apparently cleaned up the broken dishes and turned the dining room table upright, but Ceony, after hunting through cupboards for cleaning supplies—swept and mopped the floor and wiped down all the counters. She washed the dishes in the sink, dried them, and set them carefully onto their respective shelves. She browsed through the icebox to get ideas for lunch and dinner. She had milk and an apricot for breakfast.

Upstairs in the lavatory—which had the best mirror in the house—Ceony carefully curled her locks and pushed a headband into her hair. After examining herself, she took the headband out and instead pinned back the sides of her hair and set a simple olive barrette over them. Her mother had always said olive looked best with red hair, even if Ceony's hair was far more orange than it was red.

She took a kohl pencil from her makeup bag and carefully lined her eyes, then smudged some of the kohl between her fingertips and pinched her blond lashes to darken them. She thumbed a bit of rouge on her cheeks as well and changed into her second-best set of clothes: a navy-blue skirt that cinched just above her hips, and a peach-colored blouse with frilled collar, which she tucked into it. She considered, briefly, wearing her *best* clothing—a sage-green dress with short sleeves and slim fit—but she didn't want to overdo it.

Content with her appearance—even confident with it—she stepped into Emery's room to check on him. He was unmoved, but she thought his breathing sounded a bit easier.

She sat on the bed beside him and ran her fingertips through his dark hair, then traced her pinky finger over his brow. Felt his temperature. Normal. She fetched him some broth and carefully poured it bit by bit into his mouth. There was little for her to do beyond that.

Downstairs she made cucumber sandwiches and potato salad, despite doctor's orders. Enough for two, but with Emery unchanged, she ate alone and stored the rest in the icebox for later. After suffering a few stomach cramps, she cooked sausage gravy, biscuits, and asparagus for dinner. Again she made enough for two and waited until eight o'clock. Emery didn't wake, however, so she let the food grow cold while she fed him more broth and wiped his face and neck with a damp towel. She ate quickly—standing at the table rather than sitting—and afterward retrieved *Pip's Daring Escape* from her bedroom. She pulled the chair from the library into Emery's room, sat on it, and read the book with all the feeling and charisma she had. Images of the small gray mouse and his adventure through a cat-strewn garbage dump to retrieve a beloved toy played out in ghostly apparitions over Emery's torso. Still, he didn't wake.

Ceony washed her face, hung up her clothes, and went to bed late.

She rose with the sun the next day, bathed, and set her curling iron by the fire as she swept the front hall and dusted the front room, even picking up Jonto's collapsed form to reach the windowsill. Back in the lavatory she curled her hair with a little more flare and fastened it with a tie behind her left ear, so that the curls hung neatly over her shoulder. After applying some kohl and rouge, she changed once more into her peach blouse and navy skirt. She skipped breakfast and got to work on her few pieces of dirty laundry.

Her white blouse—the one she had worn through Emery's heart—was ruined, but the skirt only needed some patchwork to be wearable. She scrubbed it and hung it outside to dry beneath a clear, sunny sky and set to work on lunch. She made cucumber sandwiches once more, but ate them alone. For dinner she planned rosemary chicken.

She pulled the chicken from the icebox, a shriveled onion from a cupboard below the sink, and some dried rosemary that hung on a string opposite the dining room door. As she cut into the chicken breasts, however, her hands stilled as watery blood dribbled from the meat.

*Lira froze . . . and never moved again.*

She set the knife down and examined her hands, seeing blood where she knew there was none. *Paper*, she reminded herself. *It was a* paper *spell, nothing more.*

But paper illusions didn't have any effect on real people, did they?

She bit her lip. She still hadn't heard back from Mg. Aviosky. Did her old teacher suspect her? Had she even received the telegram?

She glanced into the dining room, to the stairs that led to the second floor, where Emery slept. What would Ceony tell *him*?

"This is nonsense," she said aloud, snatching up the knife and cutting the chicken crosswise. She seasoned and breaded it and shoved it in the oven. The aromas of home cooking and the washing and hiding of the knife helped to soothe her.

Ceony checked on Emery, and though he truly looked just like a man taking a nap, he didn't wake.

After dinner Ceony retrieved her bag and took Fennel to the library, where she sat at the desk and tried multiple Folds of paper to see if she couldn't rebuild him herself. She was still too green, though, and the connections in his body and the crisp lines of each unique Fold confused her. Even if she *had* watched Emery create the pup, she didn't think she'd be able to copy it. The spells were just too advanced.

Giving up and trying not to feel heartsick, Ceony browsed the books in the library until she found a novelette entitled *The Barn Spider*, which had line sketches every few pages for reference. She read it to Emery, but being unfamiliar with the tale, she couldn't make a single illusion appear for him. Something she would have to practice.

That night, as she slipped *The Barn Spider* back onto its shelf, the telegraph began tap-tapping. Ceony wrung her fingers together until it finished, then read Mg. Aviosky's words while biting her first knuckle.

checked coordinates stop no sign of lira stop cabinet investigating stop
hope all is well stop

For some reason, the news that the others hadn't found Lira did little to pacify Ceony's nerves. If anything, it scared her even more.

It took several hours before she fell asleep, her thoughts lingering somewhere on the Foulness coast, replaying her confrontation with Lira over and over again. Pressing two fingers to her neck, she felt her own pulse, the *poom* of its *PUM-Pom-poom* too faint to detect.

She woke late the next morning, and went about her morning routine: curling her hair, applying her makeup, getting dressed, and doing chores.

For breakfast—or rather, brunch—she cooked bacon, eggs, and toast. Enough for two. After eating alone, she counted up what groceries Emery still had and determined she would need to go to the store soon. She'd prefer not to go alone.

She went outside, the warm summer sun shining between clouds at the cottage. Beneath the eave in the backyard rested an actual garden of actual plants, not just the paper imitations. It looked well tended, though a few baby weeds had grown between mint, parsley, and what looked like radishes. Ceony picked them out by the root one by one and set the pile aside to mulch. She stuck her index finger into the soil—it needed to be watered.

When she returned to the kitchen for a pitcher, however, she heard a faint but familiar sound in the dining room—an airy sort of clap, meant to be a bark.

She felt her insides break apart into puzzle pieces and slowly set themselves together again, but with her heart wedged into the base of her throat.

Fennel ran into the kitchen yapping wildly, his paper paws skidding along the smooth wooden floorboards. He fell over once, picked himself up, and ran for Ceony's feet. Ceony, mouth in a wide O, knelt down to intercept him. Fennel licked her sleeves with his paper tongue and wagged his tail so fiercely she feared it would fly off his rump and land in the icebox.

"There we are!" she exclaimed, scratching Fennel behind his ears and under his chin. "That wasn't so long, was it?"

But she knew Fennel hadn't magically reanimated himself. Her pulse thudded loudly enough in her ears for her to distinctly make out its quiet third beat.

Two breaths later, the door to the stairwell swung open and Emery stepped out, wearing his same indigo coat but a clean shirt and pants—the gray slacks Ceony had washed just yesterday.

She stood slowly, feeling her face turn pink. He walked with a slight hunch that whispered of mild discomfort, but otherwise seemed perfectly healthy.

His eyes found hers—his beautiful green eyes—and they smiled.

"I have a distinct feeling I've missed something rather spectacular," he said. His voice was a little rough, and he cleared it before adding, "That, and I'm incredibly hungry."

"Oh!" Ceony said, pushing past Fennel to the bread box. "I can make you something. Sit down. Do you like cucumbers? But of course you do . . . They're your cucumbers."

He quirked an eyebrow, but his eyes still grinned, and the sentiment even reflected in the tilt of his lips. "I believe I'm well enough to make my own sandwich, Ceony."

But she shook her head and pulled out the cutting board and the last of the cucumber from the icebox. Emery paused for a moment between dining room and kitchen before giving up and taking a chair.

"How do you feel?" Ceony asked, her pulse still thundering in her ears. It made her hands shake as she peeled and cut the cucumber. She forced herself to slow down so she wouldn't slice open a finger.

"Like someone has been tromping around in my chest, looking at things they shouldn't be looking at."

Her knife froze mid-slice. She met his eyes and saw knowledge behind their amusement.

Her neck and ears burned. "Y-You know what happened, don't you?"

He twisted a piece of hair around his finger. "It's my heart, Ceony. Of course I would know what's in it. Most of it, at least."

*Most of it?* she thought, opening a cupboard door to block Emery's view of her blushing face. She tried to focus on cutting the cucumber. *How much is "most of it"?*

She thought of their brief conversation from the fourth chamber and worried her clothes would ignite, her skin felt so hot.

The cupboard door shut, and Ceony jumped to see Emery beside her, taking the knife from her hand and setting it down on the countertop. "But I don't know what happened before, or after," he said. His eyes dropped to her neck. Reaching out a hand, he tilted her chin up with a knuckle. Ceony realized he was studying the faded bruises there, left by the fingers of one of Lira's undead hands.

She pulled back and pushed her hair over her shoulders to mask them. "I stole your glider," she said.

"Did you now?"

She nodded. "I sent out paper birds to scout and followed them. I think she—Lira—intended to escape on a boat—"

"But she didn't." It wasn't a question. His eyes seemed determined, wondering.

Words spilled from her mouth. "I met her at the coast, in a cave. She put some sort of spell on you—on your heart—and that's how I got stuck inside. I didn't mean to 'tromp.' I had no choice."

She found herself speaking faster with every sentence, unable to look away from those penetrating eyes. "And I thought if I could just make my way to the end I could get out. She was in there, too, somehow, but not always. I tried to go quickly. I didn't want you to die.

"And then I got out," she blurted, and he nodded. So he *did* remember that part. Ceony's feet had gone cold for all the blood rushing to her face. "And she was there, and all the spells got wet and she grabbed me and said she'd take my heart, too, and—"

She stepped farther away from him, the small of her back hitting the rim of the sink. "I'm not like her, Emery. I didn't mean . . . but it happened."

His forehead wrinkled. "Didn't mean what, Ceony? What happened?"

"We both ran for the dagger at the same time," she explained, as though Emery would understand her story despite its lack of context. "I grabbed it first. I hurt her." She touched her face where the blade had cut into Lira's skin. "She bled everywhere. The paper . . . there was paper all over the rocks because of the spell you gave me. The bursting spell. And I wrote on them that she'd be frozen forever . . ."

A lump formed in Ceony's throat, forcing her voice to grow quiet. She tried to swallow it down, but doing so only made it ache. "And it worked," she whispered. "She'd still be there if they hadn't come for her. I wrote it in blood and it worked . . ."

Tears clustered in the corners of her eyes, and she blinked rapidly to clear them. "I'm not like her," she squeaked. "I'm not an Excisioner . . ."

Emery's hand on her shoulder brought her gaze back to him. How silly she must have looked, must have sounded.

"No, you're not," he said, sounding much surer than she felt. "You've bonded to paper; you can't be. It's impossible."

She stared at him, gaze moving from one green eye to the other. "But Lira—"

"Lira was not a magician when I met her," he answered, pulling his hand away. "She was a nursing assistant, which explains why things like blood didn't bother her. Don't bother her."

Ceony nodded slowly, feeling somewhat numb. "Then I'm not . . . I didn't do the forbidden magic?"

"I don't know what you did," Emery replied, running a hand back through his hair. His eyes glanced out the window behind her for a moment. "But nothing illegal. Nothing that would ever hold in a court, if that's what you're worried about. You saved my life, Ceony, unless I'm dead and I greatly misjudged what the afterlife would look like."

Ceony looked at her feet, hiding relief and a smile. "I'd be greatly upset if this were the afterlife and you were dead, Em—Magician Thane," she said. "Because that would mean I flew clear to the ocean and back for nothing."

Fennel barked and sniffed about Ceony's shoes. Emery smiled.

"Well," he said after a moment almost long enough to be awkward. He picked up the slices of cucumber and put them on the bread himself, then pulled a plate from the cupboard. Walking back to the table, he said, "Now we can finally have this meal, hm?"

"*This* meal?" Ceony asked, glancing at his bland sandwich. He took a bite of it without even bothering with mayonnaise. "Any meal I put thought into is levels above a cucumber sandwich. I could have been a chef, if you recall."

"Is that so?" he asked, taking another bite.

Ceony began to cut two slices of bread for herself, but paused halfway through the first. "Would you humor me for a moment?"

"I believe I've been humoring you since you walked through my front door," he replied.

She smiled. "Just for a moment."

She abandoned the bread and cucumber and hurried to the study, selecting a sky-blue piece of square-cut paper from the shelf behind the desk. Resting it against the desktop, she carefully Folded a half-point Fold and a full-point Fold, pulling from memory the creation of the fortuity box that had promised her "adventure" before she had even known Lira's name. With a pen she scrawled down the fortune symbols, pausing after drawing five.

She brought the box back into the dining room and showed it to Emery. "Which ones go here?"

Amusement touched his eyes—that seemed to be their preferred emotion—and he took the pen and paper from her, finishing the last three symbols himself as he chewed. Ceony committed them to memory before pinching the box in her fingers and presenting it to Emery.

"What is your mother's maiden name?" she asked.

He leaned his chin into his palm, elbow propped on the table. "You don't remember?"

"I do," she retorted, "but I don't want to jinx it. Just answer."

"Vladara. One *r*." His eyes glimmered.

She opened and closed the box seven times and asked, "What is your date of birth?"

"July fourteenth, 1871."

She moved the box back and forth. "Pick a number."

Emery remained silent for a moment, studying Ceony's face. His thoughts didn't reflect in his eyes. Before her flush could return, however, he said, "One."

She opened the flap scrawled with a square divided into three, one of the symbols Emery had drawn. She opened it, seeing blank paper for a half second before an image flooded her mind with far more strength than it had the first time she'd read his fortune.

The vision was familiar—a setting sun, a plum tree, a hill covered with wildflowers and crabgrass. A soft breeze carried on it the scents of earth, clover, and honey.

Emery sat up on a patchwork quilt beneath the tree, his hair shorter than it was now, an indigo coat folded neatly beside him. He watched the sunset wordlessly, and in his bright eyes Ceony saw contentment.

Beside him a woman lay on her side, tracing the veins on the back of his hand with her finger, spotted with three freckles. Her orange hair fell in a neat braid over one shoulder. On the other side of the tree two young boys with raven hair played on a swing, pushing each other back and forth, grabbing the ropes and laughing.

Ceony closed the flap, blinking away the colors of the sunset. The lump in her throat had vanished, and her heart beat steadily right where it should be.

"Well?" Emery asked.

"It's bad luck to know your own fortune," she said.

"I believe it's only bad luck to *read* your own," he countered.

"Best to play it safe," she said, trying to stifle a grin and failing miserably. Scooting back a chair, she sat at the table and asked, "I was wondering, though, about Prit. You hated Folding, so why did you choose to bond paper?"

"For the same reason you did," he said, leaning back in his chair. "I didn't. And it turned out well, in the end. You see, Ceony, we're more alike than you may think."

"Yes," she said, her grin spreading with full force. "Yes, I believe we are."

# AN EXCERPT FROM CHARLIE N. HOLMBERG'S
## *THE GLASS MAGICIAN*

A late summer breeze wafted through the open kitchen window, making the twenty tiny flames upon Ceony's cake dance back and forth on their candlewicks. Ceony hadn't made the cake, of course, as one should never bake her own birthday cake, but her mother was a good cook and a better baker, so Ceony had no doubts that the confection, complete with pink cherry frosting and jelly filling, would be delicious.

But as her parents and three siblings sang her birthday wishes, Ceony's mind wandered from the dessert and the celebration at hand. Her thoughts narrowed in on an image she had seen in a fortuity box just three months ago, after reading Magician Emery Thane's fortune. A flowery hill at sunset, the smell of clover, and Emery sitting beside her, his green eyes bright, as two children played beside them.

Three months had passed, and the vision had not come to fruition. Ceony certainly couldn't expect otherwise, especially since children were involved, but she ached for a wisp of the thing. She and Emery—Mg. Thane, that is—had grown close during her appointment as his apprentice and the subsequent rescuing of his heart. Still, she longed for them to be closer.

She debated her birthday wish and wondered if it would be better to ask for love or for patience.

"The wax is dripping on the cake!" Zina, Ceony's younger sister by two and a half years, exclaimed from the other end of the table. She tapped her foot on the ground and blew a short lock of dark hair from her face.

Margo, the youngest sister at age eleven, nudged Ceony in the hip. "Make a wish!"

Taking a deep breath and clinging to the crisp memory of the flowery hill and sunset, Ceony bent over and blew out the candles, careful not to let her braid catch fire.

Nineteen went out, casting the kitchen into near darkness. Ceony quickly huffed and extinguished the twentieth rogue candle, praying it wouldn't count against her.

The family applauded while Zina rushed to turn on the one electric bulb that hung from the kitchen ceiling. It flickered thrice before popping, sending a downpour of glass and darkness onto the partygoers.

"Well, great," complained thirteen-year-old Marshall, Ceony's only brother. She heard his hands slide around the table, searching for matches—or perhaps sneaking an early taste of cake.

"Watch your step!" Ceony's mother cried.

"I've got it, I've got it," Ceony's father said, shuffling toward the cupboard-shaped shadows. A few moments later he lit a thick candle, then fished around in a drawer for an extra bulb. "They really are handy, when they work."

"Well," Ceony's mother said, ensuring none of the glass had landed on the cake, "a little darkness never hurt anyone. Let's cut the cake! Do chew with care, Margo."

"Finally," Zina sighed.

"Thank you," Ceony said as her mother expertly sliced a triangle of birthday cake and handed it to her. "I really appreciate this."

"We can always spare a cake for you, no matter how old you get," her mother said, almost chiding. "Especially for a magician's apprentice." She beamed with pride.

"Did you make me something?" Marshall asked, eyeing the pockets of Ceony's red apprentice apron. "You promised you would two letters ago, remember?"

Ceony nodded. She took a bite of cake before setting the plate down and retreating into the tiny living room, where her purse hung from a rusted hook on the wall. Marshall followed excitedly, with Margo at his heels.

From the purse Ceony pulled out a flat, Folded piece of violet paper, feeling the slight, familiar tingling of it beneath her fingers. Marshall looked on as she pressed it against the wall and made the last few Folds that formed the bat's wings and ears, careful to align the edges of the paper so the magic would take. Then, holding the bat's belly in her hand, she commanded it, "Breathe."

The paper bat hunched and pushed itself up on her palm with the small paper hooks on its wings.

"Amazing!" Marshall exclaimed, seizing the bat before it could fly away.

"Careful with it!" Ceony called as he rushed toward the back hallway, to the room he, Zina, and Margo shared.

Reaching into her pack again, Ceony pulled out a simple bookmark, long and pointed at one end. She handed it to Zina.

Her sister crooked an eyebrow. "Uh, what is this?"

"A bookmark," Ceony explained. "Just tell it the title of the book you're reading and leave it on the nightstand. It will keep track of what page you're on by itself." She pointed to the center of the bookmark, where she'd overlaid a small square of paper. "The page number will appear here, in my handwriting. It should work for your sketchbooks, too."

Zina snorted. "Weird. Thanks."

Margo clasped her hands under her chin. "And me?"

Ceony smiled and rubbed Margo's orange hair, a color that matched her own. From the side pocket of her bag she pulled a small paper tulip. Green paper comprised its stem, and red and yellow paper formed its six petals, which overlapped at the edges and alternated in color.

Margo's mouth formed a perfect *O* as Ceony handed her the flower.

"Set it in your window, and in the morning it will bloom, just like a real flower," Ceony said. "But don't water it!"

Margo nodded excitedly and followed Marshall's path back to the bedroom, cradling the tulip as though it had been crafted of glass.

Ceony sat in the living room to finish her cake with her parents while Marshall and Margo played with their new spells in their room. Zina had headed to Parliament Square for a date. Bizzy, the Jack Russell terrier Ceony had been forced to leave behind upon accepting her apprenticeship, curled up lazily at Ceony's feet, lifting her head every now and then to beg for a crumb.

"Well," Ceony's mother said after her second piece of cake, "it does sound like it's going well for you. Magician Thane seems like a very nice teacher."

"He is," Ceony said, hoping the poor lighting masked the blush creeping up her cheeks. She set her plate on the floor for Bizzy to lick. "He's very nice."

Ceony's father clapped his hands down on his knees and let out a long breath. "Well, we'd better get you a buggy so you can head back before it's too late." He glanced out the window at the night sky. Then he stood, opening his arms for an embrace.

Ceony jumped up and hugged her father tightly, then her mother. "I'll visit soon," she promised. Without traffic, it took just over an hour to get from Emery's cottage to Whitechapel's Mill Squats, so Ceony didn't drop in as often as she would have liked. She felt certain she could make the trip in a quarter hour on Emery's paper glider, but he insisted that the world wasn't ready for such eccentricity.

Ceony's father called the buggy service, for which Ceony insisted on paying, and soon Ceony sat in the back of an automobile, chugging past the tightly spaced flats of the Mill Squats on a cobbled road winding between town houses. She passed the post office, the grocer, and the turn for the children's park, taking the meandering route out of the quieting city. Soon her buggy's lights were the only ones on the road. Ceony stared out the open window at the stars, which grew in number the closer she drew to Emery's cottage. Invisible crickets sang from the tall grasses that lined the road out of London, and the river running alongside it bubbled and churned.

Ceony's heart beat a little faster when the buggy pulled to a stop. After paying, she disembarked and stepped past the cottage's menacing spells, which disguised it as a run-down mansion with broken windows and falling shingles. Beyond the fence, the home stood three stories high, made of soft yellow brick and surrounded by a garden of vibrant paper flowers, buds closed for the night. A light burned in the library window. Emery had been away all week at a Magic Materials in Architecture conference, which the Magicians' Cabinet had insisted he attend. Ceony quickly straightened her skirt and rebraided her hair to smooth any loose ends.

The padding of paper paws capered behind the door before Ceony could finish turning her key. Once inside, Fennel jumped into her arms and wagged his paper tail, barking his whispery bark. His dry paper tongue licked the base of Ceony's chin.

Ceony laughed. "I wasn't even gone a full day, silly thing," she said, scratching behind the dog's paper ears before setting him back down. Fennel ran in two short circles before jumping onto a pile of paper bones at the end of the hallway. When enchanted, those bones formed the body of Emery's skeletal butler, Jonto, to whom Ceony had finally become accustomed. Still, being routinely awoken by a paper skeleton dusting her headboard had been enough motivation for Ceony to start locking her door.

"Be gentle," Ceony warned Fennel, who had taken to chewing on Jonto's femur. Fortunately, his paper teeth did little damage to the bone. She stepped past the mess and flipped on the light in the kitchen. The simple room had a small stove to her right and a horse-shoe of cupboards to her left, behind which rested the back door and the icebox. She didn't see any dirty dishes in the sink. Had Emery eaten?

Ceony thought of preparing something just in case, but a flash of color from the dining room caught the corner of her eye.

There, on the table, sat a wooden vase full of red paper roses, so intricately Folded they looked real. Ceony approached them slowly and reached out a hand to touch their delicate petals, which had been Folded of the thinnest paper Emery had in stock. The flowers even had complex, fernlike leaves and a few rounded thorns.

Beside the vase rested an oval hair barrette made of paper beads and tightly wound spirals, heavily coated with a hard gloss to keep it from bending. Ceony picked up the barrette and thumbed its orna-mentation. It would take her hours to craft something this intricate, let alone the roses.

The roses. Ceony pulled a small square of paper from the center of the bouquet. It read "Happy Birthday" in Emery's perfect cursive script.

Her stomach fluttered.

Ceony fastened the barrette behind her ear and slid the note into a side pocket of her purse, where it wouldn't wrinkle. She took the stairs to the second floor, pinching her cheeks and adjusting and tucking her blouse as she climbed. The electric light from the library drew a lopsided rectangle on the hardwood flooring of the hallway.

Emery sat at the table on the far side of the book-lined room, his back to Ceony. He leaned on one hand, fingers entangled with the dark, wavy locks of his hair. His other hand turned the page of an especially old-looking book, though Ceony couldn't tell which one. A long, sage-green coat hung over the back of his chair. Emery owned a long coat in every color of the rainbow, and he wore them even in the middle of summer, save for July 24, when he had thrown the indigo coat out the window and spent the rest of the day Folding and cutting a blizzard's worth of snowflakes. Ceony still found the snowflakes every now and then, wedged between the icebox and the counter or collected in crumpled piles beneath Fennel's dog bed.

She knocked the knuckle of her right index finger against the doorframe. Emery started and turned around. Had he really not heard her come in?

He looked tired—he must have been traveling all day to be home by now—but his green eyes still burned with light. "You're a sight for sore eyes. I've done nothing but sit in hard chairs and talk to stuffy Englishmen all week." He frowned. "I also believe I've become something of a food snob, thanks to you."

Ceony smiled and found herself wishing she hadn't pinched her cheeks so adamantly. She turned her head to showcase the barrette. "What do you think?"

Emery's expression softened. "I think it's lovely. I did a good job on that."

Ceony rolled her eyes. "How modest. But thank you, for this. And the flowers."

Emery nodded. "But I'm afraid you're now a week behind in your studies."

"You told me I was two months ahead!" Ceony frowned.

"A week behind," he repeated, as though not hearing her. And perhaps he didn't. Emery Thane had a talent for selective hearing, she'd learned. "I've determined it's best for you to study the roots of Folding."

"Trees?" she asked, thumbing her barrette.

"More or less," Emery replied. "There's a paper mill a ways east of here, in Dartford. They even have a division for magic materials, not that it matters. Patrice requested your attendance for a tour of sorts, the day after tomorrow."

Ceony nodded. She *had* gotten a telegram from Mg. Aviosky about that.

"We'll start there. It's quite exciting." Emery chuckled.

Ceony sighed. That meant it wouldn't be, but she wasn't surprised. How exciting could a paper mill possibly be?

"We'll take a buggy at eight that morning," the paper magician continued, "so you'll have to rise early. I can have Jonto—"

"No, no, I'll be up," Ceony insisted. She turned back for the hallway, but paused. "Did you eat? I don't mind cooking something if you're hungry."

Emery smiled at her, the expression more in his eyes than his lips. She loved it when he smiled like that.

"I'm fine," he said, "but thank you. Sleep well, Ceony."

"You, too. Don't stay up too late," she said.

Emery turned back to his book. Ceony let her gaze linger on him for a second longer, then went to get ready for bed.

She set the roses on her nightstand before falling asleep.

Charlie N. Holmberg's *The Glass Magician* is
available Fall 2014 from 47North

# Acknowledgments

THERE ARE SO MANY people worth thanking for the fruition of this book. First and foremost is my husband, Jordan, who read the roughest of rough drafts and who bears many a literary bruise from all the ideas I've bounced off him.

Another huge thanks for all my alpha and beta readers—Jessica, Laura, Hayley, Lindsey, Whit, Andrew, and especially Juliana, whose belief in me and my stories became a battery for my writing.

A big thanks to my family as well, and very much to my baby sister, Alex, who talks me up to all her friends.

Thank you to Lauren for reading countless query drafts and helping me solve plot problems.

Thank you to Brandon Sanderson, the best writing teacher any aspiring author could have, and to my old writing group for molding me into someone who could put together a decent sentence. You know who you are.

And of course, thank you to Marlene and David for giving me a chance, and the 47North team for making this book, and this dream, possible.

Finally, here's a shout-out to the Big Man upstairs, because any shred of talent found in these pages most certainly came from Him.

# ABOUT THE AUTHOR

BORN IN SALT LAKE City, Charlie was raised a Trekkie alongside three sisters who also have boy names. In addition to writing fantasy novels, she is also a freelance editor. She graduated from BYU, plays the ukulele, owns too many pairs of glasses, and hopes to one day own a dog. *The Paper Magician* is her debut novel and the first in a whimsical series exploring a world of magicians who animate manmade materials. She currently lives with her family in Utah.